Arctic Inferno, the sequel to Arctic Meltdown, is a timely and gripping international environmental thriller set against the background of the devastation of climate change and the melting of the polar ice cap. The heroine, Hanne Kristensen, the beautiful Danish geologist appointed Minister of the Environment and Natural Resources for the newly independent Greenland, has to maneuver through a wave of setbacks to foil both a Chinese attempt to control Greenland's natural resources and a more aggressive Russian attempt to gain hegemony over the sparsely populated fledgling country as well as to save her friend, the ousted Premier of Russia, Pavel Laptov. Her suitor, Canadian diplomat Richard Simpson, aids her in this process as well as in the design and signing of a new and more environmentally focused Arctic Treaty to save the region from complete environmental catastrophe. But at the same time Hanne's private life is complicated by this relationship, as she has to choose between Richard and her long-time lover and childhood friend, Kristi Olafson. This is an action-packed novel with lots of twists and turns guaranteed to keep the reader at the edge of their seats, but also one that brings home the realities we could be living in the very near future.

Reviews

Other Books by Geza Tatrallyay

Arctic Meltdown, (thriller) e-published on Amazon and www.smashwords.com, December 2011

Twisted Reasons, (thriller, first in 'Twisted' trilogy) November 2014, Deux Voiliers Publishing

Cello's Tears, (poetry collection) May 2015, P.R.A. Publishing

For the Children, (memoir) May 2015, Editions Dedicaces

The Expo Affair, (memoir) April 2016, Guernica Editions

Twisted Traffick, (thriller, second in 'Twisted' trilogy) October 2017, Black Opal Books

Sighs and Murmurs, (poetry collection) April 2018, P.R.A. Publishing

Twisted Fates, (thriller, third in 'Twisted' trilogy) June 2018, Black Opal Books

The Waffle and the Pancake, (children's picture storybook), September 2018, Bayeux Arts

The Rainbow Vintner, (thriller) February 2019, Black Opal Books

The Fencers, (memoir) March 2019, Deux Voiliers Publishing

Extinction, (poetry collection) April 2019, P.R.A. Publishing

Extinction Rebellion, (poetry collection) July 2020, Cyberwit

Arctic Meltdown, 2nd Updated Edition, (thriller), August 28, 2021, Black Opal Books

The Mind Spins, (short story collection), November 2021, P.R.A. Publishing

The Abyss: Poems for our World, (poetry collection), September 2022, Deux Voiliers Publishing

Arctic Inferno

By

Geza Tatrallyay

A Black Opal Books Publication

We borrow the earth from our children.

- Inuit saying

Preface

Climate change is a reality. Drought afflicts broad areas of the world, destroying agriculture and causing wildfires that burn ancient forests and grasslands. Elsewhere, torrential rains and rising seas inflict widespread flooding on communities. At the heart of climate change is global warming caused by our continued release of greenhouse gases such as carbon dioxide and methane into the atmosphere.

The Arctic is warming more rapidly than other parts of the world: some scientists say temperatures are rising in this fragile environment at least four times as steeply as elsewhere in the world. This rapid melting of the polar ice caps there and in the Antarctic are now coming to be seen by science as not just a result, but also a driving force, of climate change. The feedback loops and synergistic effect of all the aspects of climate change, however, are still not fully understood and this makes effective modelling difficult.

For example, warming in the Arctic causes the permafrost to thaw. This in turn, results in the release of the methane gas trapped in the frozen soil, which then heats up the atmosphere even more. With the higher temperatures, fires burn the forests and the taiga—the most extensive wildfires in the world in 2021 were across Siberia—and this in turn causes more heating, more melt, more methane release, yet more warming and sea level rise.

As the polar icecap in the north melts, and the Arctic Ocean becomes opened up, it becomes more attractive for countries and companies to rush in to exploit the vast natural resources in the region—both subsea and on land—and to consider using the ice-free waters as routes for shipping. The US Geological Survey estimates that 22% of the world's oil and gas reserves are in the Arctic. There are also vast mineral deposits throughout the region, and Greenland is one of the richest countries in the world for valuable rare earths. Transpolar trade routes could cut shipping times by over one-third between the Far East and the US Northeast or Europe.

Yet there is no effective legal regime in place to govern the region, as there is for Antarctica with the respected Antarctic Treaty. The United Nations Convention on the Law of the Sea (UNCLOS—which the US has not ratified, although it generally abides by) gives sole jurisdiction for resource exploitation and the right to regulate navigation and overflight to coastal states out to 200 nautical miles (370 kilometers) or the outer edge of their coastal continental shelf (whichever is greater). A further clause gives countries jurisdiction along "natural prolongations" of their shelf, but the definition of what constitutes such a prolongation has been the source of competing applications to the relevant UN committee for additional jurisdiction by the coastal nations in the Arctic. *Arctic Meltdown*, the first book in this series, is based in part on a very real and currently contented claim by several countries to additional jurisdiction of seabed resources anchored in views that the Lomonosov Ridge, which extends across the Arctic Ocean virtually under the North Pole, is a prolongation of their shelf (see map).

There are eight Arctic coastal states: Canada, Denmark (Greenland), Finland, Iceland, Norway, Russia, Sweden, and the USA. Over the years, these countries have had differing views on the overall importance of the Arctic. For Russia, it has, for many years, been at the center of their vision of who they are. The Soviet Union claimed much of the Arctic according to the "sector principle"—from the furthest point east of Siberia to the furthest point west and then up to the North Pole, everything was theirs. While subsequent Russian governments have signed international treaties and laws since then—including UNCLOS—this vision of what belongs to them still very much lives on in the mind of today's politicians. Under Vladimir Putin, Russia's military presence in the Arctic has been significantly increased with the recent creation of the Military District of the Northern Fleet, and it would be difficult for any nation or for that matter even an alliance such as NATO, to contest this view should Russia wish to enforce it. Furthermore, Putin has made it clear that any transgression of its Arctic claims would meet with an appropriate response. The view that Russia "owns" the Arctic, is certainly underscored by the frequent penetration of Russian aircraft and naval vessels (including nuclear submarines) into the jurisdictional territories of the other Arctic states, particularly Norway, Denmark and Canada.

The status of Greenland is another somewhat nebulous factor. This huge island, with a population of 58,000 largely indigenous people, has been for many years a colony of Denmark. Its international and military affairs are today still handled by Denmark of which it is considered a part, but it is on a track toward total independence, although a key limiting issue is how to finance sovereignty—Greenland currently receives a subsidy of just over $600 million equivalent from Denmark, which accounts for roughly 20% of its GDP and more than half its budget.

The Arctic Council, established in 1996 by the Ottawa Declaration, is an international forum that addresses issues faced by Arctic governments and the indigenous peoples of the Arctic. Its focus, however, has largely been limited to environmental and scientific matters. Besides the eight nations that are the member states, the Council allows for other countries to participate as observers and indigenous peoples to be represented (for example, both China and India have signed on as observers). With the invasion of Ukraine by Russia—the country with the largest Arctic coastline—the other seven members of the Council declared that they would be "pausing participation in all meetings of the Council and its subsidiary bodies." This has effectively meant that on top of the lack of a legal framework to govern Arctic issues, there is no institution that allows for and promotes coordination.

It is against the very real and disturbing background that the two thrillers in the series—*Arctic Meltdown* and *Arctic Inferno*—are set. They explore one possible way in which Arctic affairs might evolve, although with the rapid melting of the ice cap, the lack of any effective governing legal and institutional framework, and the currently increasing confrontations internationally between democratic and autocratic nations, this may end up being a naïvely optimistic view.

Let us hope though, that Hanne Kristensen and Pavel Laptov will ultimately win. The future of the Arctic, indeed the world, could very well depend on them.

Hanne's Map

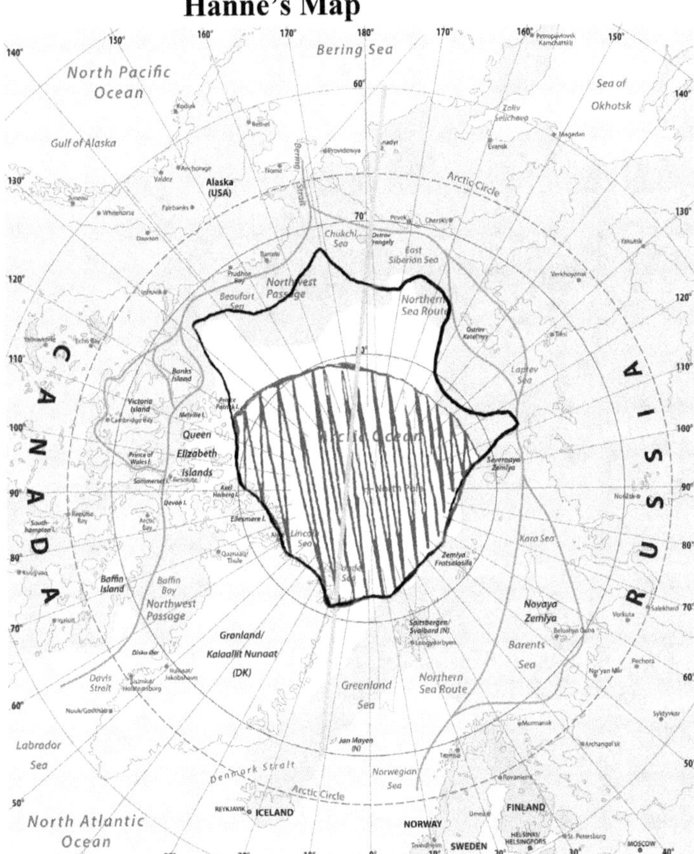

North Pacific Ocean
Bering Sea
Sea of Okhotsk
Gulf of Alaska
Zaliv Selichova
Petropavlovsk Kamchatkii
Kodiak
Bethel
nadyr
Magadan
Evensk
Providenya
Nome
Anchorage
Valdez
Alaska (USA)
Fairbanks
Arctic Circle
Dawson
Whitehorse
Juneau
Pevek
Cherskii
Yakutsk
Chukchi Sea
Ostrov Vrangely
Barrow
East Siberian Sea
Prudhoe Bay
Northwest Passage
Verkhoyansk
Beaufort Sea
Northern Sea Route
Ostrov Kotelny
Inuvik
Tiksi
Echo Bay
Yellowknife
Banks Island
Laptev Sea
CANADA
Victoria Island
Melville I.
Cambridge Bay
Prince Patrick I.
Arctic Ocean
Severnaya Zemlya
Queen Elizabeth Islands
Prince of Wales I.
Resolute
Axel Heiberg I.
North Pole
Norilsk
Repulse Bay
Somerset I.
Devon I.
Arctic Bay
Ellesmere I.
Lincoln Sea
Kara Sea
Southhampton L.
Qaanaaq/ Thule
Zemlya Frantsaiosifa
RUSSIA
Kujjuaq
Baffin Island
Baffin Bay
Wandel Sea
Novaya Zemlya
Vorkuta
Salekhard
Igloolik
Northwest Passage
Spitsbergen/ Svalbard (N)
Belushya Guba
Disko Øer
Grønland/ Kalaallit Nunaat (DK)
Longyearbyen
Barents Sea
Nar'yan Mar
Pechora
Davis Strait
Ilulissat/ Jakobshavn
Sisimiut/ Holsteinsburg
Northern Sea Route
Nuuk/Godthåb
Greenland Sea
Syktyvkar
Labrador Sea
Murmansk
Archangel'sk
Jan Mayen (N)
Tromsø
Narvik
Denmark Strait
Norwegian Sea
Arctic Circle
Umeå
FINLAND
North Atlantic Ocean
REYKJAVIK
ICELAND
NORWAY
Trondheim
SWEDEN
HELSINKI/ HELSINGFORS
St. Petersburg
MOSCOW

Chapter 1

Ottawa, Canada—Midweek, Late September, 202-

T he morning after the successful conference in Ottawa, where the groundbreaking Arctic Treaty was signed, Hanne and Richard slept in, and, as the morning light seeped in through the curtains, they slowly came to in each other's arms and relished some unhurried lovemaking. Showered, they made their way to the kitchen in the matching fluffy bathrobes he had on hand in his apartment, Richard turned on the TV, and, over the sumptuous breakfast he whipped up—cappuccinos and blueberry pancakes slathered with melting butter and Quebec maple syrup—the two lovers watched the breaking news.

Hanne was particularly interested in the rapidly evolving events in Russia. The evening before, they had been glued to the screen as CBC reported that three members of the *siloviki* who claimed to be in temporary exile in Belarus had demanded the removal of her friend, Pavel Laptov, and the return to power of the former President and FSB overlord, Andrei Gusanov. Minister Laptov, the famous polar explorer, now the leading member of the ruling troika that had replaced Gusanov in a populist coup, was, in her view, the person who had been most instrumental in bringing about the signing of the much needed, momentous Arctic Treaty. In fact, he had to stage a coup with the help of some of his senior level contacts in the Northern Fleet to remove Gusanov, who had viewed any international understanding on the Arctic as antithetical to Russia's interests. But now, these rogue members of the Russian intelligence community who supported Gusanov and wanted Laptov's removal, claimed to be in possession of enough nuclear material pilfered from several of the former Soviet nuclear sites to devastate London, Paris, New York, and Beijing if their ultimatums were not met.

The news buzz this morning was—much to Hanne's dismay—not about the treaty, but about this horrific threat of the *siloviki,* and the camera showed a crowd of reporters outside the Chateau Laurier, where Hanne knew Pavel was staying. They were all waiting to catch a glimpse of the Russian statesman with the hopes of peppering him with questions about what his reaction was to the demands of his rebelling countrymen, what he would do under the circumstances, would he agree to their demands, and so on. As the newsman droned on and on, Hanne reached for her cell phone, saying, "Richard. Don't you think this is a good time for me to call Pavel? I'm worried about him. Here, I have his personal mobile number…"

"To tell him what, my dear?"

"That   he   shouldn't   give   in.   Under   any circumstances…"

"So that we'll see New York and London blown to smithereens? Come on, Hanne, he has to surrender. He has no choice."

"Matters will evolve. The situation in Russia is changing rapidly. He needs to talk to Barlow—get the Yanks involved. Anyway, how can we be sure that these crazy *siloviki* and their friends have control of all that nuclear material? They could be bluffing, for all we know."

"Well, you wouldn't need much…"

"Okay. In any case, he should talk to President Barlow. And the other world leaders. Most of them are still here. They will all be attending tonight's Heads of State banquet hosted by your prime minister."

"My dear, no doubt your friend Pavel has come to that conclusion himself. But call him if you want," Richard said, getting up from the table. "Another cappuccino?"

"Yes, please," Hanne answered, as she punched the quick dial for Pavel. It took nine rings for the famous Arctic explorer, now a politician to answer.

"Hanne, what is it?" The Russian's voice was anxious, stressed. "I am sure if you are calling it must be urgent."

"Pavel, yes. Just don't give in to the demands of those evil FSB officers. I'm sure the Americans can help…"

"I will be talking to President Barlow at the dinner. He knows what is at stake."

"Pavel, I'm very worried for you. Are you sure things are okay back in Moscow? Your people are still in control? And is it safe for you to return?"

"I am getting hourly reports from Admiral Maslenkov and my other friends. The threat by those *siloviki* in Belarus seems to have unfortunately emboldened some of Gusanov's men—even some in the armed forces. They may be coordinating with them—but so far, we remain in power."

"Pavel, if that changes, you must not go back." Hanne hesitated before continuing. "Come to Greenland, we will look after you."

She heard Richard whisper to her: "They could always come to Canada. We will give them asylum. I'm sure I can arrange that."

From Pavel, a little chuckle, then: "My dear Hanne, that is very kind of you. But my place is back in Russia, no matter what happens."

"Pavel…"

"Now I have to run. Maslenkov is on another line."

"Keep me posted. Please, Pavel. And take care of yourself."

"Of course, dear friend. Goodbye."

And Hanne wondered whether she would see, or hear, from the polar explorer, ever again.

Chapter 2

Ottawa, Canada—Midweek, Late September, 202-

Early the next morning, Hanne said goodbye to Richard. They hugged and kissed with teary eyes, not sure when and where they would be together again. Richard promised to take some days off to come to Nuuk or Copenhagen to see Hanne and she vowed to be back in Canada very soon. But they knew that their relationship would be a difficult one to maintain since they both had such important and fulfilling careers. She, as the recently appointed Minister of Environment and Natural Resources and head of the Geological Survey for a newly independent Greenland, and he, as the one assigned to the new position of Assistant Deputy Minister for Arctic Affairs in Canada's Global Affairs Ministry.

Nevertheless, as she headed for the airport in the Uber that had come all too quickly, Hanne told herself that she would carry on like this for a maximum of two years, but then she would settle down and have children—and Richard certainly seemed to be the right partner for that. Even though marriage would likely mean giving up so, so much on her part, she lamented. But it was the right thing to do—she was not getting any younger. Somehow, they would have to manage to string it out until then. Who knows, though, life sometimes takes unexpected turns, she added as an afterthought.

With this seminal Arctic Treaty behind them—that she and Pavel had made a reality, with some inadvertent input from her ex-boyfriend, Jens, and, of course, help from Richard—there was so much to achieve to ensure that the massive oil and gas and mineral riches of Greenland were only extracted sustainably and with consummate regard for the environment. With the post-independence Chinese money starting to come in to finance much of this, and interest from Russian, European and American governmental and corporate interests, she knew she would have her hands full to make sure all the right regulations were in place and followed religiously. And she would also have to deal with all that legacy pollution the Americans had caused near the Thule airbase she had learned about when she took over her post as head of the Geological Survey… All that on top of the grave dangers posed by climate change and the melting of the polar ice cap.

Then there was this worrying backlash in Russia: after Pavel's swift, unexpected popular revolution, could Gusanov and his reactionary forces regain power in his absence? Surely not—for one, that would be the end of the Arctic Treaty. Also, the imminent elections in the USA did not bode well for the Arctic. President Barlow was way behind in the polls after only one term and the Republican Party's candidate was once again that anti-science, anti-environment, jingoistic industrialist, Ronald Stamp, who for sure would withdraw the US from the treaty. And other treaties too, judging from the past.

Hanne was deeply immersed in these depressing thoughts in the back seat when her cell erupted with the strains of the Dvorak *New World Symphony,* which she had set as the ringtone on the work phone she had been issued.

Pleasantly surprised, she saw on the screen that it was Kristi.

Gorgeous Kristi. Her best friend. Her first love, back in Copenhagen. They had experimented with the physical joys of sex already as teenagers, and just had not been able to stop since.

"Hello, Hanne. How is it going, dear? I miss you so."

"And I, you. It all went superbly, I must say. The treaty is signed."

"Fabulous. So, when are you coming home?" This reminded Hanne that when she took the job in the Greenland government, the agreement with the prime minister had been that she would get to spend some time back in Copenhagen.

"My dear, I'm just on my way to the airport. Here, in Ottawa. To go back to Nuuk. There is a lot I have to do…"

"Then…can I come and see you there? It's been such a long time…"

Hanne paused for a moment as images of Kristi's lithe body and the erotic memory of the two of them making love came into her mind and fought her rapidly developing relationship with Richard, and also—in ways that she resisted—her perception of her role as a minister. But, in spite of their promises, it would be a while now before she would see Richard again, and she knew that, in the end, she could not refuse Kristi…

"Of course, my love. Let me see…I know I'm going to be very busy catching up the first few days next week, but if you come, say…Wednesday, that would be fabulous. Let me know your ETA once you have your flights and I will be there to meet you or send a car."

"Terrific! I can hardly wait."

"Me too. Bye for now," Hanne said, as the Uber pulled up outside the Canada Reception Centre at Ottawa

International Airport. It was here where she was supposed to meet the Greenland delegation to fly back to Nuuk.

And they were there already. Prime Minister Malik Rorsen of Greenland, Hanne's boss and now friend—the gentle Inuit who had placed his trust in the Danish geologist to oversee the development of the newly independent Greenland's resources—greeted her, as, pulling one small bag, she strode over to the three men in their crisp white sweatshirts and black trousers and the single woman dressed in the traditional colorful native ceremonial attire. Hanne wondered how long it would be before she would adopt this rather exotic uniform that all female Greenland officials seemed to wear.

"Hello, Malik." By now, they had known each other long enough to be on a first name basis. "I hope I'm not late."

"No, no, Hanne. Perfect timing. We're just about to board."

"How was your meeting with President Barlow yesterday?" She remembered that Rorsen had a meeting scheduled with the US president to discuss the treaty and the future of the Thule airbase among other matters. Such as the US-caused pollution issues up there: the lingering contamination from the crash of the B-52 bomber carrying four hydrogen bombs in 1968 and the ill-fated attempt to build an under-the-ice military base and missile complex east of Thule in the late fifties and sixties.

"Very good, I must say, although the outcome regarding the future of Thule was not what we expected."

"How so?"

"We agreed that they would turn the base into a scientific center to monitor the melting of the ice cap and assist with all the environmental issues we are facing. But they will also keep a policing capability at Thule to make sure that there are no infractions of the treaty by others. Certainly, their radar—now that they are close to having it back up and working again—should be able to see if the Russians or Chinese…get out of hand anywhere. Not just militarily but environmentally as well."

"Excellent!"

"Also, I emphasized the need for them to clean up the mess they left at Camp Century, you know, the Cold War missile base they tried to establish east of Thule…and that awful B-52 issue. The crash of that plane carrying the nuclear bombs…"

"Great. What was the response?"

"I'll tell you more later."

The flight attendant came just then to get them to board, so Hanne did not have the opportunity to express her concerns of what might happen once a new administration took over in Washington. That also would have to remain unsaid until another time. And who knew—maybe it would all turn out favorably. One could still hope, she consoled herself, as she followed the Greenlanders across the tarmac to the Dash 8-200 jet that had come to pick them up, courtesy of Air Greenland.

Chapter 3

Nuuk, Greenland—Midweek, Late September, 202-

And what of the Arctic now? Hanne mused as she sat, eyes closed across from a sleeping Prime Minister Rorsen on the plane taking them from Ottawa to Nuuk. If Gusanov's counterrevolution succeeds, no doubt the Russians will abrogate the treaty and move aggressively to exploit the riches up there. Their military resources across the north were unmatched and they would pretty well have free rein. Gusanov would no doubt reiterate his claim to the entire Arctic from either end of Russia right up to the North Pole—the old Soviet, and come to think of it, Canadian, Sectoral Principle. And who knows, heaven forbid, maybe even beyond?

Also, what will happen to Greenland, her adopted homeland? Which, now that it had thrown off the colonial yoke and declared its independence, and with its tremendous natural riches, had so much hope, so much new-found energy. It seemed, though, that it was likely to become a battleground: certainly, the Chinese, whose twenty-five-billion-dollar commitment to finance resource extraction had underwritten the polar country's independence and who had already commenced mining operations up at Citronen, were set to play a role. And of course, a Gusanov regime, if the former FSB head regains power—they had already invaded once up north with six submarines, ostensibly to protect Greenland from Chinese incursion. The Americans, too, no doubt wanted in— hadn't they already made a ridiculous offer to purchase Greenland from Denmark under a previous president? Whose successor on the right now seemed like he might be reelected, if all the polls were to be believed.

Just a few days ago, she had been so full of hope, of optimism. Now, Hanne felt that had all been washed away. She knew though, that she could not fall into dejected inactivity. There was so much that needed to be done to stave off disaster for herself, her friends, her new country and the world. Where to start?

ᏉᎠᏉᎠ

After a close to four-hour trip, the Dash penetrated the low cloud cover and landed in Nuuk in pelting rain. Prime Minister Rorsen offered to drop Hanne in Qinngorput, the newest suburb of Nuuk where Hanne's assistant had found a large and bright, fully furnished apartment for her. Before leaving for the momentous treaty signing, Hanne had quickly dropped by to approve of her new digs, and the efficient Aniuk arranged to move her few belongings over from the Hans Egede Hotel during her absence.

"Great job in Ottawa, Hanne," Malik said, as she was getting ready to climb out of the car. "I'm sure you will be comfortable in your new home. When you're settled in, you will have to have Nanurjuk and me over."

"Thanks, Malik. Of course."

"And take the rest of the day to settle in. In the morning,

come by my office for a debriefing over coffee before you tackle your workload. See you then."

"Bye, Malik. Thanks for the ride."

⁊ↄ⁊ↄ

As she waited for the elevator inside the glass front of the lobby, Hanne was glad to be alone after the intense five days in Ottawa focusing on getting the treaty signed and enjoying the pleasures of her budding relationship with Richard. She had so much to do, to sort out, both in her professional life and her personal life—it was overwhelming. Never mind, she told herself: it will all work out, and yes, it was good to have lots going on, as opposed to the boring existence of some of her *confrères* back in Copenhagen.

Once inside the apartment, she kicked her shoes off, and leaving her roller bag in the hall, rushed over to the floor to ceiling windows that looked out over the port, across to the town. The rain had stopped, the sun had come out and the view all around was magnificent—the colorful indigenous houses, the dark blue fjord speckled with whitecaps, and the snow-covered peak, Sermitsiaq, looming behind. She could hardly wait to share it with Kristi, or Richard, for that matter.

After unpacking her smattering of belongings in her new home, showering, and wrapping herself in the fluffy robe she found in the bathroom—Aniuk had clearly taken it upon herself to buy some supplies to make the apartment comfortable—Hanne went out to the combined living room/dining room/kitchen area, flipped the TV on, found the tail end of Euronews and surveyed the provisions in the fridge and the kitchen cabinets. She was glad to see that they were well stocked, although some of the items she found there were not familiar to her. Most importantly though, she was pleased to see six bottles of red and four of white in a standup wine rack, with another two bottles of Argentinian Torrontes—Aniuk must have done some research on her to know this was one of her favorite *cépages*—cooling in the fridge. She cracked one open, poured a healthy dose into a wine glass she took down from the rack hanging above the island, and went back to the living room, making herself comfortable on the sofa to listen to the top-of-the-hour news, which was just about to start.

The lead story was Russia: there were reports of fighting between units of the armed forces—some supporting a freed ex-President Gusanov, who was shown ranting about the treacherous betrayal of Russia's interest in the Arctic, others supporting the troika led by Pavel that had been instrumental in bringing Russia to the table to sign the treaty and the promise of a better future for Russia, the Arctic, and the world. As Hanne uttered an involuntary, "Oh, no!" in response, the reporting moved on to Washington where the camera focused on President Barlow receiving ruling troika member Laptov. Surprised to see her friend in Washington, Hanne said to herself, "Let's hope the Americans can help, Pavel."

She thought of calling the polar explorer but decided it would not be appropriate. He was probably still in meetings or perhaps back at his hotel taking a much-deserved rest. But then she thought that, in fact, if the bilateral discussions were over, and what with the events in Russia, he may already be on his way back home. Somewhere up there in the sky—she wished him well!

Hanne picked up her phone, scrolled down to Pavel's number and without so much as a moment's hesitation, touched it with her forefinger. Sometimes, you just have to go with your instincts, she told herself.

The phone rang and rang, but this time there was no answer.

✃✄✃

Hanne decided to order in for dinner, so she could tackle some of the reading on Greenland's geology and environmental issues that she had taken on the Ottawa trip but had not found the time to get through. Besides, it would be sheer joy, she told herself, to watch night fall over the fjord and the mountains, and—if Aniuk were to be believed—the northern lights dance across the autumn sky from those enormous windows.

She had dozed off on the comfortable sofa after most of the bottle of wine and the pizza she had ordered, when the ding of her cell brought her back with a start. Orienting herself in the dark room, now only lit by the sparkle of the lights from Nuuk, she saw that it was a message from Kristi: "Arriving Wednesday 1:10 pm, GL555. Can't wait to see you!"

"I can't either," Hanne muttered to herself. "In fact, I would love to have your company here right now."

Then, suddenly feeling a spasm of guilt, and since her phone was still in her hand, she clicked on Richard's number. Her Canadian friend picked up immediately.

"Hello, Hanne. I was hoping you would call."

"Thanks. I was just feeling a bit lonely, wishing you were here with me."

"Me, too." And as she heard him say this, a spectacle of dancing colors lit up the sky. Excited, she hummed into the phone, "Especially now, Richard. Wow! The northern lights are performing a ballet for me. You should be here to see it…"

Chapter 4

Nuuk, Greenland—Friday, Late September, 202-

Over coffee in Prime Minister Rorsen's office the next morning, with the TV on low in the background, they discussed the rapidly deteriorating situation in Russia and its implications for Greenland.

"Unfortunately, it doesn't look good for your friend—Minister Laptov—Hanne."

"No, it sure doesn't. And in the end, I don't really know what the Americans can, or will do. Other than provide intelligence."

"You're quite right. I'm sure there is no way they would interfere. After all, it's a Russian internal matter. Although it will certainly affect the world in a big way, if that Gusanov takes over again."

"Yes. So much for our Arctic Treaty then…"

"Well, there's that. But also, he and his *siloviki* buddies are much more belligerent. Those six subs they sent to Citronen in early August almost caused a world war."

"Hmm. I wonder where Pavel is now," Hanne mused.

"Probably on his plane back to Moscow. But that will not end well, I am sure. Poor man."

"I'll try to reach him later. *Á propos* Citronen, I wanted to let you know, Malik, that next week, I intend to go see the progress our team and the Chinese have made on reopening the mine up there. After all that damage my traitorous Danish Greenpeace friends managed to inflict on the site earlier—of course, with the underhanded help of the Gusanov régime!" *Hmm,* she thought to herself after saying this, *I may have to take Kristi with me.*

"Yes, with the warmer climate, they might even be back in operation for a bit if you're lucky. Knowing Derek Tate, the COO of Goldenrod, he would push as hard as possible to try to make up for lost production."

"Well, even if they aren't, I want to examine it for myself to see what still needs to be done. Also, I would like to stop and see the team monitoring Camp Century. And flying over the ice cap will give me the opportunity to assess its condition. The extent of melt this summer."

"Good, Hanne. Let me know where matters stand when you get back. But, no doubt, we will be in touch before then. Oh yes, there is the Cabinet Meeting Monday morning, so I will see you there, will I not?"

"Of course. Thank you."

ოჲოჲ

Once behind her desk, after an impromptu meeting with her senior staff to catch up on all the emerging issues related to the development of Greenland's resources, Hanne settled in to read some correspondence. But, just as she was starting to look at yet another letter from a Chinese government-owned entity interested in obtaining a lease on some offshore oil and gas concession, she heard Dvorak on her phone again. Pleasantly surprised, she saw that it was her Russian friend. Eagerly, she clicked on the green "Accept" button, and said, "Hello, Pavel. Is everything all right?"

"Yes, thanks. We just got clearance to land in Nuuk. Hanne, could I ask you, please, to come and meet us at the airport to help clear the way?" The Russian sounded tired and concerned.

After recovering from a moment of surprise, Hanne said, with a smile, "Of course. I'll be there *pronto*. So glad you're coming here, my friend." She, on the other hand, was pumped: her throwaway suggestion had worked!

ᘒᘖᘒ

On the way down to the parking garage, where she had left the official car she had access to, Hanne dialed the prime minister's number. Fortunately, she got him after just a couple of rings.

"Malik," she said excitedly, "Laptov and his delegation are landing here at Nuuk…"

"Wow! They must know…"

"Yes, I think they got word after taking off that Gusanov is back in power with the help of the intelligence services and whatever segments of the armed forces were loyal to him. I'm on my way to meet them at the airport."

"Good. Let me know what I can do to help."

"Well, I was just thinking that maybe we need to extend asylum to them. At least, to Pavel. I wanted to ask you…do I have your blessing?"

"Of course, Hanne. I trust you will do the right thing."

"Thank you. I'll keep you posted."

"Why don't you bring the minister to my office. In the meantime, I will think of how we can best handle this."

"Sure thing, Malik."

ℭℑℭℑ

As she drove to the airport, a plan started to formulate in Hanne's mind. Clearly, Pavel was a marked man. With Gusanov back in power in Moscow—as the news stations had reported that morning—the rogue president in Russia would have all of his operatives worldwide out looking for the man he hated most now, the polar explorer he had lifted up to be minister of the Arctic, who had then "betrayed" him and "committed treachery" against Russia by giving away their birthright to the Arctic and leading a coup against the rightful government of Russia—at least that was how the former FSB hack would be thinking, Hanne surmised.

So, Pavel would have to go into deep hiding for a while.

And where better than in some remote part of Greenland? Surely, neither the FSB nor the less well-known SVR would have operatives in some little fishing village up in Northern Greenland? It would even be difficult for them to get there to search for him without being noticed! No doubt, Malik could help find the right place.

As for the rest of the delegation, she would ask Richard to arrange for Canada to take them in—they would certainly be more comfortable there. More importantly, it was a good idea to send them there to put the Russians off the scent—they would assume that if Laptov's plane, with the rest of its passengers flew to Canada, Pavel would be on board too. She could even have the officials doctor the paperwork accordingly, no doubt.

Satisfied, she parked in the airport's lot just as she saw

the Russian jet touch down on the brand-new runway financed by the Nordic Investment Bank. She took out her phone as she walked to the terminal and clicked on Richard's number.

"Hello, Hanne. I'm so glad you caught me. I just got out of a meeting with our prime minister. Terrible what's happening in Russia. I fear for your poor friend, Pavel…"

"Yes, in fact, Richard, that's why I'm calling. He just landed here in Nuuk and I'm about to meet up with him. My thought is that we could hide him in Greenland, until the dust settles."

"Good idea, Hanne…"

"What I'm thinking, though, is that the rest of his delegation should fly to Canada—that is, if you would have them. I'm sure they would like it better there, and also, it would help put the FSB and the SVR off the trail. These are all professional scientists or legal experts, Arctic specialists…"

"Perfect. I should have no problems arranging asylum for them all. And when the time comes, for Pavel, too, if he wants."

"Thanks, Richard. I knew I could count on you." As an important afterthought, she added, "And Richard, I love you."

"And I you, Hanne dear."

Chapter 5

Nuuk, Greenland—Friday, Late September, 202-

On the way in from the airport to see the prime minister, Hanne and Pavel discussed the developing situation.

"Boy, I'm sure glad, Pavel, that you did not go back to Moscow," Hanne repeated what she had said in the terminal right after greeting the Russian minister. "You would certainly have been taken prisoner and probably executed on the orders of that criminal, Gusanov."

"When we heard the news *en route* that his co-conspirators arrested Admiral Maslenkov and the others in my government, I had us land here mainly out of concern for my colleagues and crew. I did not want them to face repercussions. But, you know, Hanne, my place is back there. Even though conditions are very difficult there right now."

"No, Pavel. Allow me to disagree. Admiral Maslenkov and your former colleagues are, unfortunately, in grave danger. You know that. And there is nothing we can do for them now. But the world cannot afford to lose you, Pavel, at this critical time, with your environmental expertise and knowledge of the Arctic, and of course the worldwide respect you command. Without you, the Arctic Treaty would never have come together…"

"Well, so much for that," the minister retorted. "I am sure, though, this usurper will withdraw from the treaty, and without Russia, any agreement over the Arctic will have very little…bite."

"Let's see where this all goes. But Pavel, I've been thinking of what might be best for you and your people on the plane…if you'll allow me."

"I am listening…"

"I'm of the view that you—yourself—should stay here in Greenland. For the next little while anyway."

"Haa…"

"Please listen to my reasoning. I'm sure Gusanov will have his operatives out looking for you everywhere. To assassinate you. Yes, just as Stalin did with Trotsky. The least likely place the FSB or the SVR would have informers is in some small fishing village in Northern Greenland. It would even be very difficult for any operatives they might send to get there without a fanfare."

"Yes, you are probably right…"

"And you could even pursue some of your research up there, so it wouldn't be a total waste of your time. In the meantime, we can see how matters in Russia evolve. And wait for the right time for you to go back and replace that usurper."

"But Hanne…"

"Hear me out, Pavel. I've already talked to the prime minister about it, and he will extend political asylum to you and no doubt figure out where it would be best for you to lie low on this vast island. As for your crew and colleagues, I have approached Richard Simpson—you know, my friend, the Canadian Arctic diplomat—and he assures me that his government would more than likely be quite happy to grant them asylum. I'm sure your friends would be keener to start new lives in Canada rather than in Greenland. Or back in a reactionary, autocratic Russia.”

“Yes, on that point, you are no doubt right.”

“Plus, if we can have your plane takeoff from here, say tomorrow, with everybody on board, we might be able to put Russian intel off the trail. We could doctor the papers—I might even be able to get Richard to get them to announce that the entire delegation defected to Canada at this momentous time.”

“Hmm…Hanne, you have certainly thought this through,” Pavel acquiesced, as the car pulled into the government parking lot. “Thank you! You are a true friend.”

“We’ll finalize the details with Prime Minister Rorsen,” Hanne said, opening the door to get out. “He’s waiting for us.”

ოჳოჳ

“Thank you, Prime Minister, for your hospitality,” Pavel said as he stretched out his hand to the diminutive Greenlander.

“My pleasure, dear Minister,” Rorsen grabbed Laptov’s hand with both of his. “As you know from our meetings in Ottawa, I am a huge admirer, and I am very glad to be able to help in these difficult times. But come, let’s sit over here,” he continued, pointing to a low table surrounded by two armchairs and a sofa. “I will have my secretary bring us coffee and something to munch on. You must have missed lunch with all this going on.”

“Malik, if I may,”—Hanne took the floor once they were seated comfortably—“I started to set out my thinking to Pavel—the Minister—that Greenland, that is, you, would be kind enough to extend political asylum to him. And that we might find some fishing village up north for him to hide out for a month or so—or for however long, until it's safe elsewhere. The Canadians—I've already talked to my friend—will take in Pavel's colleagues and the plane's crew. They are less likely to be targeted there by the new regime in Russia."

"That sounds great, Hanne. What do you think Minister Laptov?"

"Hanne's plan is growing on me, Prime Minister—"

"Please, just Malik. And may I call you Pavel?"

"But of course. I was hoping we could use first names."

"The idea is to throw Russian intelligence off the scent." Hanne took the floor. "So, I think that you, Pavel, and the other Russians should all stay at the Hans Egede Hotel for tonight. Tomorrow morning, after you all check out together, we will ferry everybody to the airport, make a big show of your friends getting on the plane. In fact, come to think of it, I will have my assistant arrange TV coverage of us saying goodbye and the plane taking off. But I will just sneak you away and take you back with me to my apartment where you can hide. Until we find a better place somewhere remote for you to hang your hat."

"That sounds terrific, Hanne. And Pavel, I have thought about it—I think I know exactly where you can disappear the best. My sister, Biina, is married to the headman—the mayor of Qaanaaq, the northernmost town in Greenland. I will call her as soon as we are done here, and I am sure she will welcome you with open arms."

"But…"

"Also, Qaanaaq is not far from Thule Air Base and, as it happens, I talked to President Barlow about visiting it and having some discussions with the top brass there. So, this could be a terrific opportunity—and if anyone is watching, also part of our ruse. We will all fly up together.”

“But Malik…”

“Besides, I have been wanting to see my sister for so long now. And Hanne, I will need you there to discuss the environmental issues at Camp Century and the B-52 crash site…plus, this will be a great way for you to see the beauty of our island and examine more of the melting ice cap. Which you would want to do soon anyway.”

“I…I…,” Pavel started again to interject. “Yes, Malik, you are too kind. I accept your kindness and your sister’s hospitality. And, in fact I have heard that Qaanaaq is considered to be one of the first settlements severely affected by climate change in Greenland. So, it will be interesting for me to hear about the experiences of your sister and brother-in-law and others. Also, to assess it first-hand. And compare it to what we are experiencing in the Russian Arctic.”

“Good. So that is settled,” Prime Minister Rorsen continued. “But instead of Monday, Hanne, perhaps we should leave on Sunday. There is nothing urgent on the agenda of the Cabinet Meeting, nothing that can’t wait, but there is a trade delegation from China arriving Wednesday that I would like to be back for, with time to prepare.”

“That works for me.” She was thinking of Kristi arriving on Wednesday.

“It is a long flight to Qaanaaq, so we should leave on the early side.”

“Good. Then let’s aim for, say, 10 am Sunday. And Malik—I was thinking that it would be nice if you and Mrs. Rorsen could come to dinner at my place tomorrow. Saturday. We can finalize the trip details then.”

“Thank you, Hanne. That sounds lovely. It will be wonderful for Nanurjuk to meet you and Pavel.”

"Say…7 pm then. I'm going to take Pavel to the Hans Egede now and we'll meet up Saturday."

഻഻഻

At the hotel, after making sure her friend had no problems checking in, Hanne asked Pavel to summon the pilot of the plane so they could discuss the plans for the rest of the Russians to fly back to Ottawa the next morning. They agreed to meet in the Skyline bar on the fifth floor— which, even as she proposed it, brought back some unpleasant memories.

Hanne went up the elevator to wait for the two men, ordered a glass of the house white, and as she sat there waiting for the waiter to bring it, she could not help but be invaded by the horrific visions of the evening she had spent in this very place with her ex-boyfriend Jens and his Green Liberation Front buddies, and then with Locke, the handsome Australian professor she had thought she was in love with, but who had turned out to be a greedy, treacherous rapist. She shuddered, as against all her efforts to suppress the images, it came back to her how he had assaulted her in her hotel room afterwards and then how he had met a just end when he tried to do away with her up at Citronen.

Men, she thought to herself, *they can be such disgusting and self-destructive creatures!*

And then, to take her mind far away from these distressing memories, she dialed Richard to confirm whether it was go or no go for the Russians to be granted asylum in Canada.

Fortunately, he answered right away.

"Richard, thanks, for arranging this," Hanne said as the

conversation was coming to an end. "So, just to confirm, you can expect them tomorrow mid-afternoon or so. You will get a call from the pilot once they are airborne. And Richard, I'll be flying up north with Prime Minister Rorsen on Sunday and dropping Pavel off in a small village up north. Once my schedule settles down a bit, you'll have to come and see my gorgeous pad—especially those northern lights!" And then she remembered that Kristi was coming the Wednesday when she got back.

"Thanks, dear. I will, of course. I love you."

"And I, you." Hanne was momentarily overcome with guilt. Yes, Kristi was coming and, truth tell, she could hardly wait. She could not help that she liked both women and men—in different ways, of course—but, at some point, she knew, she would have to level with Richard, if things with him were going to go anywhere. Or else, make a choice. One that she was trying to put off as long as possible.

❧❦❧

On her way home from the Hans Egede, Hanne stopped off at Brugseni, the main supermarket in Nuuk, to augment what she had in her fridge for the Saturday dinner party— for one, she wanted to make sure she had some vodka on hand for Pavel, with maybe a couple of extra bottles for him to take up north in what could be an extended exile in a Greenland fishing village. Her friend would be sure to appreciate it, she knew, especially during the long, dark Arctic winter, if he had to stay through it.

When she finally got home, unloaded the groceries and alcohol, she undressed to take a hot shower. While in the stall, she heard her phone ring.

Hanne grabbed a towel as she rushed to get the cell, which was sitting on the night table beside her bed. She saw, as she picked it up, that the caller was Inspector Anders Jakobsen of the Danish police. Unexpected, but it had to be something important if he was calling like this, out of the blue.

"Hello, Inspector…Anders." They had gone to first names over a bottle of her favorite Torrontes during the investigation of the attempted strangulation of Hanne by Jens Anderson, her former boyfriend.

"Hello, Hanne…Or should I call you Madam Minister now? I never had the chance to congratulate you."

"Thank you, Anders. But I'm sure that's not why you're calling."

"Indeed. Hanne, I wanted to let you know that we and our security services have continued to follow Erik Larsen since you put us on to him…" Larsen was a friend and colleague of Jens in the Green Liberation Front, and from what Jens had divulged during his lengthy interrogation after his ill-fated attempt to strangle Hanne, there was some good evidence that they had both been recruited by the FSB. This was when the GLF team members were all held prisoner after a failed mission somewhere off the Russian coast near Murmansk aimed at filming and protesting the launch of yet another Russian nuclear submarine.

"Good…and?"

"Well, you know that instead of coming back to Copenhagen after the Citronen fiasco, he managed to slip our net when he was changing planes in Reykjavik and ended up in Belarus under the name Mikael Resnikov. From there, our sources tell us he joined forces with the Gusanov crowd as their foreign advisor and is now helping the return of those FSB criminals to power."

"The traitor!"

"In fact, we suspect that he may have been one of the three hooded *siloviki* who made that threat of destroying major cities around the world if Laptov doesn't surrender. He has likely been an undercover FSB operative for many years. But more importantly, Hanne, given that he knows you, and knowing that the Gusanov government played a dirty game at Citronen once before, I wanted to give you a heads up."

"Thanks, Anders."

"And more to the point, I have a hunch that this Erik— or Mikael—may want to…to try again to get rid of you, since you know of his past, and with your position, would view you as being in his way. So be extra careful."

"I'm grateful for your intelligence and that hunch, Anders."

"We will, of course, continue to keep an eye on him. After all, Larsen is still a Danish citizen…"

"I owe you, Anders. The Torrontes will be on me the next time."

"That's not all, Hanne, I'm afraid. Your former boyfriend, Jens Anderson, has also disappeared. From the Mental Health Center at Bispjeberg."

"Oh no, you gotta be kidding…"

"Again, we suspect the FSB was involved somehow. Maybe Larsen, too. We will get to the bottom of it though."

"Keep me informed, Anders. For sure!"

A little chuckle, and, "Of course, Hanne, but please, please be careful. I don't want to see a beautiful corpse stretched out in a coffin instead of your smiling face over a glass of wine the next time we meet."

Feeling chilled after the call, Hanne wrapped herself in the fluffy bathrobe, went straight to the kitchen and poured herself a glass of Torrontes, then took the entire bottle with her to the sofa. She wanted to take her mind off the bad news about her two former friends she had just learned from Anders but couldn't stop thinking about it. So, it would seem that both Jens, who had already tried to kill her once on the orders of the FSB, and Erik, who apparently had been complicit in that attempt and was also likely the one who had murdered Sven, Jens' and his colleague at the Green Liberation Front, had been recruited by Russian intelligence. In fact, if, as Anders had surmised, Erik had been one of the *siloviki* threatening to bomb key western cities were Gusanov not reinstated as the rightful president of Russia, he would no doubt have managed to worm his way into Gusanov's close circle. Not only was Pavel now a marked man, but she, too, would be high on their list of targets. She would have to tread carefully and watch her back even more than before.

Damn it, Hanne said to herself as she poured herself another glass and switched around the different TV channels until she came upon an episode of *Ragnarok* that she hadn't seen yet. If anything, that would take her mind off her predicament.

Chapter 6

Nuuk, Greenland—Saturday, Late September, 202-

Pavel and the Russian team of Arctic experts were already at the airport when Hanne arrived. So were a reporter and a cameraman from KNR TV. In fact, in the departure lounge of the brand-new terminal, Pavel informed her that the crew was already on board and minutes from having the plane ready for its passengers. As the cameraman was interviewing one of the scientists, Hanne whispered to her Russian friend that he should leave the building with the rest of the team through the door leading to the tarmac, but then peel off and come around to her car in the parking lot in the front where she would be waiting. And to do this all as unobtrusively as possible. Then they feigned a goodbye in front of the camera and Hanne stood for a moment and watched as the Russians all left the building.

Her plan went off without a hitch. The plane took off with Pavel not on board, and she saw no one in the parking lot when he appeared around the side of the terminal. They drove the short distance back to her apartment.

"What a lovely place you have here, Hanne! And thank you for all of this…you are saving my life, I know." Pavel sauntered over to the big picture window gazing out over Nuuk. "What a view! Gorgeous."

"Wait till the northern lights do their ballet. But I'm sure they've danced for you before."

"Not in Greenland, they haven't. It will be fun to compare."

"Come, Pavel, let me show you to your room, so you can settle in." Hanne took Pavel down the corridor and showed him the sumptuous guest suite, where he would be spending the night. "Once you're ready, come out front and we'll have a light lunch before I have to pack and then start cooking for my prime minister and his missus. And, of course, you, my dear friend, which is a delight. Dinner will be early, since we leave tomorrow in the morning."

"Thank you, Hanne."

☙❧☙

Out front, as Hanne started to throw together a salad and put out some smoked salmon and *rugbrød*, the Danish rye bread she had grown up with, she watched the report on the KNR channel. She was pleased to see that they had picked up on the departure of the Russians for Canada, including her hugs with Pavel and his leaving the terminal with his team, all following the flight hostess who had come to fetch them to board.

"You played that well, my friend," she said as she noticed Pavel watching from the corridor side of the kitchen. "I think we will manage to confuse the FSB at least for a while…as long as none of those on board ends up squealing to the Russian authorities."

"I think my colleagues are all trustworthy. Admiral Maslenkov and I handpicked them. Although I am sure you know that every Russian is for sale."

"True for my Danish Green Liberation Front friends as well, it would seem. But come, let's have a bite now."

ᏝᎧᏝᎧ

Hanne still had the TV on, but low, as she prepared a delicious variation of *bouillabaisse* using freshly caught halibut, redfish, mussels and shrimp, to be followed by her version of *rødgrød,* a Danish red berry pudding her mother had always made, but which she was inspired to prepare with the cloud berries native to Greenland. When the news came on, she turned it up and went to sit over on the couch where Pavel was reading some documents. This time again, the lead item was Russia, and the newscaster was reporting on a press conference in the Kremlin. The camera focused on Gusanov, and the simultaneous translation had him saying, "...abrogate the Arctic Treaty, which was illegally negotiated and signed by my usurper-of-a-predecessor, Pavel Laptov. We formally declare this fake Arctic Treaty null and void. Laptov and his western co-conspirators used a corrupted United Nations process and structured this supposed international arrangement to strip Russia of its natural heritage, the right to the Arctic waters and lands falling in the sector that extends from its northern shore to the North Pole. This territory has been ours since time immemorial and under no circumstances will the Russian people relinquish sovereignty. So, from this moment forward, if any ship, submarine, airplane or vehicle, or indeed intruder of any sort enters this space without our prior permission, we will consider it an act of aggression and shoot to destroy without asking questions. Russia is, always was, and always will be the preeminent

Arctic power and it will never cede this role to anyone.

"Moreover, we understand that the criminal Laptov and the gang of co-conspirators from Russia who went to Ottawa to sign this supposed treaty have asked for asylum in Canada. We hereby demand that the Canadian government send these gangsters back to Moscow to face charges of treason. Let me assure the pretender that he will not evade the justice he rightly deserves anywhere in the world, not even in Canada. There is nowhere he can hide…"

"It seems I was right, Pavel. These crooks will do everything they can to get their hands on you. But our ruse seems to have worked. Better for you to hole up here in Greenland."

"I just hope they will leave my colleagues alone."

"Richard will make sure Canada protects them appropriately, don't worry."

"I will be in his debt…And yours, of course."

❧

Hanne had just stepped out of the shower and wrapped herself in her bathrobe when her cell rang. She immediately saw it was her Canadian friend.

"Hello, Richard. I was hoping you would call."

"Of course. I always love talking to you, my dear. But I also wanted to report on your Russian friends…"

"They arrived okay?"

"Yes. And the RCMP have taken them to a safe house, until their asylum papers can be processed, and we can set them up with new identities."

"Thank you, Richard. I'm sure Pavel will be happy to hear. I knew I could count on you." As an afterthought, she added, "And Canada. You have a great country, indeed."

"Well…I'm pleased to hear you say that. It gives me hope that you will join me here one day."

"Not out of the question, Richard. But there is still so much to do before that…I'm flying up north tomorrow. To Thule and Qaanaaq. Back in Nuuk on Wednesday."

"Have a safe trip, dear. And call when you can."

"Sure. I love you."

"And I you."

ೞೞೞ

"Hanne, this is delicious," Prime Minister Rorsen complimented his minister of Environment and Natural Resources. "You have learned to use Greenland's seafood resources extremely well."

"Thank you, Malik. It's such a gift to be able to eat from the fresh bounty of the Arctic Ocean every day. And I'm very impressed—my colleagues in the ministry assure me that fishing here is done sustainably."

"Of course. As you know, that is one of the key policies of my government. You may not know yet, Hanne, but we actively manage all our fish and seafood stocks. Waste is minimal. We pride ourselves on using at least seventy per cent of any fish, shellfish or other living resource taken from the sea. For the turbot catch, in fact, it is ninety-four per cent, since only the skin and bones are discarded. And Pavel, you will see that in fishing villages like Qaanaaq, even the skin and bones are used for animal feed, so there is absolutely no waste."

"Remarkable, Malik. If only we could be such stewards of nature in Russia," Laptov observed and after a moment's pause, added. "But the chance for that now is next to zero. With this Gusanov crowd."

"Pavel, on another important matter, I spoke to my sister right after our meeting yesterday and she and her husband are delighted that you will come and stay with them. As I mentioned, her husband is the headman in Qaanaaq and there happens to be a vacant little house two doors from them that you can make your home for as long as you like."

"I am truly grateful Malik. I don't know how I will ever be able to repay you. And of course, your sister and her husband."

"So, Hanne, we will first drop Pavel in Qaanaaq—my sister is expecting us sometime in the afternoon—then help orient Pavel in his new home and we can all have dinner together. We will stay with Biina and Aani. In the morning, you and I will fly over to Thule. As I mentioned, I want to check on progress made there to repair the damaged radar and talk to Colonel Sandman, the commander there, about the plans to turn it more into a research center and an Arctic watchdog. And, of course, the difficult Camp Century situation."

"That's a plan, Malik!"

⁊⁊⁊

Hanne's guests had left, Pavel had retired for the night, and she was just finishing the cleaning up, when her phone rang.

"Ron. Ron Hall here." It was President Barlow's well-respected advisor on Arctic affairs in the National Security Council on the other end. Hanne and he had become friends in the lead up to the signing of the Arctic Treaty. He was calling late, but it was two hours earlier in

Washington. "Hanne?"

"Hello, Ron. Good to hear from you…"

"Hanne, I hope I'm not calling at a bad time."

"No…no. Not at all." She knew that it would be something important.

"Well, we're very concerned about the developments in Russia. And, of course, how they affect the treaty we so meticulously put in place. Especially this latest step…its abrogation by Gusanov…how that will impact Greenland."

"I agree. It is all extremely concerning, Ron."

"These rogue Russians will continue to pressure us on leaving Greenland, even though the President and your Prime Minister agreed to turn Thule to peaceful uses."

"Yes, we were very pleased with that."

"But they will no doubt not stop their aggression until the Base is turned back to you and we stop rebuilding the radar. Or who knows, maybe not even then…Gusanov sees Russia as the 'preeminent Arctic power' which could mean anything."

"As it happens, Ron, Prime Minister Rorsen and I are scheduled to fly up to Thule tomorrow."

"Hanne, you might want to discuss this new situation with both your Prime Minister and Colonel Sandman, the commander-in-chief up there. We have just held a session on this in the Situation Room—we will go full speed ahead to finish the rebuild of the radar and we'll be damned if we yield to any Russian pressure." Ron hesitated for a moment before continuing. "But Hanne, I wanted to mention another disturbing development at Thule."

"What's that?"

"Well, it's all very new, so we're not quite sure yet. But Sandman reported to us that since the cruise missile bombing in August and the resulting deeper melting of the icecap and the permafrost then, and the continuing thawing with global warming, several of her men have gotten quite sick, and in fact, she was wanting some of them evacuated. We don't know, but some of our people here suspect that it might be an ancient microbe that has been released by all the melting. So, Hanne, anything you can find out about this for us would be helpful. But for God's sake, be careful up there."

"Wow, Ron that is shocking! Not what I wanted to hear. Of course, we'll see what we can find out. Thanks for the heads up."

"Take care, Hanne. And thanks."

"Bye, Ron. Talk soon."

Hanne had to sit down to digest what Hall had told her. No, this was not good, not good at all.

Chapter 7

Nuuk and Qaanaaq, Greenland—Sunday,
Late September, 202-

The next morning over muesli and cappuccinos, Hanne told Pavel what she had learned from Ron.

"Yes, I am sure Gusanov is going to pursue his bellicose stance. He will be very aggressive on Thule for sure. The radar…the American listening post is a real…how do you say…bugbear…is that the word?…for him. Perhaps he would even use the opportunity of the upcoming elections in the US to take more decisive steps."

"Such as?"

"Obliterate it." He continued without waiting for a reaction from Hanne. "But tell me more about this…this microbe."

"Pavel, it seems they are not sure what it is. Just that several servicemen on the base have become very sick. That's all I know—it's early days. Ron Hall—and a few of his colleagues—think that it could be from some ancient pathogen released from the melting icecap and permafrost. But it's too early to tell. More facts are needed."

"Hmm. Interesting. It could very well be—although somewhat against the odds. We, in Russia, have had some experience with this kind of thing."

"Yes, I seem to recollect that, now that you mention it."

"This is one of the areas of research that greatly interests me…especially after the COVID pandemic."

"Well then, it seems, Pavel, that your expertise will be very useful. I'm sure the Americans will be keen to pick your brains. Maybe you should come to Thule with us…"

"We have had several instances of supposedly 'killer' pathogens escaping from the permafrost in Russia. For example, Hanne, in 2016, up in the far northeast of our country, a twelve-year old boy died, and many others had to be hospitalized with anthrax. Apparently, the boy, who was looking after his reindeer, was infected by one of his herd that had come into contact with some human or animal remains exposed when the permafrost melted. Fortunately, there is both a vaccine and treatment for anthrax. Antibiotics…"

"Lucky it wasn't something else…"

"And a couple of years earlier, a good friend and colleague of mine discovered some hitherto unknown viruses in a thirty-thousand-year-old ice core they were studying. Both these viruses revived in the lab and became infectious, but luckily for us, their targets were amoebas and not humans."

"I was not aware of that…"

"You may also have heard that a few years back, a team of American and Chinese scientists discovered twenty-eight new viruses in a melting glacier in Tibet. And more recently we have found more than a hundred different microbes in the permafrost in Siberia that are resistant to antibiotics."

"Wow!"

"With global warming, Hanne, anything is possible…"

"But you say that it's against the odds…"

"Well, that is the current scientific thinking. As an aside, scientists now estimate that the total biomass of all the microbes encased in glaciers and in permafrost may be more than one thousand times the biomass of all humans on earth. Since these pathogens—whether bacteria or viruses—tend to be broken down by the constant thawing and refreezing that characterizes the active top layer of permafrost, it is unlikely that they would be detrimental to humans. Now, if somehow such a pathogen came from a deeper part of the ice cap, it might be more possible…And although a vaccine for the COVID-19 virus was developed very fast, still, it may take a while to get to an effective treatment and a vaccine. A lot of people could die in the meantime. There is some hope in the generic coronavirus vaccine the Americans are rumored to be working on, but I am not sure where that stands. But, as we saw in some parts of the world, like the USA, not everyone is willing or keen to get a vaccine."

"Indeed, this may be a pathogen from lower down in the ice. Hall implied that there was deeper permafrost melt after the cruise missile hit the Thule radar and some of their experts think this may have had something to do with it."

"Possible…"

"In any case, Pavel, your knowledge will really be appreciated by the Americans in Thule, I'm sure. I will talk to Malik, and we'll alert Colonel Sandman that we will be bringing you along. And of course, we, too, need your expertise since this outbreak is on our territory."

"Glad to be of help."

∽∾∽∾

On the way north, when Malik learned of Pavel's

knowhow, he totally agreed that the Russian should come with them to Thule the next day. They would, nevertheless, stick to their plan of going to Qaanaaq first, to introduce Pavel to Biina and Aani, and to help him get settled in his digs. Then the next morning, they would all make the short hop over to Thule. This new plan had the bonus that they would be able to notify the Americans that the former Russian Minister for the Arctic would be coming with them.

Biina and Aani couldn't have been more welcoming.

"Any friends of Malik are our friends," Biina said, after the couple greeted them at the airstrip just outside Qaanaaq.

"Besides, we have heard so much about both of you," Aani continued. "We, the people of the north, owe you a lot for bringing about this Arctic Treaty. With climate change hitting us so hard, it is desperately needed."

"Well, unfortunately, you may have seen that my countrymen have repudiated the agreement, and without Russia, I am not sure how well it will work," the former Arctic explorer turned minister observed.

Aani and Biina took great care to settle Pavel into the quaint and comfortable fisherman's hut two-doors down from their place. They explained that its owner had abandoned it to seek work elsewhere, as the livelihoods of many here were affected by the warming temperatures. Hunting and fishing out on the ice were getting more and more difficult because of the melting. And Aani pointed to several cracks in the walls of the hut, saying, "These are a result of the thawing permafrost. Most of our homes are affected by it one way or the other. Sad, because I don't know how long we'll be able to continue to live here. Plus, there is the rising sea level to contend with…" As the Inuit couple were leaving to show Malik and Hanne to their spare quarters, Biina invited the Russian to come over for dinner as soon as he was ready.

When they all assembled again, Malik's sister greeted them with a typical Greenlandic tapas tray comprised of dried cod, paté of musk ox, cured reindeer, lumpfish roe, smoked shrimps and chunks of narwhal blubber. Aani cracked open several bottles of Greenland Northern Light Ale, the beer he favored, brewed by Greenland Brewhouse in Narsaq, to the south. The tapas course was followed by *suaasat*, the traditional soup the Inuit of Greenland have been eating for centuries.

As he placed a bowl of the thick, steaming stew in front of Hanne, Aani said, "Takanna!"

Malik translated with a chuckle. "That means, 'Dig in!' "

"This is delicious," Hanne complimented Biina after tasting the dish. "I'd love to have the recipe."

"I learned it from my mother, and she was taught by her mother. The basic ingredient is usually seal, but you can also make it with whale meat, or reindeer, or even some seabirds. You cook it with onions and potatoes—sometimes I add rice—and season it with salt and pepper. You can also put in a bay leaf if you have one."

"Or just about anything else," Malik said, laughing.

"Well, now that I live in Nuuk, I know I can get all the ingredients. So, I'll definitely give it a try, but I'm sure whatever I come up with won't be this yummy!"

Chapter 8

Thule, Greenland—Monday, Late September, 202-

Colonel Sandman was standing at the bottom of the steps in the late morning fog when first Malik, then Pavel, and lastly Hanne deplaned. Hanne was pleased to see that she and her fellow soldiers were all wearing masks—as were they, thanks to Malik handing out N95s he had left over from COVID days just before they landed.

"Welcome to Thule, Prime Minister," the petite brunette officer greeted them. Turning to Pavel, she continued, "And of course, Your Excellency, we are so honored by your presence…"

"Thank you, thank you." A nod and a smile from the Russian minister.

"Indeed, a pleasant surprise! We have been following your efforts to put this much-needed Arctic Treaty in place. And of course, your entire impressive career as a polar explorer."

Then to Hanne, "And we're so pleased to meet you, Ms. Kristensen. We have also stood in awe of your remarkable work to promote peace and sustainability in the Arctic." No wonder this lady was in charge here, Hanne thought to herself, her people skills are certainly well honed.

After touring the facility including the radar, the rebuild of which was close to finished —the work would take maybe another week, ten days at most, before it became operational, Sandman told them—they ended up in the colonel's office.

"Thank you for that informative tour," Malik said. "And thank you for receiving us so graciously. As I mentioned to President Barlow in Washington, there were a number of issues I needed to discuss with you, Colonel. And we understand that you may have some information for us on some recent developments."

"Yes, Prime Minister…"

"We had hoped that with this Arctic Treaty my friends, Pavel and Hanne, worked so hard to make a reality, that the Arctic would be a peaceful region. Much like Antarctica, with the Antarctic Treaty, on which this one is modeled. The problem is that the new populist and nationalist regime that seems to have now replaced Minister Laptov's in Russia has withdrawn from the treaty. As he will tell you, without that country, the agreement is essentially meaningless. It appears we are returning to an era where we will have a more belligerent standoff between Russia and the west. And, of course, China is a third, potentially aggressive, player that seems to have developed an interest in the Arctic."

"Yes, we are very aware of that…"

"So that means that your country certainly will not be keen on yielding this base back to us—and indeed, at least in the medium term, we may have reasons to be able to agree to that. However, we did discuss with President Barlow our mutual aim of developing a strong environmental capability here in Thule. He and I agreed that this is paramount given global warming and the catastrophic melting of the Greenland ice cap. This, and nearby Qaanaaq, are the most northerly settlements on our soil, and we would very much like to house such a facility—with a number of your scientists, and perhaps experts from other parts of the world—at, or adjacent to the base."

"Yes, Prime Minister, I am aware of that initiative. My bosses in the Pentagon and I are in conversation about how best to make that a reality."

"Good. Could we put a time frame on that?"

"Allow me to get back to you."

"Very well, Colonel."

"While we are on the topic, the other issues I wanted to discuss with you are environmental in nature as well. The first relates to Camp Century and Project Iceman, and the environmental mess that was left there by your country. I know you have been periodically monitoring it, but now, as the ice melts, we need to see some action to clean this up. We do not want the pollution encased in the ice to be carried into the sea as the thawing progresses. Perhaps I could have Ms. Kristensen, my Minister of Environment and Natural Resources, work with you—or your designate—to develop a plan..."

"I will talk to my colleagues, and we will get back to you on that as well, if we may..."

"Colonel," Hanne chimed in, "as it happens, I will be coming back up north very soon and could take a day or two to visit the site. Perhaps the appropriate individual or individuals could accompany me to the camp to take stock and start to develop a plan..."

"That makes sense," Colonel Sandman said. "Why don't we firm that up? Let my office know when you will be coming, and I will make sure the relevant people are at your disposal."

"Thank you, Colonel." One more thing for her to put in

her portfolio of things to do.

"Perhaps, Colonel, at that juncture you can also brief Hanne…Ms. Kristensen…on the matter of the lingering contamination from the crash near here some years ago of the B52 that was carrying those hydrogen bombs. And, more importantly, what you are doing about it and what still needs to be done. We need to be in the picture. This is our land. And our sea."

"Of course, Prime Minister. We will set some time aside for that."

"And lastly, Colonel, we understand from a Washington contact of Hanne's that there has been an outbreak of a mysterious infectious disease among some of your people here. That is why we, and I presume you and your compatriots, are all wearing masks now. We would like to know more about this development, and, in fact, that is largely why Pavel—Minister Laptov—is here with us. They have had a good deal of experience in Russia with malevolent microbes escaping from the melting permafrost and he might be able to help."

Hanne noticed that the colonel fidgeted in her seat before she answered. "Yes. You are right, Prime Minister. We have had several instances of my soldiers coming down with severe respiratory and gastrointestinal symptoms, accompanied with high fever and other ills. This is all very new…just the last week or so. The Pentagon flew in two medical officers, and they are doing extensive testing. We suspect it may be some kind of pathogen—it seems viral, like the COVID-19 virus, we don't yet know for sure though—that may have been released by the thawing of the permafrost. Or perhaps by some ice core drilling. Maybe even out at the Camp Century site and brought back to the base. Or with the deeper permafrost melt after that Russian cruise missile attack. Clearly, we are monitoring it closely and the affected individuals are quarantined."

"Yes, it seems like it could be some kind of virus," Pavel spoke up, after listening carefully to the colonel. "The symptoms are not dissimilar from those of COVID-19, as you point out…"

"We believe so as well," Colonel Sandman agreed. "But let's wait for the test results. If it is akin to COVID-19, fortunately now we have vaccines which hopefully could be easily adapted. Although if COVID, these must be breakthrough infections since my soldiers are all vaccinated. But certainly, with the mRNA technology now available, as I say, a vaccine against a new virus should be developed quickly, we would hope. Plus, I believe there is some good work being done on a universal vaccine against coronavirus infections in general."

"Unlikely that it is the same as COVID, even if it is a coronavirus. Especially if the melting permafrost is the origin. But, as you say, let's see." Pavel was skeptical. "And maybe there is hope in a universal vaccine, as you say, Colonel."

"Please keep us posted, Colonel," Malik weighed in. "It is of utmost importance for our people that we know what is happening, and more importantly that you take all the actions necessary to limit its spread."

"Of course, Prime Minister."

Chapter 9

Greenland—Tuesday, Late September, 202-

Back in Qaanaaq the next morning, Hanne found the farewells after breakfast difficult—first with the kind Inuit couple who had been so welcoming, but then especially with Pavel, who had become such a close friend. She had committed to come back up to Thule and possibly Qaanaaq in a few days, but she knew the Russian was now a fugitive hunted by his malevolent compatriots. Although in good shape mentally and physically, he was no longer a young man. Plus, there was this new risk from the mysterious microbe, and life in the Arctic was normally tenuous at best. So, she feared for his safety and wondered each time they parted whether she would see him again.

On the flight back to Nuuk, Malik asked Hanne to join him for dinner with the Chinese delegation the next evening. Feeling conflicted, since Kristi was arriving in the afternoon, and knowing that matters in Greenland were less formal than back in Denmark, Hanne hesitated a moment before answering, "Of course, Malik. But would it be all right if I bring a friend?"

She saw the prime minister was somewhat taken aback

though that she would want to bring a date to an official business dinner. "Sure, Hanne…"

"My oldest girlfriend happens to be arriving tomorrow and I don't want to leave her alone on her first evening in Greenland. I promise she won't get in the way of our discussions."

"Of course, of course, Hanne. I am sure the Chinese will be pleased to have another beautiful Danish woman join us…"

"Thank you, Malik."

"Hanne, we will need to be prepared to discuss—at least on a preliminary basis—how we propose to spend the twenty-five billion dollars they have committed to develop our natural resources. No doubt, they will have their own ideas, but we need to be ready to put our priorities on the table. I certainly want sustainability and the environment at the forefront of everything we have them do with us."

"Definitely, Malik. No doubt they will be focusing in the first instance on Citronen, which is already underway. I'm sure they will want to do much more though. But I'll get some thoughts together for you by the morning and we can discuss them then. By the way, who is on their delegation, do we know?"

"Well, I know it is led by a Professor Li…"

"Oh, that man! He's one of their experts on the Arctic. In fact, he is still on that UN Commission on the Limits of the Continental Shelf that awarded us the shelf along the Lomonosov Ridge." The professor had been a colleague of Lock's in Beijing, the very one she suspected of being the intermediary in buying his vote to award the sub-sea shelf rights to Greenland so that China could exploit the resources there. But that was history, and Lock would not be part of the delegation. Her Australian lover-turned-rapist was dead.

"So, it seems he views our interests favorably?" The prime minister asked.

"As long as they coincide with China's, I'm sure. I guess we will see what they want going forward."

കൈരു

For much of the rest of the trip, Hanne worked on the first draft of a paper outlining what Greenland's priorities should be in their discussions with the Chinese delegation. She would put the finishing touches on it the next morning and get some input from her staff whom she had come to trust and like in the short time since her appointment as minister of Environment and Natural Resources.

She also spent some time dozing off and daydreaming about Kristi and what they would do when she arrived. Tomorrow. Hanne could hardly wait. Too bad about the dinner—but she could not get out of it. And it was important for Greenland. They would have to indulge in their pleasures around work. Come to think of it, she had better tell Kristi to bring some evening clothes.

And then, Thursday maybe they would both fly up to Citronen together. That could be entertaining for Kristi, and it would give her a chance to be with her and to get a head start on the following week, since now she had to drop by Thule again. And Qaanaaq, too—she would want to see Pavel, how he's doing. Kristi would certainly get a whirlwind tour of Greenland.

Reminder for herself: also tell her friend to bring appropriate cold weather wear to go north.

കൈരു

Back in her apartment in the early evening, Hanne took a long shower, relishing the sensation of the warm water stroking her body. Getting out, she glanced at herself in the full-length mirror as she reached for a towel. She was pleased with what she saw: despite her heavy work schedule in recent weeks, she had managed to stay fit and maintain her lithe, well-toned curves. After she combed her hair and creamed her body—another sensual experience she enjoyed—she put on her bathrobe to go to the kitchen to reward herself with a glass of Torrontes before settling on the couch in the living room in front of her laptop to write a quick message to Kristi.

Done, Hanne found the remote to turn on the TV and clicked to KNR news.

It was all about Russia again. The newscaster was reporting on a press conference held by President Gusanov in the Kremlin demanding that the Americans return Thule to Greenland and the Chinese leave the newly independent country forthwith. "The Arctic must remain neutral!" This, from a rogue populist leader who had claimed half the Arctic—the half without Greenland—all for Russia. Were these mere empty threats, or would the Russians take action if the Chinese and Americans ignored them?

Like the last time…

Just then her phone rang. It was her American friend, Ron Hall, again. As she touched the "Accept" button on her iPhone, she remembered that he had asked her to report on what she had found out up in Thule.

"Ron, I was just going to call you. To tell you about Thule. And the virus."

"That's not what I'm calling about, Hanne. We just had Sandman's report, so we are up on status."

"Oh?"

"I just came from the situation room, and we are very

concerned about the Russians. Gusanov and his gang, that is."

"So am I…"

"Well, we think that they are unhappy about the inroads the Chinese are making in Greenland. And, of course, the rebuild of the Thule radar, which, as you know, is almost complete. We are worried that they may do something stupid…like the last time."

"You mean Citronen?"

"Yes. And trying to take out our radar."

"That's pretty serious. We came very near to World War Three, didn't we?"

"Indeed. And some of us here in Washington think they may travel down the same road again…By the way, it seems that your friend, the Russian Minister Laptov has gone missing. The entire delegation he brought to sign the Arctic Treaty has ended up in Canada and we thought he was there too…but intelligence noise tells us that Gusanov and his gang have been looking for him. Is he with you in Greenland, Hanne? Because if he is, that may be another reason for them not to be too friendly with your country. They seem desperate to find and eliminate him."

Hanne hesitated a moment but decided to be non-commital and treat the question as rhetorical. "Just for your information, Ron, I'm going back up to Citronen on Thursday and then on to Thule from there early next week."

"Good. Very timely. But be careful. And keep us informed."

"Of course. Of course. You, too, if anything comes up."

Chapter 10

Nuuk, Greenland—Wednesday, Late September, 202-

In her office, Hanne packed up quickly; she knew Kristi would already be at the apartment. Her friend had messaged, "I just landed!" as the plane taxied to the terminal at Nuuk airport. The meeting with Malik had taken longer than she had hoped, but they had honed their approach to the Chinese for the dinner that evening to his and her satisfaction. They would allow them to help speed up the on-going operations at Citronen and start work next summer on one other mine on the western coast.

Kvanefjeld, probably. Rare earths, just what the Chinese wanted more of—a global market they had already cornered, so they wouldn't want any mines not in their control opening up. It had uranium, too, another plus for the Chinese. But, sure to be the subject of intense negotiations. Though already majority owned by a Chinese company, Shenghe Resources, but the mine was still on Greenland territory. However, they would have to tread carefully because the twenty-five billion dollars committed by the Chinese to the development of the Greenland economy was what had allowed Rorsen to break away from Denmark. It would not be good to have the Chinese suddenly revoke their promise.

At the very least, Kristi would get to see her in full power mode.

ᘔᘔᘔ

Hanne fumbled with the key to unlock the front door, and when she finally succeeded, there was beautiful Kristi in her birthday suit—nothing on, naked, arms outstretched, ready to embrace her, with a huge smile on her face.

"Well, you sure took your time to get here to welcome me, Ms. Minister," her friend said with a big smile as Hanne dropped her backpack—forgetting that her laptop and all her precious work papers were in it—to eagerly hug her very first lover. The kiss was deep, their tongues explored, and hands roved all over as Hanne guided the lithe body she so lusted after into her bedroom, at the same time scrambling to undress herself. They could, it seemed, never get enough of each other.

The loving was superb, as always, and it did not take them long to reach orgasm almost in unison once they assumed the sixty-nine position. Gathering herself after the ecstasy, Hanne moved up and kissed her friend on the mouth once again before lying on her back in the big double bed.

"So," Kristi began, "you have roped me into a business dinner with some horny Chinese. Tell me, Hanne, what is my role going to be…am I your date? Can I feel your inner thigh under the table, or will I have to talk about open pit mining all night?"

"You can do both if you like, but you won't have to say much beyond just pleasant conversation," Hanne answered with a little laugh. "And, of course, looking sexy and wowing all the Chinese officials. I know, my dear, you will have no problems with that!"

"Well, I guessed that's what you would want, so I brought that little dress you really like."

"Lovely. I knew I could count on you," Hanne said, as she planted another kiss on her high school friend's lips. Then on her ample breasts. And she moved lower, as she began to fondle Kristi's nipples…

◦◦◦

The delegation was, in fact, led by the Chinese Minister of Natural Resources, Huang Changdu, and besides Professor Li, also included the Special Representative for the Arctic, officials from the Ministries of Foreign Affairs, Defense and Public Security. Representatives of China Non-Ferrous Metal Industry's Foreign Engineering and Construction Company Limited, the company active in Citronen, and Shenghe Resources—so clearly Kvanjefeld would be of interest—rounded out the nine-person team.

The two friends arrived a few minutes late at the historic Hans Egede House where official functions were held, because Kristi needed more time with her make-up than Hanne had allotted. As they were ushered into the dining room, Hanne took great delight in seeing that all the eight men and one woman in the Chinese team did a double take as the two stunning Danish beauties strutted in on their high heels, sheathed in low-cut, mid-thigh dresses. *Perhaps not entirely appropriate for a state dinner with the Chinese, but fuck it, Kristi and I go back a long way,* Hanne thought to herself as she glanced over toward Malik and her colleagues to judge how much they disapproved. *Eat your heart out. Or whatever…*

"How lovely to see you again, Ms. Kristensen," an unctuous voice addressed Hanne from among the Chinese team members. It was that despicable Professor Li, of course. "You look even more beautiful than you did when we first met at the United Nations."

"Why, thank you, Professor Li," Hanne retorted, ignoring his lascivious look.

"Allow me to introduce your counterpart in China, Mr. Zhang Changdu, now that you are the Minister of **Environment and** Natural Resources in Greenland." Hanne did not know whether this was a put down or a compliment. "And who is this lovely lady?" the Professor continued. "…Minister of…?" The sarcasm in his voice was caustic.

"My friend, Kristi, is visiting from Copenhagen," was Hanne's curt reply.

"Delighted to make your acquaintance, ladies," this from Zhang. At least he was smoother, Hanne thought to herself.

After introductions, and pleasantries over champagne and Greenlandic tapas, the two teams were seated at the longish table, the nine Chinese on one side with Zhang Changdu in the middle, the four Inuit and the two Danish beauties on the other, with Malik in the center and Hanne on his right. With the fish soup served, a silence descended on the group.

"Mr. Prime Minister, we were delighted you could receive us on such short notice," the Chinese minister opened the official part of the conversation as the white wine was poured. "Thank you."

"We are honored that you have come to visit our country," Malik replied, "and grateful for the help and financing China has offered to develop our resources. We want to ensure, of course, that this is all done sustainably and with the utmost regard for the environment and wildlife."

"We are here to spell out in greater detail, how we would like to proceed," the Chinese minister continued somewhat icily. "We would like to fast track five mines and three offshore oil and gas developments…"

"Mr. Minister, if you will allow…," Malik jumped in to show that Greenland would not be dictated to. "Ms. Kristensen has worked out this detailed plan,"—and he pushed the bound document that Hanne and her team had finished that morning across the table—"that we believe makes the most sense, taking into account both our countries' interests…"

"My dear Prime Minister," Zhang Changdu looked and sounded a mite chagrined at being interrupted, "we have very ambitious plans for our cooperation here in Greenland. This is our development plan," and he pushed a much thicker bound document across the table. "We also envisage bringing teams of engineers and experienced mining and oil and gas experts to your shores to help us achieve this plan. And we want to establish a campus of Tsinghua University focusing on science and engineering here in Nuuk with students and professors from both our countries…Professor Li has been chosen to head it up. And perhaps Ms. Kristensen and…your…her friend could teach here as well."

At this point, as Kristi sniggered, Hanne felt she had to intervene: this Chinese "plan" seemed to be the equivalent of a total takeover. They would be swamped with Chinese—probably more of them would come than the entire population of Greenland and the country would become a Chinese province. Or colony.

"Thank you, Mr. Minister. We appreciate your thoughts. However, our intent is to proceed slowly and carefully. Greenland is a new country with a small population, and we have no desire to develop more than the two mines and possibly two or three oil and gas wells outlined in our plan over the course of the next few years. We see China's commitment to help financially as one that will last for many years and not be expended in one or two years."

"Please reflect on these matters after you read our document," Zhang retorted frostily. "The commitment of twenty-five billion dollars was to carry out this strategy."

Malik saw that the conversation was getting too heated and heading in an unpleasant, indeed dangerous, direction. "Thank you, Mr. Minister. We will indeed study your plan and wish you do the same with ours. Perhaps there is a middle ground somewhere that we can agree on. But, as I said at the very outset, for us, the protection of our people, our way of life and environment and wildlife is paramount and takes precedence over rapid development. Please bear this in mind. Now, if you will permit, I will have our chef serve the special Greenlandic dessert…"

മ⁊മ⁊

After the Chinese left, Malik asked Hanne—and Kristi—to stay for a quick debrief.

"What the Minister proposes would be a total takeover of Greenland," Hanne said, still seething. "And rampant destruction of our environment. We would become a *de facto* colony of Beijing, for them to exploit as they wish. They would inundate us with so-called Chinese experts, many of whom, in fact, would be military or secret service. We cannot allow this."

"Now, now, Hanne," the prime minister said. "We need

to proceed slowly. I see that as merely a negotiating stance. We do not want to lose the twenty-five billion…"

"Malik, allow me to differ. We do not want their money if that means losing Greenland's hard-fought independence and the destruction of everything your people hold dear. This time, the "masters" in this relationship would be a much more powerful country and would not have such a benevolently paternalistic attitude toward Greenland as Denmark did. They would swamp any semblance of sovereignty and freedom this young country has won. Let alone the damage their focus on rapid development would do to Greenland's pristine environment, already so under threat with climate change. No, we cannot agree to this, at any cost."

"Well, maybe you are right. But perhaps we should try one more time with them before we give up all the money…"

"You're in charge, Malik," Hanne conceded, "but at least let's wait before we do anything until I get back from up north. I plan to leave tomorrow morning for Citronen and then Thule."

"Good idea…In the meantime, I will look at their document."

"If you don't mind, Kristi and I will be off now. I'll take this copy of the Chinese strategy with me to read on the plane." She picked up one of the extra copies of the plan Professor Li had left on the table when the Chinese left.

And as she and Kristi hurried out of the historic Hans Egede House to enjoy each other in Hanne's king size bed, Hanne had a fleeting thought: maybe these recent developments with the new virus up in Thule could be used to put the Chinese off…Hmm. Worth thinking about.

But now there was delicious Kristi beside her…and the prospect of a night of love awaited.

Chapter 11

Citronen Fjord, Northern Greenland—Thursday,
Late September, 202-

The night was magical, and neither Hanne nor Kristi slept a wink, but they both got some much-needed shuteye on the flight up to Citronen. Hanne did, however, flip through the Chinese development plan and thought more about the tactic of using the microbe-induced illnesses in and around Thule to scare the Chinese neo-colonizers off the notion of proceeding too quickly with their development plans. The idea did need more reflection though, and discussion—perhaps even with Pavel, and certainly with Malik.

Lost in her thoughts, Hanne gazed out the window and observed the surface melt on the ice—although it was no longer high summer in the Arctic, the fact that she could still make out puddles at the end of September, was an ominous sign of the warming that was taking place in the polar zone. If there were puddles, even veritable ponds, on top of the ice, Hanne thought to herself, the damage down below would be huge, and even more concerning. The icecap was degrading at an extremely rapid pace, and this did not bode well. And it meant the inevitable rise in sea level too, which would threaten coastal communities.

She was happy though, when the plane finally started to descend, and the pilot announced that they would be landing in ten minutes. It was mid-afternoon, Hanne noted, checking her watch, so there would be a few more hours of daylight, but she resolved to leave climbing up to the mine until the next day.

"We're almost there!" she said, nudging Kristi awake. "There is the little mining settlement. And…see the fjord!"

"How beautiful!" Kristi rubbed the sleep out of her eyes.

The Dash-8 just managed to pull up right at the very end of the makeshift runway and taxied back to where Hanne had noted an all-terrain vehicle waiting. As she and Kristi climbed down the steps, she recognized Derek Tate, the COO of Goldenrod Mining, the Australian company in partnership with the Chinese, getting out of the driver's seat.

"Welcome, welcome," Tate greeted them. "We're glad you have come to visit us again, Hanne." She noticed that he could not take his eyes off Kristi, so she laughed and said, "Derek, meet my best friend from Copenhagen. Kristi Olafson. She's visiting me, so I thought I would bring her along to see the country. And your operations."

"Splendid! Welcome Ms. Olafson, welcome to Citronen."

"Thanks, Derek," Hanne responded. "We won't take much of your time, but perhaps you can give us a status report sometime today and then tomorrow we can have a look around. As you know, this is such an important showcase project for Greenland…it's essential we get it right. Both from an output and an environmental standpoint."

"Yes. Of course, Hanne. But first, allow me to show

you and Ms. Olafson to your quarters. I'm pleased to let you have my little hut again and we will bring an extra cot in for Ms. Olafson."

"Please, just Kristi. And thank you."

"And Derek for me."

തൈൽ

After settling in, the two ladies joined Derek Tate and Huang Bao, the head of the Chinese team in the dining tent, where, over a beer, they were briefed on progress made at the mine. The open pit operation had been working well the entire summer, and both Tate and Zhang expressed satisfaction at the quantities of zinc ore extracted and shipped. But they showed their exasperation with the damage Hanne's and Kristi's erstwhile Danish Green Liberation Front friends had caused to the entrance of the underground mine they had been developing and hoping to bring into production during the past summer.

"The road up there is all done now, and we've reopened the entrance, but we're still finishing the clean up inside. We'll take you up there tomorrow morning, so you can see for yourselves. That bomb your Danish nationals let off was more powerful than we originally thought."

"Yes, my stupid countrymen were misled by the Russians…"

"The Russians?" The Chinese executive's interest was piqued. "Of course."

"Yes. The Green Liberation Front bombers had been given a much more powerful explosive by their Russian masters than they were led to believe. Lucky no one was killed in the blast."

"Other than the Australian Professor working with us,"

Huang Bao retorted. "That was when he died, they told me."

Hanne glanced at Kristi but ignored the comment. Only her best friend and Richard knew that she had accidentally tripped Lock as he tried to push her over the cliff and he had gone over instead, falling to his death. That had nothing to do with the blast, though.

"Let's take a gander through the camp now and we'll show you where we load the boats," Derek Tate broke the silence. "And then we can come back here for some supper."

❧❦❧

After dinner, Hanne and Kristi found it difficult to take their leave of the executive mining team—who tried everything to get the beautiful Danish women to stay. But finally, they did manage to get up and excuse themselves, and went outside in the dark to find their lodgings by flashlight. The hut—which was really no more than a glorified tent—was well heated, but the cots, placed on either side of the structure, were narrow and somewhat flimsy.

Having ascertained all that by the dim light, they looked at each other, burst out laughing spontaneously, and knew that they would not—could not—resist. As soon as they had turned the lights out—save one gas lamp—Hanne and Kristi kissed passionately, helping each other undress, and threw their parkas and other items of clothing on the floor. In her undies, Kristi then ripped the sleeping bag off her cot to cover the pile and pulled the by now naked Hanne down with her. They giggled, whispering about the strangeness of the two of them making love in the high

Arctic in a flimsy tent that could not be locked, with probably a hundred or so sex-starved men cramped in their own little spaces in the camp, perhaps watching as their larger-than-life shadows played erotically on the tent's canvas—Kristi suggesting lewdly, with a laugh, that most of them would no doubt be masturbating. The girls helped each other reach orgasm with as little noise as they could manage—other than the final release, which they hoped would not be heard in the neighboring tents—and then snuggled into their own flimsy cots for blissful sleep.

Chapter 12

*Citronen Fjord, Northern Greenland—Friday,
Late September, 202-*

After an early breakfast, by the time the sun rose, Hanne and Kristi were ready for the ride up to the entrance of the underground mine. But they were not quite prepared to be driven to the nearby helicopter pad, where a chopper was waiting for them, rotors already turning.

They ducked and climbed aboard, followed by Tate and Huang Bao, and the chopper lifted off even as the Goldenrod COO closed the door. They were delighted to see again the inlet and the vast open land and ice, dotted with human activity immediately below.

After a few minutes, Tate shouted, "There, there! That's where we're headed." Hanne could make out a dark opening in the rockface with a wide road leading up to it from the camp. She looked to see if she could glimpse the spot where Lock had gone over the cliff and shuddered when she saw the top of the ladder they had climbed to get up here the last time, right next to which her former lover charged at her. With the rush of memories, she looked away quickly as the helicopter made its rapid descent and landed on the roadway just in front of the large aperture in the rock.

It was just a few meters walk to the mine and, as they entered, Tate switched on a lighting mechanism that lit up the dark cavern.

"This is all new, and actually, we're quite proud of how rapidly the rebuild has been going. Bao and his colleagues have been tremendous to work with."

"Good teamwork, yes, Derek?" Huang's face brightened with an inscrutable smile.

"The best," was the Australian's answer, patting the Chinese executive on the back. "Hanne, you can see that we have opened up the works all the way down to the large zinc vein. Which starts there." He pointed to a rock seam of a different color, glistening greenish black, and distinguishable fifty feet or so farther in, on the ceiling at the end of the lit up "cave".

"Terrific. So, you should be able to start extracting the ore here very soon. And I see that you are minimizing damage to the environment both in here, and with your activities outside."

"Yes, well, we try to put back as much of what we can. And, at this point, we'll probably wait to start underground operations until next spring. But we'll see. It all depends on the weather now."

"It's impressive. Thank you for showing us. I will report back to the Cabinet. They'll be pleased, I'm sure."

They headed out, but before boarding the chopper, Hanne overcame her apprehensions and took Kristi's hand to lead her over to the cliffside near the head of the ladder to show her the magnificent view. But as they looked out over the fjord, Hanne's chin dropped, and she whispered, "What…what's that? What the f…no, not again," pointing to a submarine that was just that very moment breaking the surface. And then, "Holy shit!" as she gawked in disbelief at the *déjà vu,* while a second, then a third, fourth, fifth and sixth sub emerged from the deep. "Derek, Bao, come quick! See this!" But the two did not hear her yells above the din of the helicopter.

It was only when they were in the chopper and Hanne grabbed Tate's shoulder and pointed frantically to the Russian submarines that the Australian and the Chinese executives got excited.

"We must get down quickly," Hanne heard Huang say, even as Tate instructed the pilot to head to the waterfront. Their eyes remained glued to the six vessels, which by then were disgorging two rubber dinghies each, filled with probably ten armed men in every one, Hanne estimated.

The Russians were back, just as Ron Hall had suspected…but she was sure going to protest their uninvited intrusion. Or…invasion?

❧❧❧

They stood there on the beach as the first of the small boats landed and the soldiers jumped off, some holding guns pointing at them. As they approached, Hanne did a double take: she recognized the two men in front.

"Well, well, well. If it isn't my two lovely friends from Copenhagen," Erik said, with a chortle. "I figured I might bump into you, Hanne, on this vast godforsaken island— since you're now a Minister here—but I didn't expect it to be here at this mine. And for the life of me, I did not think I would see you, Kristi."

"I certainly didn't expect you, Erik," Hanne replied. "What in heaven's name brought you here? And in a Russian sub?" She looked at Kristi, knowing of the brief and troubled relationship the two had had a couple of years back. She saw that her friend was shaking.

"Well, Hanne, you may be surprised, but President Gusanov put me in charge of this expedition to rid Greenland of foreign powers and interference and to ensure that it truly is independent…"

"Oh, good lord, so is this a Russian invasion?" Hanne asked facetiously. "We don't need a Russian force to occupy Greenland to replace its former colonizers. We will choose who we allow to work with us. So please collect your men and go back to your submarines and get the hell out of our waters."

"No chance of that," Erik retorted. "You can't make me…I have Russia's full force behind me."

Hanne, in a huff, turned to the handsome soldier beside Erik, and said, "Captain Zaitsov, we have met before, too. In somewhat similar circumstances, I must admit."

"Yes, indeed, Ms. Kristensen. I am delighted to see you again." And then, snapping his heels, he said, looking at the other three, "Captain Pyotr Zaitsov of the Fourth Submarine Brigade of the Russian Northern Fleet."

"Huh," Erik struggled to take control. "It is what I said it is, Hanne. We are here to guarantee Greenland's independence from foreigners. Until our aims are achieved, we will be taking control of matters here. We also have a substantial naval force further south backing us up. In fact, a large part of the Russian navy—certainly the Northern Fleet—is now surrounding the entire island of Greenland. And I am provisional Governor, for lack of a better title, till matters are settled." The Dane paused a moment as he looked at Tate and Huang. "Hanne, who are these two men?"

"Derek Tate, COO of Goldenrod."

"Huang Bao. China Non-Ferrous Metal Industry's Foreign Engineering and Construction Company

Limited."

"Well, Mr. Huang, you are under arrest. You and your compatriots need to gather up your things and leave by the end of the day. You can fly to Nuuk and home from there. Or just swim from here if you choose…" The Dane laughed at his sick joke. "You, Mr. Tate, are welcome to stay, but must work with our men to see what needs to be done here…"

"But…" This from the Australian.

"No buts, Mr. Tate. Otherwise, you too, will be expelled." Then, turning to the ladies, "And the Misses Kristensen and Olafson will be my special guests for now. Come, we will all accompany my men up to the camp."

⌘

The mining settlement was swamped by the more than hundred armed Russian soldiers, the Chinese were rounded up and Erik ordered Hanne and Kristi to stay in the tent with a guard outside until he came back.

As soon as they were left alone, Hanne knew she had to act quickly. She would only have one chance to make a call via the radio phone on Tate's little desk. She debated over whom she should prioritize: Malik, Richard or Ron Hall? She decided on the American, although she felt badly, knowing that she should be briefing Rorsen, her boss.

Fortunately, the call went through almost immediately. Hoping the guard outside would not hear, she whispered into the receiver, "Ron. Glad I got you…"

"Hanne…"

"I don't have time, Ron, and I may have to hang up at any moment, so please listen. Six Russian subs arrived at

Citronen an hour or so ago. An invasion, once again, as you foretold. A naval force down south, apparently, too. And possibly Russian vessels surrounding all of Greenland. Supposedly in charge here this time, is Erik Larsen, a Danish traitor who was coerced into working for the Russians and has—according to what he says—been appointed provisional Governor of Greenland by Gusanov, until they rid it of all foreign interests, as he puts it. The Chinese miners have been arrested and are being sent home via Nuuk. My friend and I are under guard in the Goldenrod COO's tent—hence the radio phone. We have no idea what will happen here, but I believe Thule is under threat again and, as I mentioned, the Russians may be sending a separate force to Nuuk and elsewhere around the island. Please warn Prime Minister Rorsen. I may not be able to call him."

"Hanne, take care of yourself…"

Indeed, just then, Hanne saw the guard poke his head in, then rush into the tent, gun pointing at her, yelling something in Russian, before he came over and ripped the radio phone out of her hand and shoved her into the desk chair.

❧❦❧

Erik was back before the hour was out, with two burly soldiers carrying Kalashnikovs and Captain Zaitsov in tow.

"Now, my dear Hanne, we need to have a serious conversation." The repulsive Dane made himself comfortable on one of two chairs, stretching his legs out in the crowded space. "You know that my new boss President Gusanov sent me here, and my main mission is, as I said, to make sure that all the vile foreign colonial occupiers and interests are removed from Greenland. But he also entrusted me with one other important task: to find the traitor, Pavel Laptov. The man disappeared on his way back to Russia from Ottawa, where he tried to surrender Russia's sovereignty over the Arctic at that conference to sign some dodgy treaty you and he put together. That treaty is now dead. Haa!"

"A treaty to save the Arctic along the lines you and your Green Liberation Front friends were advocating…Before you sold out to the Russians."

"Forget it, Hanne. What the fuck do you know…" He paused a moment and looked her in the eye before continuing. "Some of my colleagues in the SVR and the FSB have reason to believe that the traitor Laptov may be hiding somewhere here in Greenland. In fact, we know he and his team landed in Nuuk on their way back and there is a television report on some local news showing you and Laptov hugging at the airport. Were you lovers with that old geezer, you whoring cunt?" He paused to chortle at his sick joke, "And then we see him leave the terminal with the rest of the Russians for the plane and whoosh, it takes off. Canadian records show him landing in Ottawa, but we cannot find him anywhere there. Unlike the rest of his team. Now, you wouldn't have helped the jerk stay here and you wouldn't be hiding him, would you, my dear?"

"I have no knowledge of any of this. I just do my job as Minister of Environment and Natural Resources here in Greenland."

"Aha! No longer, my dear. You are nothing but my prisoner now. And you know what—I think you know more about Laptov's whereabouts than you let on. After all, my sources tell me that you and he became quite good friends. If not lovers as I suggested…So why don't you be a good girl and tell your very old friend where that imposter is keeping himself?"

"I know nothing of Laptov. Or where he might be. As far as I know, he left Ottawa and is on his way back to Russia," Hanne lied, hoping that she was convincing.

"Well, my dear, I'm sure you are aware that we have ways to make you tell us what you know. Your former boyfriend, Jens—who, by the way, you will be delighted to know, is now working with our team in Moscow and is on his way to Nuuk—must have told you about some of the persuasive techniques of the FSB." Erik paused to let this sink in before he continued as he stood up. "My friends here and I are quite willing to use these methods on you, you should know. We could even, for example, start with Ms. Olafson here, couldn't we?" Erik walked over to where Kristi was sinking into her chair, sat on her lap and grabbed her by the chin. "You and I have always had a particular thing for each other, you gorgeous little thing…" His face was now very close to Kristi's and he tried to plant a kiss on her lips, but she turned her face away. "Yes, you are beautiful, at least for now, but a little workover could change that very quickly. And, no doubt, give my colleagues here great pleasure. Also, me, of course. But it would be a real shame to mark-up this lovely face…"

"Sir…," Zaitsov interrupted.

"Be quiet, Captain. This is none of your fucking business." And then to Hanne, as his hand slid down to Kristi's breasts, unzipping her fleece along the way and reaching inside. "…and Hanne, your lesbian lover's perfect body. Yes, you're surprised we know, I see. And then, yours, too. Now, have you changed your mind?" Hanne saw Kristi flinch and grimace and come close to tears, as the pervert pulled her top down and exposed much of her magnificent breasts.

Just then, one of the other Russian officers entered. "Sir, you are wanted on the radio. Urgently. The President wants to speak to you." Hanne was astounded that Erik had managed to worm his way into the upper echelons of the rogue government to this extent.

Erik molested Kristi for a few more seconds, then finally pulled his hands away. "Tch, tch, tch. Well…okay. What a shame! We'll just have to continue this latter, my dear Kristi. And Hanne. We'll have some fun with you, too." The pervert ran his right hand across Kristi's breasts, then back up to her face before continuing. "Zaitsov, why don't you take these women to the submarine—that way we can be sure they won't escape, and we will have all the time we need to get what we want from them."

Erik left with his entourage, leaving the incensed captain behind. Hanne rushed over to Kristi, who was shaking as she hugged her and helped her pull her top back up, saying, "Oh, no!" What went through Hanne's mind was the terrible episode Kristi had told her about that had ended her little fling with the Danish brute.

⁓⁓⁓

After they gathered up whatever belongings they had in the tent, Zaitsov led the way, with Hanne and Kristi by his side and the Kalashnikov toting guard following a few steps behind.

"Are you okay, Kristi?" Hanne asked, arm around her visibly shaken friend.

"Yes, thanks. But glad to leave that creep behind. Although I don't know for how long he will stay away…"

"That was uncalled for, from the…the…uhh… Governor," Zaitsov chimed in, glancing behind him to make sure the soldier was far enough behind so he wouldn't hear. "Are you all right, Miss Olafson?"

After Kristi just whispered a "Yes, thanks," he continued. "And Miss Kristensen, do I understand correctly that Minister Laptov may be in Greenland? Do you know where? I am an ardent supporter of his—I was under Admiral Maslenkov, until this new political leadership ousted and imprisoned him. I must say, I am very much a fan of the former head of the troika."

"Well, Captain Zaitsov, I'm really glad to hear that," Hanne responded, pleasantly surprised. This, of course, put matters into a different perspective. "I am a friend of Pavel Laptov's, too, and got to know him quite well during recent months. As you can gather, he's unfortunately in great danger…from Gusanov's agents."

"Yes, and I would do anything to help ensure his safety. And, of course, yours and Ms. Olafson's." Eric's vile behavior had obviously grated on him, too.

In the few moments of silence it took for them to clamber down the steep slope, a plan started to take shape in Hanne's mind. A plan that she knew would be full of danger, but she saw no other way forward. She said nothing until they approached the shore where the dinghies were beached.

"Captain Zaitsov, would you be prepared to take your submarine around the north of Greenland and help us rescue the former President?" Hanne, standing beside the captain, spoke in a whisper. "Maybe get him across to Canada? Say Grise Fjord or Pond Inlet or the base at Alert? Along with the two of us? Greenland is no longer safe, I fear."

Zaitsov did a doubletake, looking deep into Hanne's eyes. "Wuh! Ms. Kristensen, it should be possible, but it will not be easy. A dangerous mission, to be sure. But we must get the two of you away from this…this pervert. And if it also means serving Russia, so much the better."

Hanne saw that the captain had a big smile on his face as he helped Kristi and her board the dinghy. It seemed that, in spite of all the risks, he would relish the adventure. And welcome the chance to stand up for his beliefs.

On the little boat, Hanne took out her cell phone and quickly typed a message to Richard telling him about her emerging plan and asking for his help in getting Pavel to some place in the Canadian Arctic. She did not know where yet, but at least he would be alerted to what was going on. Although without the assurance of reception at Citronen, this was only a vague hope—but she had heard that Tele-Post Greenland had recently installed a network of towers and satellites making calls and the internet possible in Northern Greenland. So, perhaps the message would get transmitted when they surfaced somewhere near Qaanaaq, if not before.

Chapter 13

Immediately after Ron Hall got through to him following Hanne's call, President Barlow summoned a meeting of his key national security advisors in the Oval Office.

"So, it seems our Russian friends are up to no good," the president opened the meeting. "They have taken advantage of our blind spot, with the radar at Thule still not operational. Now that he has ousted Laptov, that bastard Gusanov has sent a force yet again to Citronen. Greenland. And it seems, some destroyers to Nuuk. And God knows what else. Ron, please, tell us what you know."

"Mr. President, I received a call from my contact in the new government in Greenland—Hanne Kristensen, their Minister of Environment and Natural Resources, who happened to be at Citronen when six Russian submarines surfaced. A force of over a hundred men landed and took control, arresting Chinese mining officials and taking the minister and a friend of hers into custody as well. She told me that the force was headed by an Erik Larsen, a Danish traitor who was coerced into working for the Russians and who has—according to what he himself claims—been appointed provisional governor of Greenland by Gusanov until they rid the newly independent country of all foreign interests. She warned us that that probably also includes getting us out of Thule. The Russians now present themselves as the guarantors of Greenland's recently won independence. A significant naval force has been sent to sit offshore Nuuk as well, it seems, and to surround the entire island."

"This is clearly an invasion," the Secretary of State, James Gilchrist, said gruffly. "What are our options?"

"The last time we held back from bombing Severemorsk, their naval base by Murmansk, after they sent a cruise missile to Thule to take out the radar. Fortunately, the situation was eventually diffused. But we did cripple one of their subs in the fjord then." This from the Secretary of Defense.

"Perhaps that is where we should start," the Joint Chief of Staff piped up. "Immediately…right now…let's take out their submarine flotilla. And send bombers to harass their naval operations off Nuuk."

"Can we not talk some sense to them through diplomatic channels?" the President asked. "James, you could call an extraordinary session of the UN Security Council to condemn these actions. And let's figure out some severe sanctions."

"Unfortunately, Gusanov is not likely to be receptive to diplomacy. Nor does he care about sanctions. The same as Putin with the Ukraine situation. It seems that he wants absolute control of the Arctic and will stop at nothing short of it." Tom Deacon, Ron's boss, the National Security Advisor, got to the point.

"Taking out the subs is not an option as far as I'm concerned," Ron opined. "My friend and other innocent people may be on those vessels as prisoners. Besides, it could start a war. World War Three. We came mighty close the last time."

"Probably not, since the subs don't really have the capacity to take on lots of extra people. Your friend and the mining staff will more than likely be kept on land. I say we take out at least one submarine now to show the fuckers." The Joint Chief of Staff looked directly at Ron.

"Well…the last time we did that, they sent a cruise missile to take out the radar. And, as we know, the personnel at Thule are currently under severe stress with some kind of viral epidemic," Ron continued. "Until we get better clarity on that, we should not do anything to endanger our people up there, in my humble opinion."

"Why don't we annihilate the whole fleet then, before they bomb Thule again?" The Joint Chief of Staff would not let up. "If we surprise them, they won't be able to do anything."

"Gentlemen, let us all cool down," the President intervened, ignoring the last bellicose view. "James, I want you to make a strong *démarche* to the Russians, if possible, jointly with the Prime Minster of Greenland, protesting their move. Weave Rorsen in, for sure. And call for a special UN session. The General Assembly. It has more impact than the impotent Security Council where Russia and China veto everything."

Then, to the Joint Chief of Staff: "Bill, we will hold off on military action for now, but do notify the command at Thule. They have to be on red alert, and we also need to speed up the repatriation of the sick from there. Pronto. Also, increase the surveillance flights over Greenland. Especially up north. And let's check out those naval ops they have near Nuuk. We need to see what's happening there. Bill, while you're at it, send a few battleships to the arena. A show of force. But avoid confrontation. Unless they engage first. Sandman should also make sure nothing is coming her way. I mean a cruise missile or something…”

“Yes, Mr. President.”

“James, give the Ruskis twenty-four hours to start moving the subs out. And the destroyers or whatever, too, if they have penetrated Greenland waters. If they don’t leave, we take them out. That will be all for now, gentlemen. Let’s get on with it.”

Chapter 14

Citronen Fjord, Northern Greenland—Friday,
Late September, 202-

As soon as the ladies followed Zaitsov excitedly down through the hatch, and the soldier bringing up the rear closed the cover, the captain turned to Hanne and said, "Igor will show you where you sleep. I am afraid our quarters are tight. I can only offer you the beds of some of the men still on shore. You can have Igor put whatever things you have there."

"Thank you, Captain."

"I will then have Igor bring you up front to the command center. I must go give orders now for us to leave. That is, if we are still keen on this rescue operation."

"Of course!" Hanne was elated. "We need to get Minister Laptov to safety as soon as possible. And we need to get away from here."

As Zaitsov quickly spouted some words at the soldier in Russian, Hanne saw the submariner's jaws drop. No doubt, he was rather surprised with what was taking place.

"I have just explained to him that we have orders to submerge and depart immediately, since there may be an attack by the Americans," Zaitsov said, with a wink, as he, too, noticed the expression on Igor's face. And to the ladies: "See you in a few minutes."

The seaman led Hanne and Kristi through a hatch and down a narrow corridor with cots slung in columns of three on either side. Several men lounging on their bunks in their underwear were dumbstruck as the two Danish beauties passed by. Just as they got to near the end of the hall where Igor stopped and pointed to the two top cots on either side, a loud siren screamed. All the men jumped up from their bunks, many uttering words Hanne could not understand under their breaths as they rushed to pull on their uniforms.

Igor said, "We go to battle stations. The submarine is descending. You come quickly."

He led Hanne and Kristi back up the corridor and through several hatches to the buzzing command center. There, Zaitsov detached himself from the screen he was looking at with several of his men and came over to Hanne. "We are on the way. Mr. Larsen will not be too happy when we disappear under water, and quickly move out of the fjord."

Just then, someone came on the radio in Russian and exchanged words with Zaitsov. Afterwards, he turned to Hanne and explained, "That was Captain Chernov in one of the other boats. The rest of the officers fortunately are all on land. He was wondering why we are submerging. I just told him I need to go around the headland to check out another part of the mining operations. They will find out soon enough that that was a falsehood, though, but by then I hope to be far away and submerged, if not under the ice. Fortunately, it will not be easy for them to reach us now that we are traveling underwater."

"Tremendous!" Hanne said, admiringly.

"But Ms. Kristensen, you no doubt realize, that we are embarking on a very dangerous mission—not only will we be hunted by my own compatriots, but I am sure the Americans and others will soon realize that something is amiss. And then there are the dangers inherent in taking a submarine through the Arctic so close to the North Pole…right around the north of Greenland."

"Yes, Captain, I do. But we have no choice."

"Of course. But Ms. Kristensen…"

"Just Hanne, please."

"Thank you. Pyotr for me then. Hanne, I need to know our destination."

"I trust you, Pyotr, for sure, but I…can we just head toward Thule for now, around the north coast, as you said? I will let you know more precisely when we get closer."

"That is…okay. I understand your hesitation, but these men are fiercely loyal to me. And when they find out the reason why we split away from the fleet, I am sure they will be supportive."

"Thanks, Pyotr. I will tell you in due course."

☙❧

Back on shore, Erik was monitoring the Chinese as they boarded their transport plane under heavy guard when Captain Kruglov, the senior naval officer in charge of the entire Citronen fleet, approached. The captain was hardly able to contain himself as he said, "Governor, the *Seminov* has submerged. Did you give them any orders? Because I sure didn't."

"No, certainly not, my dear fellow. I just told Zaitsov to take those two female prisoners on board so we could question them later. I have no idea what you do with your submarines, but I hope those two fucking sirens haven't hijacked the vessel."

"No chance of that, sir. There were several men on board who would all love to overpower those gorgeous women at the slightest provocation," Kruglov said with a smirk. "As would I."

"Well, for fuck's sake, Kruglov, get in touch with that asshole Zaitsov and see what the hell he is up to."

"Unfortunately, it is not possible to reach him from here. Now that the submarine is underwater."

"Ridiculous. Maybe then we need to chase him down, don't you think?"

"That is not so easy to do. The *Seminov* will have a good head start and we are not sure what Zaitsov's intentions are. A silent sub is very difficult to find, especially underwater. To make it worse, these new Yasen class subs have a very low acoustic signature."

"Well, for fuck's sake, we can't lose those women. What do you suggest?"

"We should not do anything rash. If I take the rest of the fleet on a wild goose chase after the *Seminov,* we will endanger the mission here."

"No, Kruglov. I want you to send two of the subs in pursuit—one south along the coast, the other north…no, no, better east, toward Copenhagen. There is absolutely no reason for them to go toward the pole. Yes, more likely they might connive to go back to Denmark, where those two cunts live. And with the Chinese out of here, if we keep three submarines, that should be good enough until further notice."

"Yes…Governor." It was clear, though, that Captain Kruglov did not agree. But at least another two of his vessels would be safe from any incoming cruise missile.

Chapter 15

Richard turned the TV on just as soon as he dropped his briefcase on the coffee table and shed his jacket. It was a little after six, so into news time, and since it was the start of the weekend, he went over to the wine rack, pulled out a nice bottle of Bordeaux and cracked it open, wishing Hanne were there to share it with him. As he poured himself a glass, his ears perked up when the newscaster focused on James Gilchrist making a statement at the State Department.

"I have just communicated with the Russian Ambassador, to tell him in no uncertain terms that we expect the Russian force that landed earlier today near the Citronen Mine in the very far north of newly independent Greenland to withdraw immediately. And we have warned the naval fleet just outside Greenland's EEZ near Nuuk, not to approach any closer. We will not tolerate the invasion of an allied country. And yet another uncalled for intrusion into our hemisphere. If the invading submarine force does not commence standing down within the next twenty-four hours, and the naval flotilla approaching Nuuk pull back, Russia will face serious consequences. We will keep you posted of developments. Thank you."

As the Secretary of State was peppered with questions, Richard's mind was filled with anxiety for Hanne—he knew that she was going up there to check on the status of the refurbishment of the mine that had been severely damaged by the rogue elements of the Green Liberation Force just a few months earlier. He remembered that she had called him once from the Goldenrod CEO's radio phone and checked on his cell whether there was any record of that. But there was no number. And her mobile phone would not likely have reception, he thought. He quickly checked for messages anyway, but nothing from her. No way to get in touch with her—how exasperating!

Richard continued to listen to the newscast and put the facts together from Gilchrist's answers that six submarines—yet again, just like the last time—had entered Greenland's coastal waters and penetrated up Citronen Fjord to where the mine's operations were. He could only hope that there had been no armed conflict thereafter and trusted Hanne's judgement and instincts. That was all he could do for the moment, so he poured himself another glass of the *petit Bordeaux.*

❧❧❧

Ron Hall was just packing up to go home, looking forward to a relaxing weekend with the love of his life, Susan, when he received the call from June Stewart, President Barlow's secretary.

"Ron, the President needs you in the Situation Room. As soon as you can get here."

Damn, Ron thought to himself, *I will be late for Susan again.* This perennial disruption of their private plans was the one thing he did not like about this job, otherwise he loved the excitement of it. His adrenalin was in high gear now.

Within minutes, he was being ushered into the basement room where Tom Deacon and James Gilchrist were already present, along with the Secretary of Defense and the Joint Chief of Staff and a few other military and intelligence types.

"Ron, good you made it. I was just being briefed on some developments. Find a place to sit. Bill, please continue." The President nodded to Bill Sullivan, the Joint Chief.

"The picture on the screen is from earlier today. To be exact, 2:16 pm. We started our continuous monitoring of the Citronen area in northern Greenland shortly after your call to the President, Ron. It shows six submarines in Citronen Fjord, just down from the mine. The next picture—" and Sullivan clicked on a remote, "—is a little over two hours later, at 4:33 pm. As you see, we managed to catch one of the subs just submerging."

"Wow! So maybe your *démarche*, James, worked!" The President banged the conference table with his hand.

"Unlikely, since it was only just before 4 pm that the Ambassador left my office…"

"Just one more picture, gentlemen," the Joint Chief of Staff continued. "Taken a few moments ago. At 6:19 pm. As you see, we only have three subs now on the surface— the other three have disappeared from view."

"It must have been our protests then…" From the President again. "They are leaving, one after the other."

"Prime Minister Rorsen made a similar *démarche*," Gilchrist mused. "But it was even after us…To me, it seems they're leaving for some reason of their own."

"Let's hope those three disappeared subs are not on a mission that threatens us even more." The Joint Chief clicked again, the screen now showing an airplane flying high above the clouds. "Subs under water become difficult to track. We have a couple of surveillance aircraft up there with MADs—Magnetic Anomaly Detectors—which will, if we are lucky, sight these submarines. But this becomes less likely if they go deep under the ice."

"Well, keep at it, and let's find out what they're up to." This from the president. "And their surface fleet?"

"They are nearing Nuuk," the Joint Chief answered.

"Unfortunately, there is no way to reach my friend, the Minister of Environment and Natural Resources," Ron chimed in. "I'm sure she would be able to throw some light on all this. What we could do, though, is suggest to Rorsen that they send a team up there to join her, ferret around and ask questions. After all, it's their territory!"

"Good idea, Ron. Let's get on it."

❧❧

Richard dialled Prime Minister Rorsen's private number, on the off chance he would pick up, even though he knew it was after 8 pm. The line was busy at first, but he tried again and let out a sigh of relief when he got through, thinking, of course, that Rorsen must be preoccupied with the Russians intruding in the north of his country.

"Prime Minister Rorsen, Richard Simpson. We met in Ottawa at the signing of the Arctic Treaty…"

"Yes, yes. You are the friend of Hanne Kristensen, my Minister of Environment and Natural Resources. I just got off the phone with Ron Hall, you know, the American official who is, I think, her friend too. He also wanted to get in touch with her, to find out what is going on up there.

I am desperately wanting to know as well."

"Yes, Prime Minister. I'm sure. And it is she I'm calling about. As you know, the Russians are back at Citronen and Hanne was up there. I'm very concerned."

"So am I, Richard. I have issued a strong statement to the Russians, as has the US. It seems that three of the submarines have left. But apparently, two destroyers and some other vessels, for all I know, are still coming toward us here in Nuuk and are just outside our EEZ. We are now waiting for the next move by the Russians. And the Chinese. Or will the US take out the three remaining submarines at Citronen? It seems all the powers are interested in little old Greenland. And we are facing the very real danger of a war on our territory among these superpowers. A Third World War…We certainly don't want that. Especially now. Climate change already gives us more than enough to deal with, and any conflict would also aggravate this. Greenland is a peace-loving nation."

"Yes. A very dangerous situation indeed. I will have Canada make a statement similar to yours in the morning to keep the pressure up. These actions are endangering our country too, and in fact, the rest of the world."

"Thank you. Hopefully, the Chinese will also make a protest. Although I don't know if the new regime in Russia will listen to diplomatic protests."

"I'm afraid you're probably right, Prime Minister."

"The Chinese had a team of miners up there who have actually just landed here in Nuuk, I was informed a few moments ago. Forced out by the Russians," Rorsen continued. "I will be meeting with their leader very soon and will certainly ask after Hanne. Maybe they will be able to tell me something. And I will send some of my people up there to see if they can get to the bottom of whatever is going on. I will let you know if I find out anything."

Rorsen sounded tired, and understandably, a mite pissed off.

"Thank you, Prime Minister. Let's hope we find Hanne safe and sound, and this can all be put behind us. And, of course, that the powers back off."

After hanging up, Richard went to turn on the CNN news, so he could listen while he took the leftover lasagna he had prepared the night before out of the fridge to warm in the oven. As he sipped another glass of the Bordeaux, he perked his ears up. The news feed was live: Wen Shaojing, the General Secretary of the Communist Party of China, had just issued a harsh statement demanding that the Russian force that invaded Greenland leave immediately, otherwise, they would face serious consequences.

Another small step, but not one that resolved anything in Richard's eyes. He had half a mind to fly to Citronen himself, but that was not an easy thing to do. Better to wait and hope he hears from Hanne. Or that Rorsen would learn something.

All very unsettling. Good that he had the bottle of Bordeaux to help console him. Although he would be drinking it alone, without Hanne.

Chapter 16

Northern Greenland—Friday / Saturday,
Late September, 202-

S o, we are now deep enough underwater that they probably can't reach or detect us," Captain Zaitsov said. "This fjord is only three miles long, and very soon we will be in the much bigger Frederick E. Hyde Fjord. And once we round the furthermost point of Johannes V. Jensen Land, we will be in the ocean and…then I hope they won't have an idea of which way we are heading."

"Hmm. You're right," Hanne mused. "They will no doubt think we are heading south. Or perhaps east, to Denmark. Certainly, with Erik…Larsen in the driver's seat…"

"Yes, that is what I am hoping. After all, why would we go to the North Pole?"

"Are we close?" Kristi asked, intrigued.

"Hmm. Maybe 750 kilometers. Kaffeklubben Island, which we will be passing later tonight, if all goes well, is less than a hundred kilometers away from where we are now. To the west and still a bit to the north." Zaitsov walked over to a digital map up on one of the many screens around the command center. "That island is the northernmost point of Greenland, at least believed to be, since very recently they thought they had accidentally found another very small piece of land further north—but that proved to be just a piece of an iceberg with some rocks on it. In any case, at Latitude 83° 39' 45", and only 714 kilometers from the North Pole, Kaffeklubben is one of the farthest north islands in the world. From there, the rest is just ocean. The Arctic Ocean." He pointed to the island on the screen with his index finger.

"Kaffeklubben? Coffee Club?" Kristi could not help laughing. "You've got to be kidding. A coffee club in the freezing Arctic?"

"That must be where Julemanden—your Saint Nicholas, Santa Claus to the Americans—hangs out," Hanne said, laughing.

"Yes. Funnily, it was named in honor of an informal 'coffee club' of geographers at the University of Copenhagen. By Lauge Koch, an explorer from your country, who visited it in 1921."

"That's something I remember from uni, now that you mention it," Hanne observed.

"We should pass by there later tonight, if all goes well." Zaitsov pointed to the digital map again. "Fortunately, with global warming, the ice has not formed yet, so we should have no problems with pressure ridges…"

"Good, and then, I see here that we will be getting close to the Petermann Fjord, where I spent some summers a few years back—201- and 201- —observing the calving of the glacier. Huge blocks of ice, several times the size of Manhattan had been breaking off from it even then. And that has continued, and we think, accelerated. We were a team observing the glacial melt on land."

"Well, well, well," Zaitsov said, with a chuckle. "We could have met then, Hanne. We were cruising underwater in the fjord, but didn't dare get any closer for fear of the danger from the breakoff of those huge blocks of ice. Actually, we were studying the impact of these calving events on the southerly current in the Nares Strait."

"We'll have to be careful, because Petermann is even more active now…," Hanne commented. "As I said, with everything going on, we haven't been able to do much work on it this year, although no doubt, global warming will have had a significant impact since I was last there. Still with a team of Danes back then. It certainly is on my to-do-list to get up here again, or at least to send a team."

"That is a pity, because it would be good to know more about where Petermann's calving stands right now…We will try to pass closer to the Canadian side of the strait to keep clear of any icebergs that may have broken off."

"Probably wise, since we want to get to Laptov as soon as possible. We don't need any unforeseen collisions with an ice island, that's for sure."

Zaitsov gave a few orders to set course and then turned back to the two ladies, "Indeed, Hanne, it's very worrying what climate change is doing to the polar ice cap and all these glaciers."

"Yes, I'm following it quite closely, as I'm sure you are too. Particularly concerning is that the degrading ice shoulder holding back the Thwaites Glacier in Antarctica is by all reports very close to collapsing completely, and if and when it does, the entire glacier will flow into the ocean, raising see level by close to a meter. It has already started, and complete collapse could come any day now. And worse still, many of the other glaciers there could also flow into the ocean afterwards, and seas would in fact rise by three meters or more. Devastating for many low-lying countries—including little old Denmark—and coastal cities like New York, London, Boston, Shanghai, Tokyo among so many others. Bangladesh too, with its hundred and sixty million people. This bigger event could also happen in the next few years…"

"And then there are the heat waves, the drought, wildfires, melting permafrost…we are facing a very dangerous five or so years. And who knows what comes after?"

"Yes, it is all really scary…"

"One of the reasons I support Minister Laptov is because he is actively trying to do something to protect the environment. Some of us in the Northern Fleet have had direct experience with its effects—the degradation to our Siberian ports, roads, airfields and buildings by permafrost melt, as well as the creeping rise of the seas during the summer. Unfortunately, Gusanov on the other hand, seems to welcome climate change and continues to promote the burning of fossil fuels. For one, he relishes the fact that oil and gas are Russia's main export products. I guess politically he thinks that the west—mainly the USA and Europe—has much more to lose because of the populated coastlines. Russia's coast is mainly the Arctic—and other than St. Petersburg, it has no major centres of population on its shores—although those on rivers further inland could suffer as well. But the overwhelming view in our country is that comparatively, we would be hurt less by rising sea levels. And then there are the claimed benefits to agriculture in a northern country like ours…but how our politicians, our people, can overlook the devastation from the wildfires and the thawing permafrost is beyond me."

"Very interesting, Pyotr…you know that Pavel Laptov and I have become close because of our similar views on the Arctic and how to protect it."

"Of course… I know. You two were the main driving forces behind the Arctic Treaty. Which now seems to be dead!"

"Well, let's not give up on it yet, Pyotr. But I did mean to ask you…" Hanne hesitated because she didn't quite know how to put what she was thinking. "How is it that you can fully support Laptov and then take orders from Gusanov and his crowd? To come and invade Greenland."

Zaitsov looked at her with a smile and said, "Well, Hanne, to answer that, it is complicated. First, I did not think the mission was to invade…or occupy Greenland. We were told simply that we would investigate what the Chinese were doing at Citonen Fjord…"

"But Pyotr, when Laptov was ousted in the coup, along with Admiral Maslenkov—who was, I believe, your boss then—how and why did you stay on and obey these criminals?"

"Hanne, I am first and foremost an officer in the Russian navy, indoctrinated to obey our senior officers. When that 'coup' happened, I was out at sea, and their removal took me, and many of my fellows, by surprise. We were disappointed that those two men we respected were removed, but that was no reason not to follow the orders of the new leaders. That happens often in our country…"

"But Pyotr…"

"Hanne, let me finish. In Russia it is not so easy to survive. I have a two-year old baby back in Murmansk and a beautiful young wife. If I had not been willing to take orders from Admiral Velikov, who replaced Admiral Maslenkov at the head of the navy, I would have been jailed for insubordination for sure. Or maybe even executed for desertion or treason. Which is the risk I am now running…"

"Yes, you are very brave…"

"In the end, I want to do what is right, Hanne. And support Minister Laptov, who is risking all to try and save our earth and a decent way of life for all."

"That's great, Pyotr…"

"You will no doubt be pleased to know that there are others in the navy who share my views and are ready to help us if there is any chance of getting rid of those in power now and putting Laptov and Maslenkov back in their leadership positions."

"Yes, good to know. We will need everyone we can get. But first things first: let's save Pavel."

"Of course…"

☙☙☙

"Wow, that is massive!" Hanne observed, blinking to clear the sleep from her eyes as she looked at the sonar screen. "You're right, Pyotr, that must be an ice island, calved from Petermann."

"I thought you would want to see it. It must be the one that broke off early this summer. I haven't heard of any other big iceberg calving off."

"It sure is big enough. Even with all the melting…Unbelievable!"

"We'll just have to steer around it. But we'll have to be careful."

"Thanks, Pyotr, for waking me up to see it. Even though it's just via sonar, I've always wanted to see a major ice island underwater. It's sure one big piece of frozen H2O. Petermann continues to be a prolific parent."

"Well, I am glad we saw it up ahead before we rammed into it," Zaitsov laughed, looking at his watch. "Hanne, we should be approaching the Thule area in the next six or so hours. Is that where Pavel Laptov is? Can you tell me now?"

"Sure, Pyotr, it is time. He's actually in a small village, one bay up. Qaanaaq. The northernmost habitation in Greenland…"

"We'll set course for it, Hanne. You can go back to bed if you wish."

"Thanks. But I'm pretty awake now."

"Let's grab some breakfast then. We'll need to fortify ourselves."

☙❧

Over a breakfast of coffee and cereal, they discussed how their approach to Qaanaaq might work.

"We'll have to act very quickly," Captain Zaitsov said. "Every moment we're up top increases the chance that we will be detected."

"That would not be good. Especially if it's your people who see us," Hanne responded.

"Well, we'll surface as close to the village as we can and you can ride in on the speedboat, find Laptov and return with him. Hopefully, that won't take much more than an hour."

"Too bad we can't alert him to be down at the water's edge."

"No, definitely not."

Just then, Igor approached. "Captain, we are just passing Hans Island."

"Oh, yes. That's the island in the middle of Kennedy Channel disputed by Canada and Denmark for so many years. Luckily, just recently, they agreed to draw a border down the middle, so Greenland didn't have to inherit that *contretemps*," Hanne quipped. "That's at least one issue off our plate. But it was a fun one, because occasionally the Canadians would land there to stake their claim. And leave a bottle of Canadian Club whiskey. The Danes— while they were still in charge—would then pick it up and leave a bottle of schnapps. Fortunately, that is as vituperative as this international conflict became."

"So, since the dispute is settled, we won't have to surface to pick up any liquor this time," Zaitsov said with a chuckle. "Igor, my orders are to pass the island very slowly. We do not want to risk being detected by anyone who might be on or near the island. And let's pass on the Greenland side."

"Yes, Captain."

"There are two more islands further along. Franklin and Crozier, if I remember. We will pass them to starboard, since they are closer in. Then it will just be a few more hours before we enter Inglefield Fjord, where you said Qaanaaq is located."

Chapter 17
Saturday, Nuuk, Greenland—Saturday,
Late September, 202-

Malik, the call is for you." Nanurjuk brought the Prime Minister's cell phone over to him from where he had left it on the kitchen counter.

"Thank you, dear." Rorsen touched the green icon and put the phone to his ear.

"Prime Minister, this is Panut Akerolik. I am the duty officer at the airport. I wanted to report that two Russian military helicopters are approaching and have requested permission to land."

"Thank you, Panut." Rorsen hesitated a moment, thinking quickly that the helicopters must be from the destroyers supposedly just outside the Greenland EEZ. Or had these vessels come closer? In any case, he could not really refuse to allow them to land. They probably would anyway, and there was very little he could do about it.

"Grant them permission but keep any passengers…under surveillance." Rorsen was keenly aware that if even just ten armed soldiers jumped off the choppers, they would be able to take control of the airport. "Bring their leaders to my office and report back to me please as soon as you know more."

"Of course, Prime Minister."

ℰℐℰℐ

Rorsen had just arrived at his desk when his mobile rang again.

"Panut Akerolik here, Prime Minister. The Russian visitors are on their way. I took their names—a Vice-Admiral Ogarov, a Captain Petrov and a Dane, Jens Anderson. The nine soldiers and the two pilots with them are staying here at the airport. I must say, things are a bit tense. Only Anderson speaks any English. And, of course, Danish."

"Thank you, Panut." Rorsen pressed the red icon to end the call, wondering why such a high-level Russian delegation was visiting—were they going to ask him to surrender? What? And what was a Danish civilian doing with a Russian military force? Had their previous colonial masters linked up with the aggressive Gusanov regime against the newly independent country? That would no doubt compound his problems. And a Jens Anderson— wasn't that the name of Hanne's former deranged boyfriend who had tried to kill her after the last Citronen fiasco? The very same person they had handed over to the Danish police? Rorsen made a mental note to ask Hanne the next time he saw her.

Fifteen minutes later, the delegation of three was shown into Rorsen's office. After welcoming them, he offered coffee out of courtesy and had them sit where just a few days earlier, the now deposed head of the Russian government, Pavel Laptov, and his own minister of Environment and Natural Resources, Hanne Kristensen, had sat. *Hmm, Hanne, who had almost fallen victim to this creep Anderson*, if he was correct. *How ironic,* he thought to himself! But he would have to be wary…

"Thank you, Prime Minister, for allowing us to land," Jens spoke after they were all ensconced in their seats. "And for seeing us."

"Of course. How can I help you gentlemen?"

"As you are no doubt aware, Prime Minister, Russia has been very concerned about the continuing foreign influences in your newly independent Greenland." It was Jens who spoke again. "We know that your full nationhood was hard fought and a long time coming,"—Malik thought he sensed a tinge of facetiousness in the Dane's tone—"but also that there are many foreign interests vying to get at your largely untouched natural resources. And, we fear, also to use your territory as a base for potential military aggression…"

"Let me assure you that we are quite happy with our independence and able to manage it on our own. And we will never be the base for potential military aggression, so long as we are in control. We are grateful for your concern but do not need any help. By the way, Mr. Anderson, are you, a Dane, the head of this…Russian delegation?"

Jens blushed a little before saying, "My Russian colleagues do not speak Danish or English. But yes, I have been empowered by President Gusanov to speak on his behalf."

"What can I do for you then?"

"Prime Minister, we must request that you fly with us forthwith to Thule to make a formal public demand that the USA leave your territory. We would therefore like you to instruct that one of your Air Greenland planes take the four of us up there immediately…"

"Impossible, Mr. Anderson."

"Yes, possible." Captain Petrov pulled out his MP-443 Grach semi-automatic pistol and pointed it at Rorsen. "Now. Do it." So, this Petrov did understand and speak English, in spite of what the Dane had said.

"And no one is to know about our intentions," Jens interjected. "You can tell your wife that an emergency has arisen, and you have to go up north. We absolutely do not want the Americans to know before we land there. You need to make up an excuse to visit the base without telling the Yanks we are on the plane with you. Otherwise, you, your wife and children, and their children will die."

The three intruders watched as Rorsen made his four calls. The first one was to Air Greenland, the second to his wife. Just before he picked up the phone to make the third call, he said to his unwelcome visitors: "I am calling Colonel Sandman, the head of the base at Thule. I will tell her that I am coming with a small team to follow up on the environmental issues we discussed. You will be pleased because that should not create any suspicions."

Malik was relieved when he did not get through to the Colonel but was asked rather to leave a message. He was afraid that she might bring up the raging virus—and that could have far-reaching consequences. These crazy Russians may come up with the notion that they should bomb Thule to eradicate this new microbe and the American base at the same time. And besides the many deaths, that would certainly lead to substantial melting of the ice cap—not something that would be good for Greenland. Or indeed the world.

Somehow, too, a plan was starting to formulate in his mind that maybe it wouldn't be bad to take his visitors to Thule and possibly expose them to infection. Of course, he would have to be careful, wear a mask like the last time— fortunately, he still had a packet of them from COVID days in his desk, which he furtively pocketed—and, of course, also try to socially distance but leave the intruders to their own resources.

Yes, let the Greenland virus fight for Greenland.

His fourth call was to get his car.

৫১৫১

On the way to the airport, Jens's cell rang. "Erik, where are you?" He asked in Danish.

Malik could overhear both sides, and clearly understood, since he spoke the language of Greenland's former colonizers.

"Still at Citronen. But Jens, that stupid former cunt of yours, Hanne, has disappeared, along with her bisexual friend Kristi—you know, the bitch I was banging for a while back home. It seems they left here in a rogue submarine, and we have no idea where they went. Keep a lookout for them." Shocked by what he was hearing, Malik nevertheless kept his cool.

"We're on our way to Thule with Malik Rorsen, the Prime Minister." Jens glanced over at Malik, realizing just then that he understood the conversation. "Erik, it doesn't make sense for you to come to Nuuk once you're finished up at Citronen. Can you join me there, in Thule? As the appointed Provisional Governor of Greenland, it would be good if you were present when we air the demands."

"Good idea, Jens. I'll get the Goldenrod corporate plane to fly me there. If I leave soon, we should arrive around the same time. But, in the meantime, you should get that Ogarov to radio the submarine fleet they sent to Thule to arrive then, too. They should certainly be within striking distance by now."

"Perfect. I'll see you soon. In Thule."

∽∾∽∾

Nanurjuk was worried. She puzzled over Malik's call—he had never been so cagey in any of his communications before. And he had told her about the Russian helicopters landing at the airport, so there must be something afoot. Something disturbing, not right. She hesitated about what to do but finally decided that she would try to get in touch with Ron Hall, the American official she remembered her husband talking to about some security issues.

When she was put through to Hanne's friend, Nanurjuk told the presidential advisor about the landing of the Russian helicopters and her husband's call. And that she believed he left rather suddenly for Thule without really explaining why.

"I appreciate you reaching out to us, Mrs. Rorsen. And giving us the heads up," Hall said. "We will notify Thule and have them be on the lookout. Don't worry, we will get to the bottom of this. We'll definitely keep an eye out for your husband."

As soon as he hung up with Nanurjuk, Ron called the president to brief him on the situation. Barlow, in turn, instructed his Joint Chief of Staff to focus several of the surveillance planes already in the air over Northern Greenland on incoming traffic to Thule and to brief Colonel Sandman on the circumstances.

Chapter 18

Northern Greenland—Saturday, Late September, 202-

Zaitsov was in the command center with the two women.

"We're approaching Qaanaaq now. We will surface very soon. I do not dare go any closer in these shallow waters." The captain pointed to the map on the screen that showed the depth gradients for the bay. "We will launch a rubber dinghy, and I will send Igor and two other men with you." Hanne nodded her assent as the Russian continued. "Kristi, you should stay here with me. But from the moment we surface to when you get back, Hanne, you will have to be very quick. An hour, maybe two at most, on shore."

"Pyotr, I will try to be fast," Hanne responded. "But there is no guarantee that Pavel will be in his little hut. Or indeed in the village. Remember, he's first and foremost a polar scientist and explorer, and likely to be out on the ice somewhere. And he's had no indication that we're coming to spirit him away."

"Well, I will instruct Igor to raise a flag when you return to the dock. We should be able to see it through the periscope, and then come up to get you. In any case, now we are all systems go, so get ready, Hanne."

☙❧

Hanne could feel the sub rising in the chilly waters of Inglefield Fjord as she followed Captain Zaitsov to the hatch. She heard a sudden rush of water as first the sail and finally the full vessel cut through the surface. Zaitsov waited a few minutes to open the lid, then poked his head through and climbed up on top of the submarine, extending a hand to Hanne. As she emerged and relished breathing the fresh Arctic air, she could see the little Inuit fishing village nestled on the shore below the plateau with the ice sheet behind it and prayed that Pavel would be at his temporary home, or if not, at Biina's. But she didn't have more than a moment to take in the scenery as several of Zaitsov's men were already launching a rubber dinghy further down the sub's hull and maneuvering it in her direction. When they reached the metal ladder leading down from the hatch, Zaitsov said, "Okay, Hanne, time to go search for Minister Laptov. God speed! And be careful."

It took the little boat no more than ten minutes to reach the shore, and by then a number of Inuit fishermen had assembled on the pier to greet the visitors. Hanne was not sure what to make of the situation as she looked at the men and then at Igor but was delighted when the tallest of the locals addressed her in Danish, saying, "Ms. Kristensen, I am pleased to see you again. Welcome."

She deftly jumped out of the boat and onto the dock as she said, "Whew, Aani, I can't tell you how glad I'm to see you. Do you by any chance know where Pavel is? We've come to take him away…"

"Hanne, yesterday at dinner, he said he was going out on the Qaanaaq ice cap today. My son, Aput, had offered to take him on his dog sled. They left very early this morning."

"We need to find him. His life is in danger, and we have to get him away. The submarine you saw surface out there is a friendly Russian one. The captain and the crew are working with us. Please, will you help?"

"Well, Hanne, I can go out with you on the ice cap to look for them. I have an idea of where Aput might have taken him."

"Thank you, Aani…"

"Come, let's go in my truck. We will drive up to where my snowmobile is parked and then go out on the ice to search for them. I am sure we will find them."

After confirming the plan with the flag, Hanne took leave of her Russian companions. Then, as she followed Aani to his pickup, she turned her cellphone on, hoping the message to Richard she wrote still in Citronen would transmit, if it hadn't already. And that he might have answered. But so far, no messages. Aani drove up a dirt road to the village from the dock and continued up a steep slope to the plateau. It took them another ten minutes or so to reach the top and to a spot on the ice-covered land where several snowmobiles were parked.

"I see that my hunch was right. This is where they started from," Aani said, as he climbed out of his pickup and pointed toward his snowmobile. "That is my machine. But see, those are their tracks. The dog sled leaves a pretty good trace to follow."

"Good," Hanne said, "hopefully, we won't need long to find them." It took Aani no time to rev up the engine, and they set off at a rapid pace. Hanne delighted in the fresh air and open space after the closed, claustrophobic conditions on the submarine, and the shining midday sun helped brighten her mood. But she was astounded to see the number of melt pools on the ice surface, most of which the dog sled had avoided on its outward journey. Climate change was indeed taking its toll on the Greenland ice cap. The minutes ticked by though, and she felt a sense of relief when Aani finally turned and said, "There, Hanne, up ahead. That must be them."

Hanne strained her eyes but with the sun's glare reflecting off the ice, could not see anything. After a couple of minutes of staring ahead, though, she finally made out a few little black specks and hoped that indeed, Aani was right.

ↄ◦ↄ◦ↄ

Hanne jumped off the snowmobile and ran to Pavel, who was stunned to see his beautiful Danish friend out on the ice cap.

"Pavel, we have to get you back to Qaanaaq immediately. Your life is in danger. Gusanov's forces are looking for you. A friendly submarine—actually, one of yours, under Captain Pyotr Zaitsov—brought me here and we will whisk you away. Probably to Canada."

"Captain Zaitsov? Pyotr Zaitsov? A remarkable officer. I remember I was there when Admiral Maslenkov awarded him the medal *For Service in the Submarine Force.* But…"

Aani, who was as resourceful as his prime minister brother-in-law, came over after talking to his son and said, "Yes, Hanne, you and Pavel must take the snowmobile. You just need to retrace our steps to the pickup. Aput and I will return to the village with the slower dogsled and take his van."

"No, no…" Hanne started to protest, but immediately understood that what he was suggesting would be the only way for them both to get back quickly. And hearing what she thought was the roar of a plane come closer, she looked up at the sky and indeed, saw a speck in the distance.

"You will need these," Aani reached the keys to the truck over to Hanne, as he too, turned his eyes to the sky. "Hmm. That is odd. There are no scheduled overflights today at this time." Pavel, who was saying his quick goodbyes to the two Inuit who had so generously contributed to his stay, also looked up.

The plane was now more visible, and then, in a flash, Hanne recognized it. "Shit! Excuse the language, but that's the Goldenrod plane from Citronen. What's it doing here? And where is it going?" But she had a sinking feeling that it was her wicked Danish compatriot, Erik, who had commandeered it and was on the search for her—and ultimately Laptov.

"Pavel, this is not good. We have to get going. Now. Let's move!"

She hopped on the driver's seat of the snowmobile, waited a moment until Pavel settled in behind her, and took off like a rocket following the tracks Aani had made on the way there.

Chapter 19

The Air Greenland plane carrying Prime Minister Rorsen, Jens and the two Russian naval officers taxied down the runway toward the small terminal at Thule. The two Ruskis eagerly gawked at the plethora of airplanes and other military equipment positioned around the airfield.

As Malik descended the staircase and put a mask on, he saw that another plane was coming in to land behind them. It must be the one carrying that Erik, Jens's compatriot, the Dane had talked to earlier, flying in from Citronen. But he was glad it was Colonel Sandman, also wearing a mask, who greeted the visitors on the tarmac. "We are honored to have you come and see us again, Prime Minister…"

"Thank you, Colonel Sandman." And noticing that the colonel was more interested in his guests, two of whom were in Russian military uniform, Rorsen continued: "Allow me to introduce Jens Anderson, representing the newly formed government in Russia, Vice-Admiral Ogarov, who is in charge of all the Russian naval forces in the area, and Captain Petrov, the commander of the task force of the Russian navy off the shores of Greenland at

Nuuk." Malik had to restrain himself from adding "that has just invaded my country."

"Gentlemen, welcome. I am sorry I was not notified about the visit of such distinguished officers of the armed forces of a brother nation. To what do we owe the honor?" Sandman asked, somewhat facetiously.

It was Jens who answered, just as the other aircraft touched down. "Colonel, perhaps we should wait until our colleague joins us from the incoming plane. But I see you are all wearing a mask. Is COVID still an issue here?"

"We were advised a few hours ago—surprising, I must say—that Derek Tate, the Goldenrod CEO, was flying in. I was not aware though, that he would be a colleague of yours or your Russian companions." Sandman continued with her sarcasm.

Malik jumped in to add: "In Greenland we are still concerned that foreign visitors might bring the virus to us. We are extra careful." He didn't elucidate which virus, or that it could be the other way around, but never mind. And then to Colonel Sandman: "I believe it is a close confidante of Mr. Anderson's we are waiting for. Hopefully, the purpose of their mission will be made clear very soon. To all of us." The Dane gave the Prime Minister of Greenland a surprised look. Of course, he had understood his entire phone conversation with Erik.

"Please, in the meantime, let us make ourselves comfortable in my office here. I will instruct one of my men to bring your friend along."

Just then, a youngish-looking officer rushed up to Colonel Sandman, and said, "Colonel, there is a matter that requires your immediate attention." She turned and followed the soldier out of earshot, and the others could see that they both stared out into the fjord. As all eyes followed, six Russian submarines surfaced, one by one, menacingly close to shore.

After giving a series of terse orders to the officer, Sandman rushed back to the group and, in a raised voice, addressed the more senior of the Russian visitors. "Vice-Admiral, what is the meaning of this invasion?"

"Could we please discuss this in your office, Colonel?" It was again Jens who answered.

"By all means. This way please." Sandman could hardly stifle her anger. "But we want some answers fast."

☙☙

The atmosphere inside the small room was tense as Erik was ushered in a few minutes later. After brusque introductions, the new arrival addressed Sandman. "Colonel, could I please have just five minutes alone with my colleagues? And then, of course, I will explain our mission to you."

Colonel Sandman was fuming but agreed reluctantly. "Very well, Mr. Larsen, but five minutes. Not a second more. This is already an intolerable situation." *But*, she thought to herself as she closed the door behind her, *at least, that will give my pilots a chance to carry out the scramble orders I just gave when I saw the submarines surface. Yes, before those goddam Ruski subs launch a cruise missile at us and destroy us and all our planes.*

As Malik stepped out into the corridor, he extracted his phone from his pocket and saw that there was a new message from Panut Akerolik. He had heard a bleep just as Erik came into the room and was puzzled why the duty officer at the airport would be calling him again. It said: "Please call. Something serious has come up."

He moved a little further away from Colonel Sandman

and the other two officers who were in any case all deeply engaged in a conversation, no doubt about the strange visitors. Malik clicked on the number and put the phone to his ear. It took only one ring before a voice answered, "Panut Akerlik here. Prime Minister, thank you for calling back. I wanted to bring to you attention something potentially important that has been transpiring here at the airport in the few hours since your departure. Several Air Greenland and airport officials seem to have come down with some apparently very serious infection. The symptoms resemble the COVID-19 illness a few years back…"

"Interesting…because the same thing has happened up here at Thule. In fact, it started even before my last visit here. They were surmising that it was perhaps some microbe released by the melting of the permafrost…You and your colleagues need to mask up. Please tell everyone. And stay away from those affected."

"Well, that may explain it, sir. I believe the two pilots and the two stewardesses who accompanied you and your guests and stayed overnight at the base are among the sick. In fact, it may have been they who infected the others. They are all in the isolation unit at Queen Ingrid's Hospital now. Eleven people so far. The doctors are assuming it is a coronavirus and taking precautions similar to those we implemented for COVID-19. As are we, as you say, until we have clarity."

"Thank you, Panut. Please keep a watch on the situation and let me know. By the way, what happened to the Russian soldiers and pilots you were holding at the airport? I thought that was what you might be calling about…"

"They left a couple of hours ago. Actually, sir, two of the four officials I had watching them are among those in the hospital. So, I hope the Russians did not get the infection, whatever it is…"

"Thank you Panut. Keep me informed of any new developments."

"By all means, Prime Minister."

As Malik hung up, he thought, *well, maybe it would be good if those Russians did get sick. And infected the whole bloody lot of them on those destroyers. Or whatever the vessels they have offshore Nuuk are. Hallelujah, the Greenland virus is coming to our rescue! We just have to make sure we can keep it away from ourselves.*

♥♥♥

As soon as Sandman, Rorsen and the other two American officers in the room left, Erik burst out. "Goddammit! Jens, as we were flying low over the ice near Qaanaaq, I saw what I am absolutely certain was that stupid cunt Hanne Kristensen tooling around on a snowmobile. And who do you guess was with her? Laptov, that fucking old geezer we've been trying to find."

"Are you sure?" Jens couldn't believe his ears.

"Yes. And do you know what?" Erik addressed the two Russians in their language. "I think it was that asshole…that renegade colleague of yours, Vice-Admiral. Captain Zaitsov, he must have commandeered one of your subs to bring that bitch—lamentably a compatriot of mine—to this side of Greenland, to find Laptov. The decrepit old jerk must have been hiding in Qaanaaq or something. Admiral, you need to give orders to blow that wretched village sky high. And find that fucking sub of yours before they steal Laptov away from under our noses again."

Ogarov and Petrov quickly conversed, and the captain

rushed out of the office, pulling his phone out of his pocket. As Petrov passed him, Malik wondered what they had discussed in there. He hoped the scurrying about didn't mean that they had found out where Laptov was hiding, and that they would send a force to Qaanaaq. Or worse still, send a cruise missile there.

Or could it be that some members of the invading troops had become sick with some viral infection?

℘℘℘

"Colonel, we're here to demand that the US announce forthwith its impending withdrawal from Thule, indeed from all of Greenland's territories." Erik dove into a statement of their mission as soon as the door was closed, and everyone was seated in the small office. "If you are not prepared to do this, we will have no choice but to destroy this entire facility. It is unconscionable that your country continues to occupy a piece of Greenland's territory for your own military purposes, and I am sure the Prime Minister here agrees. After all, Greenland is now an independent country, not a colony of a capitalist empire. We have a force of six nuclear submarines positioned in the fjord and they are ready to release the necessary missiles to achieve our aims if you do not comply willingly."

"Mr. Larsen, I'm sure you will understand that I can make no such statement without discussing it with Washington. Such an exchange may take a few days, and usually a matter with such profound implications involves diplomatic consultation. Not just military invasion."

"Colonel Sandman, these are abnormal times, and we do not have the luxury of several days. By the orders of

President Gusanov, I have the discretion to give you only twenty-four hours to consult with whomever and in any case, we do expect a positive reply. Please note that significant Russian naval and air forces are positioned all around Greenland, and should you not comply, I am afraid that we will have to ensure your departure—and that of other foreign intruders—by force. Greenland may well become scorched earth in the process. The blood of the people of this country, Colonel, will be on your soul."

Sandman reflected for a moment, then nodded to her two fellow American soldiers in the room, who pulled out their arms menacingly. "Well, my dear Mr. Larsen, let me assure you that if there is any hostile activity initiated by the Russian forces you cite, you and your three colleagues will be the first casualties. Oh, and by the way, we have a squadron of planes in the air ready to release their weapons to rid the waters of your submarines as soon as there is any sign of aggressive activity from them or from any other Russian source."

She paused to make sure that her statement had the desired effect before continuing. "The four of you will be my guests—under armed guard of course—until this Sicilian stand-off you seem to have engineered is resolved diplomatically. And it is very unlikely to be in twenty-four hours. So please step outside this office and follow my armed colleagues to the quarters you have been assigned. Oh, and before you go, I need you to place all arms and communications equipment on the table."

With the drawn automatic pistols of Sandman's compatriots pointing at them, the two Danes and two Russians—faces scowling—had no choice but to obey. It was only as he left the room after being patted down by one of the soldiers that Jens considered that they may have grossly miscalculated.

Chapter 20
Ottawa—Saturday, September, 202-

Richard was content with the terse but strong speech Prime Minister Juneau had just made to the press on the steps of Parliament, protesting the Russian incursion into Greenland. Although the bureaucratic machine had inevitably watered down his first draft, the statement made it clear that Canada would not tolerate any incursion into its territory or maritime zone, and that it viewed it as its obligation to come to the defence of its neighbour, Greenland, even though the membership of the newly independent country had not yet been ratified by all of NATO's members. Richard did smile though, as the thought came to him that if the other countries in the alliance did not join—and certainly without the USA—Canada and Greenland would not stand a chance against the military might of Russia. Even though in their invasion of Ukraine a couple of years back, their military had exhibited surprising weakness, but then again, the forty-four million Ukrainians fighting for their homeland, heavily armed, trained, and supported by NATO, were no doubt a tougher enemy.

He clicked on the remote to turn off the TV screen

gracing the wall opposite the desk in his office in the newly renovated Lester B. Pearson Building and reached over to where his iPhone was resting on a charger, remembering that there had been a chirp while he was watching the press release, indicating that a message had arrived. Yes, probably from Hanne.

As he opened the Message App, he was delighted to see that the incoming blurb was indeed from her. Short, but succinct, it read: *Just departing Citronen in renegade Russian sub, around north of Greenland to ferret Pavel away. Can we bring him to Canada? Where in northern islands best? Coming from Qaanaaq. Need your help please. Lv, H.*

That explained the time lag shown on the message: she must have sent it yesterday, just before the submarine submerged, hoping that her mobile had reception. And it came now, because they must have surfaced, very probably near Qaanaaq, if indeed she had reached where Laptov was hiding. Richard was glad that Greenland's Tele-Post had put in the network of towers and satellites to blanket the immense island—truly a feat of gigantic proportions. Canada certainly had something to learn from Greenlanders. Of course, the efficient Danes, too, he smiled to himself.

And he could not be more amazed by the woman he was in love with. How did she manage to convince one of the submarine crews—or at the very least, an officer in the Russian navy—to commandeer one of their subs and take her around northern Greenland, in the hopes of finding a fugitive former head of state running from the Russian armed forces and intelligence operations? An incredible woman, she was, his Hanne. Her bravery, strength of character, loyalty, cleverness—you name any positive quality, and she had it without par. Oh, and not to forget her beauty and sexiness—yes, the loving with her was truly unequalled. How he missed Hanne!

But what should he respond? He already had clearance to offer the Russian minister asylum in Canada—as he had done with the rest of the Russian delegation for the treaty signing—so that was not an issue. Where should they land? He simply had to be there when Hanne and Laptov came on shore. He had visited many of the Inuit villages on his inaugural tour when he was first appointed Assistant Deputy Minister for Arctic Affairs, and they were all very remote. He had to find somewhere on the coast and, if possible, with some kind of military presence. Of course, also a decent airfield. And not too far from Qaanaaq, if possible.

Then it hit him. Pond Inlet, of course! It was the one spot that had all the desired qualities.

He quickly composed a message back to Hanne: *"Pond Inlet. Can you get there?"*

He hoped that she would have reception, whether she was in Qaanaaq or somewhere else. When he saw that the message had sent, he had the brilliant idea of dialing her cellphone. With shaking fingers, he pressed the green button when her number came up, and it took a while before he heard a dial tone, but he could not get through. He was supremely disappointed and worried for her.

But, he thought to himself, as he opened his laptop, *my Hanne is a very clever girl, and she will no doubt figure out that Pond Inlet is the best place for them to land. So, I should probably get up there as quickly as possible to help. Even if they end up in some other village, it will be easier for me to get there from Pond Inlet than from Ottawa. And, in the meantime, perhaps she will get my message...*

Richard buzzed his secretary, to ask her to get General Wippinger, the head of the Royal Canadian Air Force, on the line. Fortunately, Richard had met the officer several times and he knew that the General would be following the emerging events in Greenland very closely.

"General Wippinger, Richard Simpson here." He did not want to waste any time on pleasantries. "Would it be possible for one of your planes to get me to Pond Inlet ASAP? It is of the utmost importance. I have some reason to believe that a Russian submarine will be landing there in just a few hours with the fugitive former head of state, Pavel Laptov, accompanied by Greenland's minister of Environment and Natural Resources. We need to make sure we protect them from the forces the Gusanov regime is arraying against them."

It did not take much for Richard to persuade General Wippinger, and within the hour he was on his way to the airport, in high spirits because he would soon be seeing the love of his life. *When this is all over, I'm going to ask Hanne to marry me*, he decided then and there in the government car taking him on the first leg of his journey.

Chapter 21

*Northern Greenland and Washington D.C.—Saturday,
Late September, 202-*

Once Malik and Colonel Sandman were left alone in her office, she addressed the prime minister without trying to mask her anger. "The audacity of this new Russian government is beyond belief. They have once again brought us close to World War Three. And it could well be a nuclear engagement this time…"

"They seem to be getting bad advice from those two renegade Danes, among others. The two are the very ones who were involved in that terrible bombing at the Citronen mine several months ago," Rorsen commented. "We locked them up and extradited them to Denmark, but they must have escaped along the way."

"Well, we can certainly keep them behind bars, even though we might have to release the Russian naval officers once this situation is diffused. If it can be de-escalated. In that respect, I am going to call my superiors now and discuss next steps with them. Prime Minister, I would be honored if you joined me on the call. Your participation would no doubt bolster our case and help determine appropriate steps we can take."

"I'd love to, Colonel. Thank you. That would certainly make it easier for us to coordinate our actions."

❧❧❧

Nanurjuk was just leaving the Hans Egede House where she had spent some time with the staff to prepare for the annual cabinet dinner, when she saw the imposing fleet of Russian naval vessels position themselves offshore Nuuk. Her jaw dropped at the size of a couple of the ships as she stopped momentarily to take it all in. Then she resumed her walk back to the residence as fast as she could possibly move her tiny legs—only a few more minutes away—so that she could call Ron Hall. She knew that he would be the person her husband would reach out to at the time of such a national—no, international crisis.

But just as she got to the rise leading down to their waterfront home, she saw the two mother destroyers spawn myriads of rubber landing dinghies full of soldiers, all teeming in the bay and speedily making their way to the shore. "This is an invasion," she muttered to herself angrily, as she felt her heart speed up. "Oh my, poor Malik! My poor country!"

As soon as she closed the door and was in the quiet of her own home, she found the number of the American official she knew was her best bet to get some action and pressed the dial button.

❧❧❧

Sandman's assistant placed the call to her boss at Peterson Air Force Base in Colorado Springs. While they waited, the Colonel quickly opened an innocuous looking laptop hidden in the corner cabinet she had used to record the brief conversation the two Danes and two Russians had while they were left alone in the room. She quickly replayed it—the audio was very revealing, but before she and Malik could discuss it, her call was patched over to the White House situation room.

"Colonel Sandman?" To her surprise, President Barlow's voice boomed over the speaker phone. "Glad to have you on the line. The Joint Chief of Staff, the Secretary of Defense, The Secretary of State and other key officials in my administration are present, and Colonel Johnson is tapping in from Peterson. Colonel Sandman, I understand the Russians have a substantial naval force near Thule, as well as surrounding key parts of Greenland. We are in a very dangerous situation. Please brief us and tell us your thoughts."

"Mr. President," Sandman responded respectfully, having liked the man the one time she met him when she was appointed to her current role, "I have the Prime Minister of Greenland, Malik Rorsen, with me, sir..."

"Delighted, Malik, I'm glad you're on the line. I was very happy to meet you in person a few months ago. I must say, Greenland is certainly becoming the focal point of international affairs these days."

"Thank you, Mr. President. Yes, indeed it is. And, not necessarily in a good way. But as we discussed with Colonel Sandman, I hope this conversation will make it easier for us to coordinate our positions. Our country is being invaded by the Russians, and we need your assistance now more than ever."

"Could you please elaborate, Malik?"

"Mr. President, Colonel Sandman will no doubt report to you in greater detail, but there are, we believe, six Russian submarines just off Thule, well within our waters.

This is after I was coerced by two senior Russian officers and their renegade Danish spokesman to fly up here to participate in this demand that the USA withdraw immediately from the shores of Greenland and return Thule to us. A small helicopter force landed in Nuuk, and the two Russians are, if I remember correctly, Admiral Ogarov, the commander of all Russian forces in the Greenland theater, and a Captain Petrov, the head of a naval task force of three or four military ships just off the capital. I believe as many as six submarines were seen up in the Citronen mine area, and from these, a contingent of several hundred men have landed and effectively taken over the mine, evicting the Chinese, who were working with us. The Russians now occupy that sector. Most distressingly, my Minister of Environment and Natural Resources, who was up there when this invasion took place, has disappeared along with a friend. There could also be Russian vessels near our other main ports."

"Hanne Kristensen?" Ron Hall could not help jumping in. "Do we know how?"

"Well, Mr. President," Colonel Sandman continued the narrative, "from a surreptitious recording we made of what the two Danes and the Russian officers said to each other when we left them alone for five minutes at their request, it would seem that a Russian submarine under the command of Captain…Zaitsov is his name, I believe— more than likely loyal to the previous Russian government under Pavel Laptov—may be taking her around the north of Greenland to rescue the former leader of the troika who was hiding out near here at Qaanaaq."

"Yes, Mr. President, at the request of Ms. Kristensen, I arranged to give Mr. Laptov asylum in our country, knowing he was in great danger from Russian operatives…," Malik interjected.

"It seems from all the intel we have, that the Gusanov regime is trying its utmost to find and liquidate Minister Laptov. They see him as a continuing major threat to their legitimacy," the head of the CIA chimed in.

"Which he is, of course. The majority of Russian people support him, according to our intelligence. But it is a brutal regime," the President agreed. "So, do we have the latest on Laptov and…Kristensen?"

"One of the Danish renegades who had commandeered the Citronen plane to fly to Thule claims to have seen them from the air on a snowmobile out on the ice on their way back to Qaanaaq. If this is true, the Zaitsov sub must have reached Qaanaaq with Ms. Kristensen on board, and if all went well, both she and Laptov are by now on it and out of reach underwater." This from Colonel Sandman.

"But surely the Russian subs and planes in the area will be on the lookout for the AWOL submarine. And ready to take it out," President Barlow observed.

"Do we know where Zaitsov and co are headed?"

"Our best guess is to one of the northern Canadian settlements."

"Ron, will you get on the hooter with our Canadian friends and warn them of the precious cargo that may be coming their way? We need to understand how they will guarantee their safety. If they can't, we may need to step in."

"Yes, Mr. President."

The discourse was interrupted by the Joint Chief of Staff, who removed an air pod from his ear as he took the floor. "Mr. President, I'm just getting reports from the surveillance craft over Nuuk, that the Russian destroyer force offshore there has moved into Greenland waters and that several hundred men have landed. Effectively, Nuuk, the capital of Greenland is now occupied."

"Malik, did you hear that?" the President stood up and took several steps. "This is an impossible situation. Gentlemen, let us consider the best response to it."

And to the Joint Chief of Staff, "Bill, get some planes in the air and subs underwater to look out for Laptov and the fugitive submarine. We must not let the Ruskis get to them first." President Barlow turned to the Secretary of State. "James, issue a *démarche* from me to the Russians to the effect that their aggressive moves against Thule and Greenland are intolerable, and unless they remove their forces from Greenland's territory and maritime zone within twenty-four hours, it will be considered an act of war against the United States and will result in appropriate retaliation from us."

"Mr. President, may I make a suggestion?" Malik seized the moment. "I am wondering if you would support an initiative for me to make a statement denouncing this hypocritical Russian aggression at the UN General Assembly. I know it is now in session, and our newly independent country—I guess I should say supposedly independent country—has just been accepted as the hundred-and-ninety-fourth member state—indeed, with the strong support of Russia and China. I think it would be a tremendous slap in the face for both if Greenland's first intervention in front of this august world body would be such a statement criticizing their attempts to subjugate us."

"Great idea, Malik. I think you should prepare your comments and come to New York to make the statement. In fact, as you say the General Assembly is meeting this coming week, I believe—" and Barlow looked at Gilchrist, who nodded, "—yes, that is correct, you are right, my Secretary of State has just confirmed it, so it would be a good time. We will also convene a special meeting of the Security Council to address this horrific transgression of your sovereignty—it goes against the founding articles of the United Nations. Although with Russia and China both permanent members, and able to veto everything, any resolution coming out of the session will only be symbolic. In any case, I will try to make a point of being there on Monday or Tuesday to support you. We will also coordinate our response with you, should this latest ultimatum not yield results."

"Thank you, Mr. President. That will all be very helpful."

"And Colonel Sandman, will you make the arrangements to fly the Prime Minister to New York and confirm the arrangements to us?"

"Of course, Mr. President."

"Thank you, both. We will see you in New York, Malik, and keep in touch, Colonel Sandman."

⍣⍣

"Put her on the speaker," President Barlow said, "but you do the talking, Ron. At least, in the beginning, to make her comfortable. Then we can all join in." Ron connected his cell to the Situation Room's speaker system.

"Mrs. Rorsen, thank you for calling…I am always keen on hearing from you."

"Mr. Hall, something terrible is happening here in Nuuk. Two Russian battle ships and some smaller vessels have parked just offshore Nuuk, and even as we speak, they have disgorged boats with many hundreds of soldiers who are making their way to shore. Greenland is being invaded…"

"Yes, Mrs. Rorsen, we are aware of these terrible developments. We are, in fact, assembled in the

President's Situation Room watching the events in your country unfold. I am sorry to say that not only is Nuuk under attack, but similar landings are underway in Kangerlussuaq, Sisimiut and Ilulissat. Thule, too, is under pressure from a Russian submarine force. And the Citronen mine up north, of course, was already occupied some days ago."

"Mr. Hall, is my husband all right, do you know?"

Barlow jumped in. "Mrs. Rorsen, this is President Barlow of the United States. You are on a speaker phone, and just moments ago I spoke with your husband and Colonel Sandman, the commanding officer at Thule. The Prime Minister—your husband—will be coming to New York to make a statement of protest in front of the United Nations General Assembly. Colonel Sandman will be flying him to New York directly from Thule, and we will make sure he gets in touch with you as soon as he gets there. I hope to be in New York to meet with him and hear his speech and coordinate further actions. Until then, Mrs. Rorsen, we would appreciate if you could keep us informed of any developments in Nuuk. Stay safe and well, and my people will be in touch."

"Thank you, Mr. President. I am deeply grateful to you."

"No, it is we who are in your debt for letting us know of these latest incidents. We thank you very much indeed."

"Mrs. Rorsen, I will call you as soon as we know more or if there are any changes in the plans," Ron Hall interjected.

"Thank you," Nanurjuk answered. "And if there are any developments here, I will let you know."

Chapter 22

Northern Greenland—Saturday, Late September, 202-

Hanne drove Aani's pick-up like a maniac down the steep dirt road that led to the village and then slowed down a bit to make sure she found the dock where she prayed that Igor and the two Russian submariners were waiting. She hoped they would put up the flag even before she reached them, to signal their impending arrival to Zaitsov, and more importantly, that the captain or one of his men was watching the shore through the periscope.

She breathed a sigh of relief when she turned down the road leading to the pier and saw the rubber dinghy tied up with one of the Russian mariners waving the flag. She pulled up right where the dirt road met the wooden dock and said to her companion, "Pavel, come quickly. We must get on that rubber dinghy immediately. Down there, where you see the flag. Sorry, but we don't have time to collect your things at Aani's. Look, the submarine is surfacing at this very moment—," and she pointed out into the fjord, "—and they will not stay above water for long."

The two ran down the jetty and jumped in the dinghy, with Igor already revving the engines as the Russian holding the rope saulted in behind them.

☙❧

Once safely in the sub, with the "whews" and "welcomes" out of the way, and the vessel already in the process of submerging, Captain Zaitsov congratulated Hanne on her quick return and successful extraction of Pavel. He warmly welcomed the Russian minister and assured him personally that he and his crew were strong supporters and were ready to do anything to protect him from the renegade Gusanov regime. Simply put, they were ready to follow his orders.

"Yes, Pyotr, but what you don't know is that I'm quite sure we were spotted from the air," Hanne interjected. "I saw what I'm quite sure was the Goldenrod plane fly low over us. But it must have been Larsen who had commandeered it. There's absolutely no reason why Derek Tate or any of the others from Citronen needed to be on this side of Greenland. Or indeed would be allowed to take off by my renegade Danish compatriot. So, it could only have been Larsen himself."

"Hanne, I think you may be right," Zaitsov agreed. "When we were periscope depth, we had our radio on just to listen, and we picked up some traffic on the command's frequency. The commander of our fleet, Vice-Admiral Ogarov, is at Thule and just met with Larsen who told him about the sighting. So, they know we are here."

"What is Larsen doing at Thule? And your commander?" Hanne asked anxiously.

"Well, it seems that the new government in my country, apparently with Larsen and another one of your renegade Danish friends leading them by the nose, is putting severe pressure on the Americans to leave Thule. And for all foreigners—Chinese, Danish, American—to pull out completely from Greenland."

"Great. You mean give Russia free reign? Just replace one colonizer with another," Hanne said facetiously.

"Mother Russia seems to be taking this very seriously. From the radio traffic, it appears that, on the orders of the Gusanov government, a significant part of our Northern Fleet is positioned in key strategic places around Greenland, and landings have already been made in important towns. In fact, Nuuk seems to be now in Russian hands, as apparently are the main airports throughout Greenland. Citronen, too, of course. And the threat is that if the Americans do not withdraw from Thule, the usurpers in my country will devastate Greenland, destroying all human life, if you can believe it. They could unleash a nuclear Armageddon for all we know."

"God, that would be tantamount to genocide! And an ecological disaster. On top of what we are already living now…"

"Yes. But it seems that Gusanov and his cronies are willing to go to any lengths to gain control of the Arctic. And that now includes Greenland."

"Which, as of a few months ago, is an independent country…"

"Hanne, before we get on to that, where are we heading now? We have to move quickly, because I am sure one or more of those subs off Thule will soon be searching for us. Gusanov stills considers Minister Laptov a huge threat to his legitimacy. And rightly so. I believe the majority of Russians indeed support you, Mr. Minister," Zaitsov said, glancing at Pavel. "As do I and some of my close confidantes in the navy…"

"Yes, Pyotr. I have given it some thought and believe

we should head for Pond Inlet," Hanne answered. "On Baffin Island. It's a little farther than Grise Fjord across on Ellesmere, but it's bigger, with better communication and transportation links. It has a better landing strip and is closer to mainland Canada, so we should be able to get Pavel to safety more quickly."

Zaitsov went over to a screen showing a map and entered the names of the settlements. "Good, Hanne. I agree with you. I see that Grise Fjord is just over 360 kilometers from here and Pond Inlet 580 or so. So, we could be at Pond Inlet in twelve, fourteen hours—it's just four hours farther than Grise Fjord."

"The main point is that it will be easier to get Pavel away from there. And I see from Google that at Pond Inlet, there are some Canadian military personnel who could help us. As soon as we have communication links to the outside, I will call my Canadian friend to have him set things in motion. We will be in good hands there, I'm sure."

It was then that Laptov, who had been silent throughout this exchange, and who had also been looking at the map on the screen, piped up. "No, my friends. Why would I go to Canada? My place is back in my country. I would like Captain Zaitsov and his submarine to take me back to Russia, if that is possible. After all, I am still officially the internationally recognized head of state, and as you, Captain, have just said, I still have strong support there. I believe that we must do everything we can to oust this criminal regime before it is too late. The fate of the world hangs in the balance."

Zaitsov and Hanne looked at each other, stunned, and Hanne eventually broke the silence. "Pavel, I fear for your safety, but I confess deep down I cannot disagree with you. If we could safely get you back to Russia, and if you could muster the support you have, and if that movement is strong enough to get rid of Gusanov and his cronies, it would be better for the world. And certainly, for the Arctic. But that is a lot of ifs…And a huge risk for you."

"The voyage is possible," Zaitsov said. "But we will have to go back the way we came. Around the north of Greenland again and then I guess head to Severomorsk. Going south, it is much longer, plus it seems that we would run into the ships and submarines of our navy. Even so, it will be a long journey—probably close to four days I would guess. And not without danger, but at least our countrymen will not be expecting us to be going back the way we came. As you said, Hanne, they probably believe we will go on to Canada. And Minister Laptov, once we are in Russia, I think I can get many of my fellow naval officers, who I know are your supporters, to join us. That will be a start."

"And a very good one, thank you, Captain. Let's do it!" Pavel was genuinely enthusiastic.

Hanne thought for a moment before interjecting. "In that case, Pyotr, please can you take us—Kristi and me—back to shore please? I know it is added risk, but I believe that a lot can happen to my new country in four or five days, and as a Minister, I cannot be literally off radar, underwater, for that long. Just as Pavel's place is in Russia, mine is here…"

"But Hanne, here in Qaanaaq…," Pavel interjected.

"Don't worry. As you are aware, I know important people here and they can help us get back to Nuuk or wherever the action is."

"Your Prime Minister is actually in Thule," Zaitsov observed, "judging from the radio reports we heard."

"So much the better. I will try to link up with him there…"

"Well, let me go and give the orders. But we will have to make it quick…"

"Thank you, Pyotr. For everything. You have been very good to us," Hanne said, surprising the captain with a hug.

And facing Kristi, with a tear in her eye, "Let's go get our things from out back."

After she wiped her eyes, Hanne turned to Laptov. "Pavel, good luck to you! And keep me in the picture. It's very brave of you to go back to Russia, and I sincerely hope you will come out on top. I will try to collect your things from your little cottage and get them to you eventually somehow."

"There is nothing there I cannot do without." The Russian took a step toward her and embraced her, adding, "You are an amazing woman, Hanne. Good luck to you, too. And thanks for everything. I owe my life to you."

Chapter 23

Northern Greenland—Saturday, Late September, 202-

As the rubber dinghy approached the shore for the second time that day, Hanne was glad to see that the fishermen were still there, even though it was the end of the working day. When she and Kristi hopped up on the dock, she was even more pleased when she caught sight of Aani and his son just walking away from the pier, up toward the parking lot. She sprinted after them, shouting, "Aani, wait up!"

"Hello, Hanne. What brings you back so soon?"

"Change in plans." Hanne paused to catch her breath. "We succeeded in getting Laptov away, but I have things I must do here in Greenland. And I need your help, please."

"Of course. What with?"

"I need to get to Malik as quickly as possible. I know he needs me." And then she thought she better introduce Kristi. "Oh, Aani, Aput, this is my friend Kristi. She's with me." She noticed that Aput stared at Kristi with mouth agape.

"Good to meet you, Kristi." Aani glanced at her, then he too, looked her up and down before continuing. "Malik is in Thule. I just had a call from Nanurjuk, who is back in

Nuuk. My brother-in-law is going to New York to make a statement in front of the United Nations General Assembly. Big deal speech, to protest the Russian invasion. The commander of the base is flying him there, probably with an escort of several planes, given the circumstances."

"Then I need to get to Thule before Malik leaves. I will call Colonel Sandman and ask her if she could send a plane to fetch us. Hopefully, I can still catch them. Could I use your phone, Anni, please?"

"Getting her to fly you to the American base could be dangerous, with all the Russian submarines and planes watching take-offs and landings. Plus, they might not have an airplane that can land here. I think it would be better for you to catch the regular Air Greenland flight tomorrow that goes to Pituffik—Thule's commercial airport. It is now getting late here anyway, and I am sure Malik will not be going anywhere today." Aani pulled up his sleeve to look at his watch as he said this. "But here, take my phone, and call him or the Colonel just to be sure and to arrange matters."

"Thank you, Aani. I knew I could count on you. I'm sure you're right…"

"Come, you can do that on the way home. You and your friend…Kristi…will stay with us tonight." And, with a broad smile on his face, he added, "You're in luck, Hanne. I know Biina has been preparing your favourite Inuit meal: *suaasat,* the fish stew you enjoyed so much the last time you visited."

"Amazing. And thank you!"

ℰᏗℰᏗ

On the way to Aani's place, Hanne dialled Malik's number. Fortunately, the prime minister picked up.

"Hanne, are you alright?"

"Yes, Malik. Thanks. I am in Qaanaaq now, but I want to get to you ASAP. There is a lot we need to talk about."

"Terrific. I will be going to New York tomorrow, to make a statement of protest at the United Nations. Of course, I am keen on seeing you and having you join me. Colonel Sandman was just readying arrangements to fly me there, but we will wait for you. Should I ask her to send a plane to get you?"

"Aani suggests that I take the Air Greenland flight tomorrow morning to Pituffik. Can you arrange to have someone meet us? By the way, Kristi is with me—we can all fly to New York together. Is that okay?"

"Very good. We will catch up on the flight then."

"Excellent."

"Yes, there is a lot to talk about and we need to do some important planning. I am glad my favorite minister will be with me to plot our path forward in these difficult times."

"See you soon, Malik. Bye."

She was about to hand the phone back to Aani but thought of Richard. For all she knew, he was on his way to Pond Inlet, so she had better call him too. *Maybe she can stop him, perhaps even get him to come to New York. Oh, but that would only complicate things with Kristi. Never mind on that, but she needed to tell him of the change in plans with Pavel going back to Russia now.*

Richard didn't pick up, so she sent him a message. "Change in plans. Going to NYC with Malik, who will protest Russian invasion at UN." *Yes, that was enough for now.*

ɞɷɞ

Settled into their seats the next morning on the short Air Greenland flight, Hanne hugged Kristi.

"Well, at least we should have a little private time in New York. I have missed your touch, my dear…"

"And I, your whole gorgeous body! I can hardly wait."

"I will be working, though. This is not just a lark," Hanne said with a smile. "Greenland has been invaded and I have a lot on my plate."

"As long as you promise that we will make love in Central Park at least once, I will be happy."

"How about at least three times in our hotel room?" Hanne responded with a smile. "You are incorrigible, you…"

"Well, I might settle for that…with no less than five orgasms each," Kristi said, stealing a kiss.

Chapter 24

*Thule, Greenland and on a flight to New York—Sunday,
Late September, 202-*

So, Hanne and Kristi, you certainly have been through a lot since the last time we saw each other," Malik greeted the two women. "But welcome, and as I said, I am very glad you are here. Safe. We have a lot to talk about. Everything that has happened, is happening, and where we go from here."

"Yes, I feel the same way. Plans certainly have changed along the way. And they keep changing."

"That's for sure! You were just going to Citronen to check out progress up there, weren't you…and then you were going to head over here to Thule to discuss some of those environmental issues with Colonel Sandman…And now we are faced with this invasion by the Russians."

"Yes, I think a meeting was in my schedule," the Colonel said with a chuckle. "But as you say, events have certainly overtaken all our planning."

"Well, since then, at least Kristi and I have seen a lot of my new country…"

"And the inside of a Russian submarine, to be sure!" Kristi said, with a little laugh, "As we rounded the northern shore of Greenland…"

"Yes, to get to Qaanaaq to ferret Pavel away," Hanne continued the story. "With the help of a friendly Russian submarine captain. Actually, one of Minister Laptov's supporters."

"So where is Pavel now?" Malik asked.

"On his way back to Russia in the submarine. Hoping he'll be able to raise enough support to be reinstated as the leader of the country."

"Wasn't the fallback Canada? Of course, we will give him all the help we can with our UN speech. He is a brave man," Malik said. "If he could be reinstated, that would be great for us. He would no doubt call off this insane invasion. And respect the Arctic Treaty he worked so hard to put in place with you and signed on behalf of Russia."

"Ladies and gentlemen, I see Lieutenant Sawyer coming toward us," Colonel Sandman interrupted. "He's the pilot who'll fly you to New York. It must be time to board."

"Thank you, Colonel, for all your hospitality and help," Malik said. "I am sure we will meet again."

∽∾∽∾

On the flight, Hanne sat down beside her boss, and Kristi got the hint. She recognized that this would be a good time for her friend and the prime minister to plan the next steps and start thinking about what to say to the General Assembly.

"I am looking forward to making a statement at the UN," Malik said. "After all, we won our independence from Denmark with promises of support from China and Russia, and now it is their governments that are wanting to dictate to us. Worse than before. Intolerable."

"Yes…"

"President Barlow probably will be coming to New York. We will discuss matters, especially how we can get these Russians to leave without major loss of life and environmental damage."

"Malik, I think there is also a very important environmental cause here that we must uphold, one that will certainly make our case stronger."

"I think I know what you are getting at, but what exactly do you mean?"

"Well, that our country—like much of the world—is going through terrible stresses as a result of climate change. And we want to preserve our pristine environment to the extent possible, but if we have one or more superpowers trying to force us willy-nilly to open up mines and oil fields that they can benefit from without the care that we take—which is what is really behind both China's and Russia's interest, other than to get rid of the American presence at Thule—we cannot do that. It goes against the principles Greenland has stood for as a country, as well as against those of the UN, and more importantly, against a secure future for humanity."

"Very good, Hanne. But as you were speaking, I was thinking just now that I should make the political protest in no uncertain terms, and then immediately after, you should come up to the podium to make a statement along those lines. That would be a phenomenal one-two punch that the members of the General Assembly would no doubt have to support, don't you think?"

"I like it, Malik, and I'm happy to do it…"

"Also, you are known around the corridors of the organization, and from all the reports, you carry a lot of respect for someone so young…and beautiful."

"Thank you, Malik. But…there's one slight problem: I have nothing appropriate to wear to appear in front of such an august body."

"That's not an issue," Malik said with a chuckle. "You will have time to do a little shopping tomorrow, and you can certainly charge a new dress or two for such an important occasion to the government budget. This could be make or break for our independent Greenland."

"I'm grateful, Malik. Perhaps I should try and put my thoughts on paper and show them to you…"

"Good idea, Hanne. Let's both work on our speeches and then we can compare notes later."

Chapter 25

*Lotte New York Palace Hotel, New York—Sunday
Evening, Late September, 202-*

Checking in at the Lotte Palace Hotel in New York—frequented not only by many rulers, potentates and diplomats, but also the choice of President Obama several administrations earlier for meetings in the city—Hanne held Kristi back to let Malik go ahead. Although it probably did not matter, she just did not want to have him overhear that she and Kristi were going to share a suite with a king size bed. Once he had checked in, she said, "See you in the morning, Malik. Breakfast—what time?"

"Yes, I am quite tired, and in need of a good night's sleep. You're right, it's best to have room service tonight. We can enjoy dinner together tomorrow, once we are all prepared for the session. And how about breakfast at 9:30 am—that should be long enough to rest our tired selves? And then no doubt you will want to head out to look for that dress."

"Thank you. Yes, that makes sense. See you then in the restaurant."

ဆာ

Once up in the luxurious room, Kristi rushed over to the picture window that gave out onto a stunning view of St. Patrick's Cathedral, while Hanne struggled to pull out a five dollar bill to tip the bellboy who had brought their meagre possessions up and showed them to the room, wondering if this would be enough. This done, she rushed over and hugged Kristi from behind, turned her around and gave her a deep kiss. When she surfaced, she looked into the eyes of her lover and friend, "Okay, Kristi dear, I'm so glad we can now be alone. It's been some time…But here's the deal. Why don't we quickly unpack our meagre belongings, then take a shower together—with perhaps a little love making thrown in—and then, while you order us a nice room service dinner, I will need to make a few calls. After that, we will have a romantic *diner à deux*—perhaps, if you're a good girl, Kristi, leading to a little more loving—after which I probably need to do some work. How about that for an action-packed evening, love?"

"Hmm. Pretty good. Except you forgot that after you do a little work, we'll need to do a lot of loving, so we can reach the minimum number you promised, with five orgasms each?"

Hanne laughed and then gave her another deep kiss, which ended up with the two frantically helping each other undress and Kristi pulling the by then naked Hanne onto the king size bed. So, they already managed to depart from Hanne's program by indulging in their first loving session and first orgasms before the unpacking and the shower, which, needless to say, was also peppered with lots of touching and feeling.

൏൏൏

Sated, and dressed only in the Lotte Palace's luxurious bathrobe, Hanne went back into the living room of the suite and made herself comfortable on the couch with her cell phone. She mulled over whom she should call first, and decided it needed to be Richard. To let him know where she was and why, and all that had happened since they last communicated.

Richard answered after only two rings. "Hanne, dear, oh, I'm so glad to hear from you. I was so worried…" The reception was not good, and he sounded very far away. Which she knew he was.

"Hello, Richard. I'm very happy to hear your voice, too. Where are you?"

"Pond's Inlet. I was hoping you would be coming here with Pavel Laptov, just like you had indicated. But Hanne, where are you? And where is Laptov?"

"Richard, I'm sorry, but the plans changed along the way. I sent you a message. Laptov wanted the submarine we had commandeered to take him back to Russia. So, there was no reason for me to go to Canada…other than, of course, to come see you. With so much going on though, I really had to get back to Greenland."

"And that's where you are now? But I heard that the Russians are occupying much of your new country. Haven't the bastards surrounded it with a massive naval force?"

"Well, no. And yes, and yes. I went to shore still in Qaanaaq and met up with Prime Minister Rorsen in Thule. Then we flew to New York—the Big Apple is where I'm right now—to protest the invasion by Russia and the less blatant pressures from China, during the General Assembly session at the United Nations. And, of course, to meet with American officials."

"Good for you. Why don't I come there?"

Hanne paused a moment and thought to herself: *not a good idea.* She was already juggling too much as it was. "Richard, we'll be leaving New York in two days. You'd barely make it here."

"Then can you come and meet me in Ottawa?"

"I need to go back to Nuuk with Malik..."

"Hanne, that is very dangerous. Into the viper's pit...no."

"Yes. I must..."

"When will I get to see you?"

"Soon, Richard...soon. I will call you from there. I miss you, too."

"Well, dear, I'll look into arrangements to come to Nuuk. I may need to rescue you from the bloody Ruskis. Or the Chinese. Or both. Fuck, all those bloody superpowers."

Richard rarely swore, so Hanne thought she had better leave it at that. "I will call you from Nuuk, Richard. I love you."

"I, too. But be careful, Hanne. Please. I want to marry you and make children with you." There, he had blurted out his resolve.

Hanne gulped at this. *This was definitely one huge step. Was he asking me to marry him?*

"Richard..."

"We'll talk about it in Nuuk. See you soon."

Holy...shit! Hanne thought to herself, *it was all happening so fast. And with everything else going on, how am I going to sort out my personal life?*

⌘

It took Hanne a few moments to recover from Richard's

somewhat uncustomary, over-the-phone proposal, but she knew this was not the time to think about it. Very soon, though, she would have to make some tough decisions…

A call to Ron Hall was of paramount importance, she knew. So, she scrolled down and clicked on the American's number. He did not pick up, so she left a message: *"Hello, Ron. Am in New York, with Prime Minister Rorsen to make a statement of protest at the UN. We need to talk. Please call ASAP."*

While she waited, she checked the newsfeed on her cell phone and saw that the main story was the escalating tension in Greenland, with different pundits speculating on why the country's prime minister was now in New York. Boy, they had just arrived, and the journalists had already picked up on it? That sure was quick!

Kristi came in when she heard the silence from the living room, to tell her that she had ordered seared ahi tuna for dinner. "What wine would you like with it, my dear? A Pinot Noir would go well don't you think?"

"Sure, whatever you like, and thanks." She was still distracted by her call to Richard, but just then the strains of the *New World Symphony* could be heard emanating from her phone, loud and clear, and she nodded to Kristi, as she answered, "Hey. Hanne Kristensen."

"Hanne, I'm so glad you called. And that you are in New York. I'm coming up there tomorrow, so we'll need to schedule some time. How are you?"

"Well, Ron, things could be better for little old Greenland…that is, huge young Greenland."

"Yes, we were just in the Situation Room discussing how we should proceed following on our ultimatum. Now that we haven't heard from the Russians, and the twenty-four hours we gave them is just about over…"

"Ron, you might want to consider some of the most

recent developments in Greenland before you take any aggressive action. I'm sure you understand, but we would prefer no bombs landing on our soil. Or our icecap, for that matter. And no fighting either. No loss of life and no environmental damage."

"Yes…we want to coordinate with your Prime Minister…"

"Good. But Ron, we should also take into consideration the virus that we are struggling with up in Thule. What you don't know is that it was carried to Nuuk. The good news, though, is that we believe that some of the Russian invaders now have it as well, and it is spreading among them. The Chinese may have contracted it too—all mostly we think by contact at Nuuk airport. Perhaps we should think about letting this Greenland virus join in the fight for us…"

"Hmm. Interesting thought. But you no doubt also want to make sure it doesn't infect your people. You know, Hanne, hot from the labs, we now have a new vaccine that supposedly is super effective against coronaviruses of all kinds. We are just testing it for this new virus since some of the men from Thule were flown here, and we are optimistic that it will work for this one too. Although, of course, it is early days and to be sure, we would need to do a lot more trials and observations over more time. But we do know it is safe, with no downside."

"Ron, that is very exciting news. Just thinking aloud, you know that Greenland's population is only 58,000 or so—if we could very rapidly inoculate all Greenlanders and let the virus take its toll among the invaders, that could certainly weaken and scare them, I think. It would then make it easier for you to threaten and take more aggressive actions militarily if need be. And back in Russia, it could bring into question the wisdom of Gusanov's invasion, and perhaps boost support for Pavel Laptov."

"That is brilliant, Hanne. I will brief the President and my colleagues. And I'm quite sure we can have 58,000 doses available for your people…"

"We're going back on Wednesday…is there any chance we could have the vaccines by then? We'll need to figure out how to get it to all the remote communities, but I believe Greenland managed it well for COVID. The Inuit are extremely resourceful."

"Excellent. I will make this a priority here. And thank you, Hanne."

"No, thank you! If this works, that would be phenomenal…"

"Indeed. I'm going to run now but see you…tomorrow. Unless getting the vaccines somehow prevents me from coming."

 උ෧ණ

Hanne shouted to Kristi—who seemed to be back in the bathroom, presumably getting ready for their romantic dinner—that she had one more call to make. She was very excited about the promise Ron had made regarding the vaccines and wanted to pass her thoughts and the news along to Malik so that he could think about how best to execute the plan. They would just have to get the word out to all the communities in Greenland to be on standby and then have a number of planes fly around the large island delivering the vaccines and medical professionals to inoculate the entire population. *The whole exercise could be carried out in just a few days,* Hanne thought to herself, *and should be done anyway, occupation or no occupation.*

Unfortunately, Malik did not pick up—either he was on

another call or asleep already. *Never mind, good enough to discuss it tomorrow.* Pleased with herself, Hanne jumped up from the sofa and yelled to Kristi, "Okay, here I come! I'm ready for our romantic evening…"

Chapter 26

Lotte New York Palace Hotel, New York—Monday,
Late September, 202-

Hanne woke slowly from a deep sleep, and only when she reached out and touched Kristi's flesh did she remember where she was. They had perhaps had too much to imbibe the night before, ordering another bottle of the delicious Penny Royal 2015 Anderson Valley Pinot Noir after they had easily polished off the first to accompany the ahi tuna—having already toasted themselves with two flûtes of a Bollinger 2009 champagne before dinner—and then sipping a Pierre de Segonzac VSOP Grande Champagne cognac as they started necking on the couch. But their consumption had been over several hours, and she did need to get her mind off all the heavy issues she was dealing with—including that out-of-the-blue telephonic proposal by Richard—she rationalized to herself, plus she had stayed away from alcohol for a good week before. And, of course, it all made Kristi just that much more delicious!

How was she going to be able to give this up? Kristi?

Marriage and kids with Richard seemed so…so idyllic. But then again—she dared not think it…conventional?

Fortunately, just then, Kristi opened her beautiful big blue eyes and they lit up with her magical smile when she said, "Hanne, this is the best, isn't it? We'll always have each other, won't we?"

With tears in her eyes, Hanne could only respond by hugging her friend, and as she moved toward her, she saw that the alarm clock over her shoulder read 9:03. She got on her knees on the bed, naked, and pulled Kristi up, saying, "We gotta get moving here, girl. I agreed to have breakfast with Malik at 9:30. In twenty-seven minutes!"

"Aw, you mean we can't do it again?"

"Not till later," and she pushed her friend out of bed. "And only if you're lucky, you sex addict. Now let's get moving. We can't go downstairs like this, smelling of…of orgasm and looking so…so dishevelled."

"But it's my favorite look for you," Kristi protested. "And that aroma on your skin is the best perfume ever."

∽∾∽∾

Stepping out of the elevator at 9:38, Hanne looked around, not knowing which of the Lotte's eateries Malik would be in. She guessed the elegant Villard Restaurant, because the evening before, she had noted that they had a sumptuous breakfast menu.

So, the two headed toward the posh venue, and indeed, Malik was already there at one of the tables off to the side, sipping on his morning cappuccino. As Hanne and Kristi followed the *maître d'* over to join him, all eyes in the restaurant focused on the two Danish beauties.

"Good morning, Malik," Hanne greeted the prime minister, as she sat down. "I'm sorry we're a bit late, but I think we all needed a good night's sleep."

"Well, I am very glad you are rested, Hanne." Malik smiled, and then, as Kristi sat down, added, "Hello, Kristi."

"Good morning, Malik."

"Shall we get the ordering out of the way before we knuckle down to business?"

"Yes. Thank you, Malik," Hanne said, as she opened the menu.

When the waiter came a few minutes later, Hanne ordered the smoked salmon on a bagel and a cappuccino, while Kristi, saying, "I am ravenous!" went for the more substantial *shakshouka*—a delicious lamb merguez sausage, poached egg, roasted tomato and feta cheese on a toasted baguette—along with a double espresso macchiato.

"So, Malik, I have some potentially interesting news to report," Hanne started as soon as the waiter left. "I tried to call you last night, but you didn't pick up."

"Yes. I called Nanurjuk and then I had a videoconference call on my laptop with several of your minister colleagues to assess the situation back home."

"Good. I hope everything is all right."

"Yes, given the circumstances. But what is this interesting news you have for me?""

"Well, Malik, yesterday, I talked to my friend, Ron Hall, President Barlow's national security advisor for Arctic affairs. He hopes to be here later today, so we can speak to him directly, but one of the exciting things he said is that the US has a brand-new vaccine that protects against all types of coronavirus infections. And they now know definitively that the Thule virus is of that type, so are optimistic that this new vaccine could be highly effective against it. We discussed that perhaps they could get us enough doses so we can inoculate most of our population while we let the virus rage among the invaders. With some Russian soldiers being brought down by this invisible enemy, it could throw the occupying forces into disarray. And it might even help Pavel regain control back in Russia, as Gusanov's unnecessary invasion of faraway Greenland becomes discredited."

"Hmm. Interesting thought. Certainly, worth mulling over," Malik answered. "Your friend is coming to New York for the UN session, isn't he? So why don't you ask Mr. Hall to join us for dinner? Then we can consider it further and firm things up. This could be factored into the response…"

"Great! I'll do that as soon as we're done. What time should I tell him? And where?"

"Hanne, I asked the hotel to make reservations for the three of us and a good friend, Kirima Hanseraq, our newly appointed representative to the United Nations, at nearby La Grenouille. A well-known French restaurant that comes recommended. For 7:30. I am sure they will have no problems accommodating one more person."

Over their breakfast, Hanne and Malik discussed what they would say the next day in front of the General Assembly, after which the prime minister again urged Hanne—and Kristi—to get some dressy clothes for the session. They were delighted to respond that that was what they would be doing the rest of the morning.

❧❦❧

But the plans changed as soon as they arrived back in their room to prepare for the shopping expedition. While Kristi went to the bathroom, Hanne called Ron Hall's cell to invite him to dinner that evening.

"Great, Hanne, thanks. But right now, can you join your prime minister for a videoconference with President Barlow? We need to figure out the response to the Russians. We are about to call Rorsen. He just messaged that he's back in his room now."

"Okay. I'll see you online then in a few minutes. Bye."

And then to her friend as she went into the bedroom: "Kristi, my dear, I'm afraid you'll have to shop for both of us. I have to join Malik for a videoconference with President Barlow."

"Well, bull-hooey, Madame Minister. Aren't we important, now?"

"Kristi, please. No kidding, can you get me a nice and relatively conservative dress—something appropriate to wear for a speech in front of the UN General Assembly? Maybe a suit of some kind? You know my size and what I like. Here's my credit card—I have to go now. Thanks, love."

⁊

Malik was already on the call when she walked in.

Barlow was talking. "Well, I was saying, Malik, what I am ordering our military to do for now is, first, to send vessels to block the fjords and harbors that the Russians have penetrated, and second, to maintain constant overflight of any areas where Russian troops have positioned themselves. Not just with one plane, but several bombers and fighters at the same time. The idea is to scare them—no, to make it clear to them that if they initiate anything against you and/or us, there will be severe repercussions."

"Thank you, Mr. President."

"In the meantime, we will supply you with this new coronavirus vaccine—sufficient for you to inoculate your entire population. Fortunately, enough has been produced for that, I think. We will not mention any of this to the press, and you should not talk about it in your speech tomorrow. As Ms. Kristensen, I believe you suggested, we should wait until the virus weakens the invading forces and perhaps then move in some troops if necessary to clean things up."

"Excellent. Thank you," Rorsen responded.

"Can you get one of your planes to Boston to pick up the vaccines, say, Tuesday pm? The production facility is just south of there, I'm told. Then, it can get you in New York and fly you back to Nuuk on Wednesday with the vaccines."

"Sure. That all sounds doable. Thank you."

"You can discuss the rest of the logistics with Ron, who I believe will be meeting with you later today. I'm still planning to come to the General Assembly session tomorrow, my schedule permitting. I have a lot on my plate right now, so we'll just have to see."

❧❧❧

After the call, Hanne went up to her suite, and since Kristi was not back yet, she decided it would be a good time for her to work on her speech for the next day.

She knew she should keep it short, but she wanted to make the point vividly that Greenland was—even more so than the rest of the world—going through major environmental stress because of climate change, and that the foreign troops on its soil only made this situation worse. These invading forces were there to coerce

Greenland to cede its natural resources to the foreign powers who wanted to exploit them rapidly for their own gain, which would just result in more environmental degradation and destruction of the Inuit way of life. Extracting and burning more oil and gas was certainly not what the world needed right now, nor did Greenland welcome the prospect of foreign heavy machinery digging on its land or drilling through what ice remained, or into its undersea territories. The illegal Russian occupation and Chinese pressure to exploit these resources should be condemned in no uncertain terms by the UN General Assembly. And, no doubt, everybody should see through the fact that both Russia and China had been vociferous supporters of Greenland's independence from Denmark— even offering guarantees and huge financial incentives— exactly for this reason. To gain access to its resources.

Hmm. There that says it all. On top of Malik's protest and call for a vote to condemn the invasion and the pressures these two superpowers were putting on Greenland, with her speech following the prime minister's, she could not see any outcome possible, other than one in favor of Greenland. And that was why they had come.

Satisfied, she looked at her watch and saw that there was still lots of time, so she could definitely fit in a workout in the Lotte Palace's sumptuous gym. Just then, though, as she started to change into her exercise wear, she heard Kristi burst in through the front door, and within seconds, her gorgeous friend was in the bedroom, carrying several shopping bags in each hand and flipping them on the bed.

"How nice, were you undressing for me, my love?" Kristi asked, taking Hanne's almost naked body in with pleasure.

"No…just changing into my Lululemons. I thought we

should go and do a workout, Kristi. To keep that body of yours beautiful. And well-toned and fit for good sex."

"Well, we should perhaps first model these lovely clothes I bought—that is Greenland bought—for us. We might still have time to exchange them if you don't approve."

"Good idea. And good timing, dear."

"Tadaa," Kristi said as she pulled a short burgundy jacket and a skirt to match out of one of the bags marked Bloomingdale. "This is a very sober outfit for Greenland's minister of Environment and Natural Resources…Designed expressly not to show off any of her wares to all the sex-starved diplomats at the United Nations."

"Lovely," Hanne said with a smile as she held up the clothes.

"And here is a top to wear under the jacket." Kristi whipped out a white silk bouse. "Try the ensemble on, dear. And the shoes…" She dumped a pair of burgundy high heels out of a fancy shoe box, as Hanne had already pulled the tight-fitting skirt up and was buttoning the blouse.

Seeing her friend dressed to the hilt, Kristi said, "Wow, the Minister does look gorgeous, doesn't she? Go check yourself out in the mirror." The bathroom door had a floor to ceiling mirror on it, and when Hanne saw her reflection, she swivelled around with a very satisfied look on her face.

"Thank you, Kristi, you did well. Now let's see you!"

Kristi stripped down to her underwear, then struggled into a more colorful and very sexy tight-fitting red dress with a forest green top that they both found equally pleasing. "Wonderful, Kristi. We shall stun all those diplomats and get them to vote for whatever we put in front of them, I'm sure."

"Fabulous!" Kristi said, as she embraced Hanne.

After one quick kiss, Hanne said, "No, Kristi. We're not doing our usual exercises here in the bedroom. We're going to go to the gym now, so let's put on our Lululemons."

ↂↄↂↄ

Back in the room, exercised and showered, the two friends relaxed in the hotel's luxurious bathrobes with a glass of wine in front of the TV to catch the six o'clock news. The invasion of Greenland and the continuing tensions inside Russia were the lead items, followed by the now daily reports on climate change-related horrors: the collapsing ice shoulder that held the Thwaites Glacier in Antarctica back, which was causing sea levels to accelerate their rise, making large parts of Bangladesh and several islands in the Pacific and Indian Oceans already uninhabitable, indeed swamping some fishing villages in Greenland, then rain instead of snow in their country accelerating the melting of the icecap, continuing wildfires devastating primeval forests in Siberia, Australia, California and Brazil, tornadoes destroying homes in the US Midwest, millions starving across Africa, Asia and the Middle East as agriculture was hit hard by drought and so on. *It does not bode well for the future of the world,* Hanne thought. *We simply have to get the Arctic Treaty back on track.* Although deep down, she knew it was probably too late.

When the news petered out, she said, "Okay, Kristi, we better get ready! Dinner with Malik and Ron Hall awaits."

"Should we wear our new outfits?" Kristi asked.

"Of course. We can break them in—model them for

these two friends. Let's do it!"

Chapter 27

*La Grenouille Restaurant, New York—Monday,
Late September, 202-*

Malik had made reservations at La Grenouille, an upscale French restaurant near the Lotte Palace, and he and Ron Hall and Kirima Hanseraq, Greenland's newly appointed representative to the United Nations, were already there as the *maître d'* led the two Danish beauties through the maze of dining guests to the table in the corner. Both gentlemen stood up and double cheek kissed the arriving ladies, while the *maître d'* and an attending waiter pulled the chairs out for them. Malik made the introductions, and Hanne was struck by Kirima's beauty. Somewhat younger than Malik, hopefully, she was equally talented. Greenland needed someone competent and strong to represent it at the UN.

"Well, Ron, I'm so glad you made it," Hanne said, as she sat down.

"So am I," the American answered. "We were just discussing with Prime Minister Rorsen and the Ambassador how lucky we all are to have you working with us. You are one impressive woman, Hanne."

"Yes, indeed. I second that," Malik agreed. "And

Hanne, I know this may not be the appropriate time to say it, but I just want to express the appreciation of all Greenlanders for what you are doing."

As she felt Kristi put her hand on her thigh under the table, Hanne fidgeted before saying, "Thank you, Malik and Ron. I'm delighted to be working with you and serving Greenland—and I hope the world, too—as best I can."

Just then the waiter came over with the menus, and Malik suggested they order before getting down to business.

Hanne decided quickly, choosing the *foie gras* terrine, followed by the lobster tail with raviolis, and then closed the menu, looking around the posh restaurant while the others finished making their choices. *This is certainly better than what we would be eating in Greenland, even at the best restaurant in Nuuk. So may as well live it up. And perhaps it is some small recompense for the tireless work I'm doing for Greenland.*

And how wonderful to be able to share it with Kristi! With this thought, it was she who stroked Kristi's naked thigh with her hand.

The ordering out of the way, Ron got right down to the business at hand. "I managed to procure fifty thousand doses of this new vaccine that is so effective against the new Thule virus to send to you now, with the same number of second shots to come within a couple of weeks' time. The first batch will be delivered to Logan Airport tomorrow afternoon by 3:00 pm, so your crew can pick them up any time after that. These are among the first new combination mRNA and viral vector vaccines that work against all coronavirus infections. So we are very optimistic that it will be effective against this Thule virus as well. An added advantage is that it does not need to be refrigerated and therefore is easy to transport."

"Fantastic, thank you…Ron," Rorsen said. "May I call you by your first name? And I am Malik. Yes, I have arranged for an Air Greenland plane to be in Boston tomorrow afternoon, as the president had suggested."

"Great. It will be important to get the doses into arms as quickly as possible, since it does take several days to reach maximal efficacy. Including all of yours, of course."

"You leave that to us, Ron. I have already put my cabinet on standby, and they have mobilized an army of nurses and doctors to do the inoculations. We put the word out around the country—in the Inuit language, so the Russian invaders cannot understand—that it is key for all Greenlanders to get inoculated as soon as the vaccine arrives in their village. We will not have any vaccine deniers like in your country, Ron, I can assure you."

"I'm sure you won't," Ron said with a chuckle.

"I'm happy to help with the inoculations," Kristi piped up. "Including yours and Hanne's as soon as we have access to them."

"Yes, Kristi is a registered nurse back in Denmark."

"In, fact, I knew you would want to be vaccinated as soon as possible, so I have enough doses for you and the flight crew back in the room."

"Good idea. Thank you." This from Malik. "The hardest part will be to get the vaccines through the airport without the occupiers knowing."

"For that very reason, I've taken the liberty of ordering the supplier to mark the bottles as 'formaldehyde,'" Ron said.

"Brilliant." This from Hanne. "You always think ahead, Ron. And Kristi and I will do our best to distract any Russians at the airport. I'm quite sure their soldiers will not know who I am, as I believe my two renegade Danish ex-friends are still being held by Colonel Sandman in

Thule. In any case, I'm sure they would be more interested in questioning me about Pavel Laptov's whereabouts than on any boxes marked 'formaldehyde.'"

"Nevertheless, I am seriously worried about how safe it is for you to come with me, Hanne," Malik remarked.

"Don't worry, Malik. We know how to handle ourselves, Kristi and I. And if need be, we can just tell them the truth, that Laptov is under the sea in a submarine somewhere—it will take them days to find him, and by then he will have arrived at his destination."

"But be careful, Hanne," Ron said. "Let me know if there is any trouble, and we can accelerate matters at our end. Send in the troops…"

"Most of the boxes will actually be left on the plane, which, once refuelled, will then ferry them to Kangerlussuaq, where they will be separated into smaller parcels to fly to the other population destinations in Greenland," Malik said.

"Well, that all sounds like you have everything in hand," Ron remarked.

"And then we'll just have to wait for the virus to do its thing with the Russians," Hanne said. "As it is a highly infectious little bug, it could weaken their forces rather rapidly."

"We certainly hope so." This from Malik.

"You'll have to keep us apprised of how it is all progressing, and when the best time for US forces to land is—if indeed that will be necessary," Ron added.

"We will see. We will see." Malik was not certain that this plan of joining forces with the virus would work, but it was the best they could do against the invading enemy. Especially if they wanted to avoid massive environmental damage.

Or enemies, if one were to add the virus itself—even

though, also at first an ally, they still had to make sure in the end they vanquish it, he thought to himself. *How complicated life can be!*

Just then, the waiter brought the ordered dishes and poured the rosé Malik had selected. After several bites amid exclamations all-around of how delicious it all was, Malik asked, turning to the Greenlandic beauty, "Now, as to tomorrow, Kirima, where should we come?" "Should we meet you at one of the entrances?"

"Yes. I suggest we meet at the entrance to the United Nations Headquarters building at 45th Street and 1st Avenue, Prime Minister," Ms. Hanseraq said. "I've informed security that you and Ms. Kristensen would be joining me for our newly independent country's first appearance at the General Assembly as a United Nations member state. Out of courtesy, I've also set up a brief meeting with the Secretary General, Sung Chi Park, and the current President of the General Assembly, Hele Mägi, to introduce you. They both very much wanted to meet you. Ms. Mägi is Estonian and is especially very supportive of Greenland."

"Excellent, Kirima. Thank you. What time should we be there?"

"Well, the session normally starts at 9:30 am, so if we meet at 8:30 that should give us ample time to meet with both the General Secretary and the President of the current sessions."

"We'll be there!"

☙☙☙

Back at the hotel, they all stopped off at Ron Hall's room, where Kristi administered the vaccine to Hanne and

Malik, and then showed Hanne how to do her. Malik took the rest of the doses for the flight crew of the Air Greenland plane that would fly them back to Nuuk.

Hanne and Kristi said good night and thank you to Malik and Ron, and then made their way to their suite. As Hanne closed the door behind her, Kristi, stepping out of her high heels, said, "You know, love, I hate to say this…but I think I had better not come with you to Greenland. I really have to get back to Copenhagen…after all, I have a job there, and the two weeks of holiday I took will be done on Wednesday."

"Oh, dear," Hanne came over and hugged her. "I hadn't really thought of that, with everything going on. But to tell the truth, also when tonight Malik said that he's concerned about me going back to Greenland, I was actually more worried for you, just thinking about how that creep Erik manhandled you up at Citronen…and what you had told me before about him."

"No, it wasn't so much that…" Kristi looked away.

"No worries, dear, I agree with you," Hanne held her tight. "You need to get back to Copenhagen. And I will come there soon, I promise. I, too, will be owed some vacation after this Russian affair."

And then, they shared a long and passionate kiss. When they came up for air, Hanne said, "But this isn't our last night, my dear. We still have tomorrow."

"All the same, Hanne, we're going to make it a night we will both remember…," Kristi said as she unbuttoned Hanne's silk blouse, the burgundy jacket having already come off as they made their way into the bedroom…

And within moments they were both naked, in each other's arms on the king size bed, on the verge of ecstasy.

Chapter 28

United Nations Headquarters, New York—Tuesday,
Late September, 202-

Tuesday morning, Malik, Hanne and Kristi made their way to the delegates' entrance of the United Nations Headquarters building at 45th Street and 1st Avenue, where Ambassador Kirima Hanseraq was already waiting. They were met there by two UN officials who led them to the office of the president of the General Assembly, Hele Mägi.

"Delighted to meet you, Prime Minister. And I am so happy that you can be with us for Greenland's inaugural participation in the General Assembly," the Estonian welcomed Malik. "Allow me to just call Secretary General, Sung Chi Park to tell him that you are in my office," she said picking up the phone on the desk. "I know he was keen on meeting you as well, and it will save time for us to double up on the meetings."

When the president of the General Assembly put down the phone, Malik said, "Thank you for your kind words, Ms....Mägi." He was not sure how to address the rather good looking official other than by her name. "I am so pleased that you could meet with me—and please allow me to introduce my Minister of Environment and Natural Resources, Hanne Kristensen. And, of course, you know Ambassador Hanseraq."

Sung Chi Park arrived a few moments after the call, and once the welcomes and introductions were repeated, Malik continued: "As this is Greenland's first appearance on the world stage after our long fought for independence—which, unfortunately, seems to be already under threat from some of the most powerful members of the United Nations—I thought it would be fitting that I come and make a statement. Indeed, Ms. Mägi, assuming you would have no objections, I would be grateful if I could do it right at the outset of the session. I would also like my Minister of Environment and Natural Resources, to have a brief opportunity after me to communicate some interesting and important perspectives."

"Why certainly, Prime Minister, as the head of our newest member state, I am sure…all our members would welcome a statement from you. And from your Minister. I shall make some brief opening remarks and, of course, introduce you both. So that's settled."

"Excellent. Thank you." This from Malik.

"Now, I think we should probably go to the hall. Our session will be starting shortly." Ms. Mägi continued.

Hanne sensed that the General Assembly's president may have felt she was going out on a limb for them. But as an Estonian, she would certainly know what it was like to have to face down a malevolent superpower, and more specifically, the Russian bear.

⁕

Hanne was nervous as she followed the ambassador and

the prime minister to Greenland's assigned desk in the second row between Greece and Grenada. She took the chair behind Malik, and as she sat down, saw there was a commotion when President Barlow entered the chambers and made his way to the USA's desk—which, for this session, happened, by chance, to be in the front row, just in front of, and to the right of where they were sitting. The president exchanged nods with Rorsen and gave him a thumbs up sign, to boost Malik's confidence, Hanne thought. Her spirits rose seeing the support they were getting from the Americans, and she experienced a wave of gratitude for her friendship with Ron Hall. Just as Hele Mägi entered and proceeded to the podium, Hanne's roving eyes finally found Kristi in the gallery and she waved to her discreetly.

The General Assembly president's introduction of both Malik and Hanne was short and to the point, and there was an audible rustle in the auditorium when the prime minister of Greenland—the first Inuit ever to appear in this forum—stood up and made his way to the rostrum.

When the noise was finally replaced by silence, Malik began: "Madame President, Secretary General, and distinguished heads of state and delegates. I am deeply honored to be present here at Greenland's inaugural participation in this august body, indeed, our first appearance on the world stage. And grateful that you have given me this opportunity to make a brief statement to introduce our newly independent country. Distinguished delegates—and I am sure many of you represent countries that have had similar struggles—our nation has worked hard over long years to gain complete autonomy as a self-governing state, and it was only very recently, when one of your committees awarded Greenland jurisdiction over large tracts of its territorial waters that this became possible. I am proud to say that Greenland is now one of the richest countries per capita in terms of natural resources, and our intent is to underpin our independence by using these judiciously, slowly, and with maximal regard for the environment and our traditional way of life. Several countries represented here have shown interest in helping us in this process and have encouraged our efforts to gain independence with different kinds of inducements and guarantees—including financial ones. Of course, we appreciate all these initiatives. But I, and my government, are adamant that we are not going to do, or allow anything to be done, within our territory that would in any way be detrimental to our fragile environment and the traditional Inuit way of life—which are already under severe stress from climate change. Madame President, I would therefore like to ask this august body to consider passing a resolution upholding and guaranteeing Greenland's resolve to do just that, and condemning the actions of any and all member states that seek to do otherwise…" It was at this point that the Chinese delegate got up with a huff and walked out of the room. But Malik soldiered on as this was happening, "…and militarily seek to interfere in our affairs, as one member state is currently doing." This is when the Russian delegate pushed his chair back noisily and strutted toward the exit, following his Chinese colleague. "Indeed, I would urge this body to condemn, in no certain terms, the invasion of our territory by Russian forces and demand their immediate withdrawal. Thank you, Madame President, and now I will yield the podium to my Minister of Environment and Natural Resources, Hanne Kristensen, to add a few words of her own."

As some in the auditorium cleared their throats when Hanne got up to go to the stage, she heard what she thought was pleased whispering which made her somewhat self-conscious. But never mind, she was used to it, and after adjusting the microphone, started into her prepared speech.

"Madame President, and distinguished delegates. I want to underscore the critically important point for our nation—and indeed for the world—that Prime Minister Rorsen just made. As much of the rest of the world, Greenland, too, is already experiencing significant environmental stress because of climate change. The ice cap is melting and some of our coastal villages are encroached upon by sea level rise from the thawing of our glaciers, as well as those elsewhere—we know that the Thwaites Glacier in Antarctica is now already critically in a melting stage, as are so many of the earth's other glaciers. The warming seas are affecting the ecosystems around our island with grave consequences for the traditional fishing and hunting lifestyle of our native peoples. Elsewhere in the world, climate change is resulting in severe wildfires, starvation causing drought, violent storms, and drastic flooding. Given all this trauma to our land and seas, it is intolerable that foreign troops—Russian soldiers on our soil and Russian naval vessels in our waters—are making this situation far worse. These forces are there to coerce our young nation to cede its natural resources so the invading country can exploit them rapidly for its own gain, which would just result in more environmental degradation and destruction of the Inuit way of life. Extracting and burning more oil and gas is not what the world needs right now, nor does Greenland welcome the prospect of foreign heavy machinery digging on our land or drilling through what ice remains, or into our undersea territories. This illegal Russian occupation, and also the Chinese pressures to exploit these resources, must be condemned in no uncertain terms by this august body. Coincidentally, I also want to bring to light the fact that both these superpowers have been vociferous supporters of Greenland's independence from Denmark—even offering guarantees and huge financial incentives, and, as we have seen, military occupation—exactly for this reason. To gain access to our resources. Again, this is intolerable, and against the very charter of the United Nations. Madame President, we ask for a vote to condemn the illegal actions of these two superpowers."

When Hanne finished and left the podium, one could hear a pin drop in the large auditorium. But by the time she was back at her seat there was deafening applause from most quarters, except, of course from the Russian and Chinese desks, which were by then respectively occupied by only one low level staffer each.

After a few moments of pandemonium while Malik and Hanne collected their papers, Hele Mägi went to the dais, and in a calm voice, said, "Thank you, Prime Minister Rorsen and Minister Kristensen. I will have my staff work with you and your representatives to present a motion to this body for a vote when it meets tomorrow, if that is agreeable."

But as the General Assembly's president made the statement—and Hanne knew that Ms. Mägi was favorable to their cause—she wondered whether it would indeed come to pass, given that such a resolution would be to condemn two of the most powerful members of the United Nations.

❦❦❦

"You were brilliant," Kristi hugged her when they met up outside the meeting salle.

"Indeed, Hanne." Malik agreed. "You couldn't have

been clearer. Thank you."

"So were you, Malik," Hanne returned the compliment. "But I was wondering just now if the resolution will ever come to the floor."

"Yes, I was asking myself that too. The interests arrayed against us are very powerful…"

"But at least we will have made the point," Hanne continued. "And the international press will certainly pick it up and run with it. Greenland is the underdog, and they will generate a lot of global sympathy. That is already a huge victory for us, and an embarrassment for Russia and China on the world stage."

"You are right. I think we achieved what we came here for."

Just then, as they were walking down the corridor, an aide came running up to them from behind. "Prime Minister, Madame Minister, President Barlow would like to have a word. Would you mind coming with me?"

They went with the official, who led them to the US delegation's office. As they entered, Hanne saw Ron Hall with President Barlow, with a man she recognized as James Gilchrist, the Secretary of State, and a woman of color she took to be the US ambassador to the UN, Abigail Thompson. Barlow greeted them, "Welcome, my friends. Well done, you said it as it is and embarrassed the hell out of the Russians and the Chinese. They will have lost a lot of credibility internationally. Friends to boot, I'm sure. And they will lose even more, once the Security Council has its session."

"Thank you, Mr. President…"

"So, when the virus weakens the occupying forces and we come in to help you get rid of them, our intervention will be viewed favorably, I think." This from Gilchrist.

"Let's wait and see," Malik said. "In any case, Mr.

President, we appreciate your support. And, of course, all the vaccines you are sending us, so we can inoculate our people."

"Let's hope that helps and the virus runs rampage on the bloody Ruskis." This from Barlow.

"Yes, we know already that at least three of the four men who were up at Thule with you, Prime Minister, have caught a really bad case of it. The fourth one probably too, but he is asymptomatic apparently. And we've had Colonel Sandman release Captain Petrov to the Russian submarine force in the fjord up there. He was very, very sick and pleaded to be allowed out of captivity, so we complied, knowing that he would spread the virus on whatever sub he ends up on. Perhaps a mite immoral, but hey, 'all's fair in love and war' as they say. And that is the strategy, isn't it? To get the virus to fight at least some of our battles…"

"Yes, indeed. Well put, Ron." This from Barlow again.

"Admiral Ogarov and the two Danes are still in our hands, since we need hostages," Ron continued, "As I said, at least two of them are in a pretty bad way too. We have them quarantining up there."

Hanne wondered whether her fellow Danes would survive—one was apparently not affected—but continuing on from what Ron had said, *they deserve it, the bastards*, she thought to herself.

⁊

Hanne, Kristi and Malik went back to the hotel to collect their gear. In the lobby, Hanne and the prime minister agreed to meet in an hour's time to go to the airport, since the Air Greenland plane was already at La

Guardia, and Malik was eager to get back home with the vaccines. As soon as the elevator door closed behind Rorsen, Hanne embraced her girlfriend and said, "Boy, I'm going to miss you!"

"You're not rid of me yet, girl," was Kristi's answer as she kissed her on the mouth. The elevator door opened just then, and Kristi tugged Hanne out by the hand, saying, "We're going to have one last session, dear, so hurry up!" They literally sprinted down the hall, and as soon as they were inside the suite, they both started stripping their clothes off as quickly as they could. Kristi was naked first and jumped on the unmade bed; Hanne was on top of her in no time and the two were all over each other. After a deep kiss, Hanne moved lower, licking Kristi's breasts, midriff and smooth mons pubis, before entering her friend with tongue and finger, bringing her to orgasm within moments. She moved back up for a kiss, but Kristi shoved her on her back and proceeded to do the same for her.

And they still had some naked time caressing each other in the shower before they got dressed and packed. Only when they gave each other a final hug did the tears come: with Hanne going back to occupied Greenland, there was no certainty as to when they would see each other again.

Chapter 29

Nuuk—Tuesday evening, Late September, 202-

It was already dark as the Air Greenland plane came in to land at Nuuk Airport. Hanne felt a sense of relief when it finally touched down, and she was able to clamber down the steps to *terra firma.* This was now home after all, and she had a lot on her plate. She was, however, unnerved by the two helicopters sporting Cyrillic lettering parked on the tarmac, and, as she followed in Malik's footsteps toward the terminal, she raised an eyebrow when she saw the pair of soldiers carrying Kalashnikovs near the door who both ogled her as she passed them. The occupation had begun, but at least so far, it was passive.

Glancing back, though, she was pleased to see that the baggage handlers put only two of the cartons of vaccines on the cart and covered them with their luggage and then a tarp—presumably, the instructions Malik had given the pilots had been transmitted to the ground crew. The remaining boxes of vaccines would remain in the hold of the plane and continue on the hour-long trip to Kangerlussuaq, from where they would, in short order, be distributed and flown the next day to the other villages with airports on the huge island, and then carried further to even smaller settlements by boat, dog sled and whatever means of transportation possible, until all Greenlanders had a vaccine in their arms.

The terminal was mostly deserted, although there were a few more Russian soldiers lounging around, but they just gazed at them with a bored look as Malik's driver waved at them, and then beckoning to the baggage handler carrying their luggage, led the VIP passengers out the front. Once in the waiting car and on their way, Malik said, "Well, that was easier than I thought it would be. I am sure the airline or the air traffic controllers informed the Russians of our arrival, so they must have known who we are."

"Yes, Malik," Hanne said, thinking aloud. "But with the two Danes and Admiral Ogarov being held by the Americans up in Thule, it would seem that their chain of command has been broken. Which, I'm sure is a good thing for us. And, in spite of the Ruskis occupying our country, they have no means to communicate with us—no Russian soldier speaks Inuit. Nor for that matter, Danish, and I believe very few even know the odd word of English."

"Well, even if their occupation is passive, it is disturbing and a huge annoyance to have these Russian soldiers around."

"It is early days, Malik. I think for now, they just want to rid the country of the Americans and the Chinese. And takeover or destroy Thule. Soon enough, though, they will start meddling, and once they get a better handle on things, they will start exploiting our resources and putting in bases. I'm sure their intent is to stay for the longer course. Unless, of course, our plan to have the virus weaken them and then the Yanks come in to push them out, somehow works."

"I think you are right, Hanne. But we don't have much time. Tomorrow, I will reinforce the need for all Greenlanders to get vaccinated with a personal message broadcast all over the island in our native language. We will have to brief the cabinet, and, of course, see what the international reaction is to our UN appearance."

"I will also try to track down Laptov. And talk to Ron Hall to find out what they have learnt about what the Russians are up to, and any feedback to our statements this morning at the UN that they may have gleaned."

"Good, Hanne. So, I will call a cabinet meeting for eleven am. That will give us time for these other matters." Just then, the car pulled up in front of Hanne's building.

"See you then," Hanne said, opening the door. "And thanks for the ride."

"No, thank you, Hanne, for joining me on this trip. You are a great friend. Not just for me, but for Greenland."

෧෨෧

When Hanne opened the door to her apartment, she breathed a sigh of relief. Good to be home. But she knew she had a lot to do, on both her professional and personal lives. She already missed Kristi, who was always so much fun to be with, and such a great lover. And that reminded her—she had promised to call Richard. She would get to that as soon as she unpacked and cleansed herself after the long trip.

Showered, hair wet, but in her comfy bathrobe, she went into the kitchen carrying only her cell phone, and opened a bottle of red, then carried it with a glass into the living room where she made herself comfortable on the sofa, pulling her legs up under her. Once she had poured herself an ample glass, she clicked on the remote, just to have the evening news on in the background, and then proceeded to call her Canadian diplomat friend. He answered after two rings.

"Richard? Hi, Hanne."

"Oh, Hanne, how lovely to hear from you. I've been waiting for your call. Is everything all right?"

"Of course…"

"You and Prime Minister Rorsen made such an unbelievable splash with your speeches at the United Nations. Bravo!"

"Thank you, Richard. I haven't yet seen the reaction…"

"Well, let me tell you, the international press picked it up, and the forcefulness of your comments has been applauded worldwide. You were amazing. The Russians and Chinese have come out defensively, both saying that all their actions have been in support of Greenland. It will be rather difficult for them now to do anything your government doesn't condone…"

"Terrific…But we'll see."

"There are calls from pretty well every corner of the globe for the Russians to withdraw their forces."

"That doesn't mean they will pay attention to them. Look how they ignored international reaction when they annexed Crimea in 2014. And even worse, when they invaded the rest of Ukraine in 2022. Killed so many civilians, destroyed the country and its economy, forced half the population to leave their homes. Mariupol, the Donbas, Bucha. Crimes against humanity. Ugh. Terrible."

"But at least in your adopted country it hasn't become a bloody war…with cruise missiles, bombings and all…"

"Well, not yet," Hanne responded, "and we don't plan to let it come to that…That would be devastating for our country."

"Hanne, please be careful. The Russians are nasty customers."

"I know that, but I think, Richard, in all fairness, as you say, this is quite different from the Ukraine. We have a small population, minute inhabited centers and an immense country with substantial untapped resources. However, if this invasion develops, it's very unlikely to become bloody and destructive as in the Ukraine, I can tell you that."

"Well, you never know. Hanne, I just don't want you to get hurt. I love you and I want you as my wife."

And there it was again. The proposal. Like the last time, she was too stunned to respond, but fortunately, Richard ploughed on.

"Hanne dear, I will ask you formally when we are together, but I did want to make a reservation to be able to spend the rest of my life with you."

Hanne burst out laughing, "Well, that's lovely, Richard. And let's do discuss it when you come. But only after we make passionate love." As she said this, she reached inside her loosely tied bathrobe to touch herself.

"I can hardly wait. I will try to make arrangements to get away next weekend and come for several days. How's that—will you be around?"

"Of course, I will be waiting for you with bated breath, my love." She was getting rather aroused as she said this.

"Till then, then. I love you."

"And I, you. Good night." Her breathing was getting heavier, as she rushed to press the red hang-up button.

And just then, the Aurora Borealis erupted in a magic dance across the night sky, and Hanne knew she was getting close to climaxing with visions of Kristi's perfect breasts and Richard's hard member alternating in her mind.

Chapter 30

Nuuk—Wednesday morning, October 1, 202-

Hanne spent a restless night, in turmoil over Richard's proposal. She liked the idea for the long term—after all, she had always desperately wanted to experience the joys of motherhood, and she had concluded some time ago that Richard would be the perfect mate for her. Gentle, loving, smart, great body and, largely under her tutelage, now a good partner in bed, too. And likely to be a wonderful father, it would seem.

But how would she be able to give up the intimate bond—and the fabulous sex—she had with Kristi? After all, they had been together forever, and by now, were almost like one person, one being.

Could she continue to have both? She had always pushed this notion away, but the more she thought about it in the dark, the more she saw this as a possible avenue. Why not? At least, to try, for a while. Kristi would no doubt be okay with it, or would be easily convinced, she thought, but what about Richard? It was so…so…alien to today's societal norms…And he was a bit conservative in some ways.

In the old days, though, and in other cultures, wasn't

bigamy okay? Well, yes, but here in modern western society, having more than one spouse was certainly frowned upon and indeed mostly illegal. But surely, there would be ways around this "technicality"?

And, on a wilder note, didn't people have threesomes? Richard could marry her, and Kristi could live with them, or adjacent to them, without marriage…or something like that. They could get together whenever. Then there were all those wild communes in the seventies…Of course, Richard, no doubt, might even like the idea, once he got used to it.

But would she mind Richard having sex with Kristi?

Of course not, she told herself. *I'm open minded. It might even be fun to watch.* Would she become jealous of Kristi? Yes, what if Richard preferred her best friend to her? And Kristi became pregnant with his child? What then?

Tough questions, but surely, this was all something to think about!

In any case, marriage right now would be difficult—as she had already decided—given her job. Richard's, too. For one, where would they have their household? Nuuk? Ottawa? Copenhagen?

She had to think out of the box.

Or not at all, not right now. There was too much else to worry about. The Russians. The virus. Climate change. The melting polar icecap. Just to start on the long list…

∽∾∽

She awoke from her deep slumber with a start to the chime of her phone alarm—fortunately, having set it. Otherwise, she would have slept till noon, she was sure, as she rushed to the bathroom.

Hanne's morning routine was efficient: after her shower, with just the towel wrapped around her midriff, she went into the kitchen and pressed the button to brew the coffee, and while it was making, she went back in the bathroom to comb her hair and put on her bathrobe, then re-emerged to tip some muesli in a bowl, add some raisins and walnuts, cut up a banana, and pour some milk on her cereal and into the coffee cup when the brew was ready. She took both items into the living room on a tray, then settled in her usual position on the couch, with legs drawn up under her, and flipped on the morning news.

The report was about the successful mission of Prime Minister Rorsen and his minister of Environment and Natural Resources to the United Nations, and the very favorable global reaction. As Richard had said, the world had received the interventions of Greenland's special delegates at the UN with praise, and from all around, there were condemnation and calls for the Russians and the Chinese to leave the island. The reporter went on to say that the USA, the European Union and a host of other countries were coordinating serious sanctions against Russia and its leadership unless its troops, aircraft and vessels departed from Greenland's territory.

And then a breaking news flash interrupted the report, showing President Gusanov with his security council and a voice translating to English: "Russian troops have landed in Nuuk and other key towns in Greenland in order to safeguard the newly won independence of Greenland and to ensure the departure of all alien occupying and/or…meddling forces. More specifically, the Chinese and American military. Our action was completely in line with the charter of the United Nations which safeguards the sovereignty of all states, even brand-new ones such as

Greenland. The condemnation of Russia's actions in the General Assembly by the USA and other nations is in violation of the charter, and the sanctions being imposed by a number of countries are illegal."

Hanne tuned out, not interested in such rhetoric, and started looking at some papers, but just a few moments later, she was shocked to attention, when, in a radical departure from diplomatic norms and his previous statements, Gusanov particularly singled out "…that warmonger and bisexual slut, the American-Danish plant, Greenland's Minister of Environment and Natural Resources…" for being an enemy of the Inuit and all other peoples. He went on to say that unless she resigned immediately of her own free-will, his government would demonstrate to the world what a fraud she was and ensure her arrest.

Hanne shook with rage as she held herself back from throwing the just-filled glass of wine at the TV, rather gulping it down, then refilling it with more.

How dare he? And how did he know about her sexuality? Probably from those assholes Jens and Erik…They must have told him. But when? And, so what?

Her first thought was that she should hand in her resignation to Malik that very morning before the cabinet meeting began. Yes, that would solve a lot of things…she could then marry Richard and move to Ottawa, get Kristi to come there, and have her cake and eat it too.

But then…what about the Arctic, Greenland, all the environmental causes—everything she had been working for? No, she had to fight. And being smeared by these Russian assholes could be something she could turn to her advantage.

Yes, back to work now…

సించి

It was a good time to call Ron Hall. That would take her mind off all this awful slanderous stuff, concentrate on what needed to be done. Plus, she had promised Malik that she would follow up with the American.

Fortunately, the call to his cell went through right away.

"Hello, Ron. Hope I'm not disturbing."

"Hi, Hanne. Of course not. In fact, I was about to call you. Wow, I just heard Gusanov's despicable comments. Ridiculous, and totally unacceptable for him to go after you like that. Especially with the positive reception from everywhere else."

"Never mind. Best to ignore it. But Ron, I wanted to let you know that we got all the vaccine through without a hitch. It's being distributed throughout Greenland even as we speak, and our people should have their first shots very soon thereafter. Malik is making a speech this morning that is being aired nationwide to make sure every eligible Greenlander participates. So, all is proceeding to plan."

"Excellent."

"Do you have any news from Russia? Other than Gusanov's despicable lecture…"

"No. Have you heard from Laptov?"

"No, but I will call him when we hang up."

"Well, let us know what he says. Also keep us in the loop on the vaccination program. We'll monitor the Russian forces around Greenland and try and get some intelligence on whether the virus is making any inroads…"

"Great, Ron."

"But Hanne, we should not ignore Gusanov's comments. They mean that your life is in danger. And you are now in Russian occupied territory. Those brutes could be coming after you any moment."

"Hmm. I hadn't thought of it like that."

"You need to find a way to get away. Out of Greenland. Now."

"Thanks, Ron. I will keep you posted."

"Hanne, no, this is important. Should I send an extraction force?'

"Let me think about it. I will get back to you."

☙❧☙

The conversation with the American had certainly nonplussed her, and yes, she would need to do something. Because, dead or in prison, she would be useless…for all of her goals. Professional or personal.

But before anything else, she needed to talk to Pavel. She dialled his cell and was pleasantly surprised when he answered right away.

"Hanne, good to hear from you…great timing."

"Pavel. Where are you? I thought…"

"We have just surfaced near Severomorsk…"

"Wow! You made excellent time."

"Yes, we did. Captain Zaitsov is the best. In fact, he has already been in touch with many of his colleagues in the Northern Fleet and they overwhelmingly support our cause. Including, he says, apparently a Captain Kolnikov, Pyotr's best friend, who commands one of the navy's vessels off Nuuk. You might want to watch out for him, Hanne."

"Of course. Thanks for the lead. Good to know that a Russian here is on our side. So, then, Pavel, what is the next step?"

"Zaitsov says that now that they know we are back here,

offshore Russia, his friends are going to move on Murmansk, where Admiral Maslenkov is in prison, and demand his release. This will be the first step in our side regaining control. I will only make landfall once he is out of prison. And then we will regain command of the entire Northern Fleet and Maslenkov will give the order for Russian forces to leave Greenland. If all goes well…"

"But Gusanov is still in control in Moscow. In fact, he has just viciously denounced me and wants me killed. The Americans claim that his operatives are looking for me. They are trying to help and want to send a force to extract me. Ron Hall—you met him, Pavel—says it's not safe for me in Greenland until all of your countrymen have left.

"Hanne, as I said, as soon as Maslenkov and I are back in charge, we can give the order for the Russian forces to depart from Greenland and to leave you alone. But until then, the situation remains highly dangerous. Even then— if they do not obey. So, I agree with your American friend, you need to leave. Now. We do not want you dead."

"Thanks, Pavel. I will try…but keep me informed on what is happening with you and Russia. Good luck to you and your friends. The world needs you to win!"

"And you too, Hanne. We are in this together."

Chapter 31

Nuuk—Wednesday, October 1, 202-

As soon as she got off the phone with Pavel, Hanne called Ron Hall again.

"Ron, just talked to Laptov. The situation in Russia seems very fluid. Fortunately, much of the Northern Fleet appears to be with him and they are getting ready to free Admiral Maslenkov, who is in prison in Murmansk. However, the odds are still stacked against them succeeding, and until they do manage to overthrow Gusanov's government, Greenland and the rest of Russia remain in the rogue president's hands. Pavel, too, advises me to get out. Leave Greenland."

"Tentative good news re Laptov. As I said on our previous call, though, we can send an extraction force, Hanne. You just need to give me the go ahead. And we need to coordinate on where to get you. Figure it out soon though, because those guys are brutal."

"Yes, I know. Thanks. I need to talk to Malik. Get his advice. He can also help with any arrangements." She was more and more convinced that Ron was right. She had to get out.

"Take care. Bye for now."

⋯

Hanne felt overwhelmed. There was so much to do, though, here, in Greenland, so much that she had come back for, but now her life was in danger. Plus, she had just agreed with Richard that he would come next weekend—she had to call him to tell him about the latest.

But first, she had to talk to Malik. Get his views. And help.

Richard, too, but that could wait.

She tried Malik's mobile. But he did not pick up. She noted the time on her cell phone, saw that it was just before eleven, and chastised herself, "Christ, the cabinet meeting! It's about to start. He must be on his way there." She had hoped to catch him before the meeting but decided the best now would be for her to head over to the Inatsisartut, the unicameral parliament of Greenland, where the prime minister and his cabinet normally met. She could join in at least this one last time and try to talk to Malik after.

On the way, she tried Richard again, several times, but he did not pick up.

⋯

The prime minister saw that already all the members of his cabinet, except Hanne, were seated around the table as he entered the room. He wondered if his minister of Environment and Natural Resources was staying away because of those disgusting comments made by Gusanov, but then, just as he was about to close the door, he saw her rush, breathless, toward him. "Hanne, I am pleased to see you…"

"Malik, I need to talk to you," Hanne said, looking him in the eyes as he ushered her in. "Perhaps after the meeting. I need your advice and help on something important."

"Yes, we'll talk right after."

Door closed, everyone seated, he cleared his throat and started into his usual opening statement, "Ladies and Gentlemen, my fellow colleagues…"

His comments were interrupted by the ruckus of the door being violently kicked open, as five armed Russian soldiers, led by one carrying a pistol who was obviously in charge, stormed into the room. So, not all the Russians had been infected with the virus, was Hanne's passing thought, even as she was stunned and suddenly very afraid. She saw Malik stand up, push his chair back, as he yelled indignantly, "What is the meaning of this intrusion?"

"Captain-Lieutenant Botkinov, Prime Minister. I am here to inform you that we are taking you and your colleagues into custody. You all need to do as I say." Looking around, the officer continued: "Ahh. And I see our beautiful Danish friend, your Minister of Environment and Natural Resources, is here. How lucky, because we are especially on the look out for her."

"You leave my people alone. You can do what you will with me, but don't touch anyone else," Malik retorted angrily.

"Well, my dear Prime Minister, I have my orders. And the very first thing is to get you to make a phone call to your bloody American friends to get them to release our commanding officer and the two Danes they are holding up in Thule. We know you are in cahoots with them."

"I can't do that…"

"Prime Minister, before you get entrenched in your refusals, let me tell you what we have in mind. It must be pretty clear even to you that we are in control of Greenland now. But we are prepared to let all of you go free and, in fact, resume your previous roles. Other than the Danish impostor there." And he nodded at Hanne as he said this. As Botkinov and the other soldiers looked her over, Hanne could not help but think that this Botnikov—unusually for a Russian soldier—spoke very good English (more like American, maybe Texan), even though he seemed like a real bastard.

"First, though, we want the Americans to release Admiral Ogarov and the provisional governor for Greenland appointed by President Gusanov, Erik Larsen, and his partner, Jens whatever. You will be allowed to play prime minister going forward, but for all consequential decisions you will have to get the agreement of the new governor and do his bidding. If the three are not released, and if at any time, you deviate from the governor's instructions, everybody here will be taken out and shot, one by one until you comply. And of course, we will start by having some fun with that sexy Danish woman, is that clear?"

Malik saw all his colleagues blanche at this last statement but did not answer.

Botkinov continued: "I take your silence as a yes for now. You will talk—now—to the American assholes to release the three I mentioned being illegally held up at Thule. After that, we will see. And if you don't, and they don't agree, as I said, we will have a little entertainment with the lovely minister of Environment and Natural Resources and then take you out one by one and shoot you. Starting with her and finishing with you. Now what shall it be?"

And when Malik hesitated, Botkinov gestured to his men, who eagerly moved toward Hanne and roughly pulled her to her feet. One of the soldiers twisted her around and grabbed her by the breasts, pushing her toward the door. It was clear that Malik had no choice, so he said in a seething voice, "Fine, Captain. Have your men leave my colleague be. When she is released and sitting down again, I will do what you ask." Botkinov nodded and the soldiers shoved a trembling Hanne back in the chair.

"So?" the captain stood in front of Rorsen.

Malik pulled out his cell phone from his pocket, saying, "All right, I will call my contact in Washington to transmit your proposal. In any case, a decision to agree may take some time, as it would no doubt have to be made by the President. But my friend is close to Mr. Barlow, although he is a very busy man."

Botkinov hesitated a moment, then said, "Tell the bastards we want an answer within two hours, or we start on Plan B. Which, just to remind you, is killing first the tasty young lady over there, after amusing ourselves with her of course, then one by one the rest of your cabinet every hour after that, finishing with you." And then with a smile he added, "Of course, I'm sure buggering you will not be as much fun as fucking the bitch, so I might just leave it up to one of my sex-starved men."

⋐↻⋑

Shocked, Malik had scrolled down to Ron Hall's number and pushed the call button.

"Hello, Ron? Malik Rorsen here."

"Hello, Malik. I'm so glad you called because…"

Malik interrupted, with a "Ron, we have a situation here." He thought that Hall might be thinking that he was calling about Hanne's plight or maybe the vaccine, but he wanted to keep the focus on what needed to be done immediately. "Some Russian troops have taken my cabinet and me into custody. They are demanding the release of Admiral Ogarov and the two Danes being held in Thule and wanting action within two hours. Otherwise, they start killing us one by one until we agree. Starting with Hanne. They are serious, not to be taken lightly."

"Jesus Christ! Let me talk to the President." So, Hanne was there, but a captive like the rest of them. Extraction would be more difficult now, the president's advisor concluded.

"We don't have much time, Ron."

"I get it. I'm sure though, one of the conditions from our side Barlow will insist on, is that Thule not be bombed if we do release those prisoners. But weren't the three really ill with that virus?"

"Yes, but perhaps that is not known by the Russians down here."

"Good. I will get onto the President right away. So, Hanne is there? With you? We want to make sure you're all safe."

"Thanks, Ron. Yes, and yes. I will hear from you shortly then?"

"Of course." Ron seemed to get the message.

⸙⸙

Malik hung up and turned back to Botkinov.

"As I said, my contact is high up in the administration and he will try his best, but you are not giving him much time. In any case, it seems in return they will want a commitment that you will not bomb Thule."

"Well, we can see—perhaps we can agree not to for a while. Or some other solution. In any case, the priority is the release of the three."

Botkinov stood up, said something to his soldiers in Russian, then turned back to the forlorn looking cabinet members sitting around the table: "We are going to go over to Hans Egede House now and we will keep you there until the three men are released. Before we do that, I want all of your cell phones, here on the table. Now." He watched as all ten Greenlanders and Hanne reluctantly complied, and one of the soldiers in the room collected the hardware.

"Now march! Fall into a single file and we will escort you over on foot. It's just a short walk as you know." He personally pulled Hanne to her feet and pushed her forward as the others got up. They all knew there was no arguing with this brute.

⊱⊰

Once ensconced at the historic venue, which now served as a prison for the Greenland cabinet, Hanne chided herself for not getting in touch with Richard to let him know what was happening, particularly the danger she was now in. She hoped that Malik's last conversation with Ron might lead to rescue, not just for herself, but also for her colleagues. However, she knew that an open American intervention could lead to all-out war, and that was to be avoided at any cost for now. They would just have to see where their strategy with the virus and now this demand for the release of the three up in Thule would lead and hope that they would be able to escape from the Russian occupiers at some point along the way. Although that bastard Botkinov had intimated that even if the US president agrees to release Ogarov and the two vile Danes she had come to hate, she would not be allowed to go. But still, for now, there was nothing she could do but wait and hope. And, as the clock ticked, Hanne could see that everyone in the room became more and more fidgety, as did she. She knew that she would be first to be taken away.

Two and a quarter tense hours had passed when Botkinov burst in through the front door of the historic house to announce that, "Well, well. Your American friends have indeed backed down. My commanding officer and the two Danes are on their way here, courtesy of a special flight on an American plane. They should be here in a couple of hours. So, most of you can go home now, other than you, Prime Minister, and the Danish whore over there. We will see how the Admiral and the Governor will decide to proceed. On second thought, you can go home too, Prime Minister, but I will send one of my soldiers with you. And you are all to stay at home—I will be checking on you, and I want no contact with anybody but your spouses. And children if you have any. But the Danish bitch stays here under guard. And which one of you is the Minister of Health?"

A middle-aged woman Hanne had only met a few times tentatively raised her hand.

"What is your name?" Botkinov asked, going right up to the woman.

"Mari Malakiassen."

"Well, Ms. Mala-whatever, we will meet you in the hospital with my boss and one of the Danes. Apparently, they are not well. You will ready the emergency services to be ready to give them the best care possible."

Hanne's ears perked up and she was glad to hear this. Her eyes locked with Malik's—it seems that their strategy with the virus was working! Also, she was desperately hoping that Malik would think to help arrange a rescue for her, perhaps even firm up the plans for her extraction from

Greenland that Ron Hall had been talking about. She was glad then, that while the others were being escorted out, Malik, who was beside her, whispered in Danish so the Ruskis would not understand, "Don't worry, as soon as I am at home, I will work on getting you out. We will find a way." And then Botkinov looked at him and slammed his pistol in his stomach, saying "No talking, you old fool. Or I will keep you here as well."

സ്ക്ക

Malik walked fast to get home and was glad that the Russian soldier who accompanied him stayed outside. Once inside, Nanurjuk embraced him, even as he said, "Dear, I need to make a couple of calls. Can I use your cell—mine was confiscated by the Russians, and I am worried that our fixed line may be tapped."

"Sure, my love, I know it will be important. These are difficult times. Let me know if I can do something," his wife handed over her phone, gave him a peck on the cheek, and left the room he used as a home office, closing the door behind herself.

Malik lost no time to call Ron Hall.

"Malik, I have been trying to reach you. We have agreed to release the Thule prisoners. Two of them need serious medical attention."

"Yes, thank you. I know. The Russians have co-opted my Minister of Health to ensure they get good care in our hospital. They, and the other Dane, are on their way to Nuuk, we were told."

"Yes, that's right, and they will be landing in a little over an hour now, if I am correct."

"Well, this Captain-Lieutenant Botkinov who was in

charge of our arrest said they will be met at the airport and accompanied to the hospital. But Ron, we need to get Hanne away. Her situation is precarious, especially since she is in Russian hands. We will need your help."

"I know, Malik. I need to make a few calls. Including to her friend, Richard Simpson. Perhaps having the Canadians alongside will make it easier. But the trick will be getting her out of Russian captivity. Let's both think and talk in a few hours."

"Good. This is important. We can't let any harm come to Hanne. And I am afraid if we cannot get her out, she will be transported to Russia—where who knows what will happen. Or just plain murdered, supposedly 'while trying to escape'. The usual Russian lies."

"Malik. Good luck. I will be in touch." And the American signed off.

Chapter 32
Ottawa—Wednesday, October 1, 202

Worried to death about Hanne, Richard was feeling very antsy as Prime Minister Juneau finally wound up the cabinet meeting he had called to discuss the Russian invasion of Greenland and what Canada's response should be. As he walked out of the Parliament's cabinet room, he noticed that Hanne had tried to call him several times, but alas, he had been sitting with other senior officials listening to the briefing on the increasingly dire situation in the neighboring Arctic country. The discourse had only served to increase his concern for Hanne.

Richard had his cell out and finger poised on the green icon to call her and did so as soon as he was in a location in the Centre Block where he deemed he might be able to have a relatively private conversation. But Hanne did not pick up. He tried again, and then again, but with the same result. Even more anxious now, he knew he needed to calm himself and think, so, as he went down the front steps of the Parliament, on this beautiful fall day, he decided to walk back to his office in the Lester B. Pearson Building, all the more so to try and figure out what he should and could do about Hanne's situation. He chose to stroll along Lady Grey Drive, close to the Ottawa River, to enjoy the views, and to give himself maximum time to think and calm his nerves.

Yes, he needed to get to Nuuk. As soon as possible, and find Hanne. But since the Russian occupation, commercial flights had been curtailed, and in any case, even if there still were flights, it would be rather convoluted for him to go from Ottawa, via Toronto and Keflavik in Iceland—a two-day operation to get to the capital of Greenland.

Was there another way?

Well, just a little while ago, he had cajoled his friend, General Wippinger, the head of the Royal Canadian Air Force to get him to Pond Inlet on an emergency basis, so, surely, he would be able to do the same now, he told himself. This was in many ways even more of an emergency, now that the Ruskis had landed in Nuuk.

And Hanne's life was at stake!

Although the Russians would not be keen on seeing a Canadian Air Force jet over Nuuk in the air space they now controlled. They might even shoot it down. Nor would they be keen on a Canadian government official arriving at the airport at this point in time. Hmm. There had to be a way, though.

Richard was just approaching the entrance to the Ottawa Rowing Club as he was having these thoughts, and just then, his phone vibrated.

Eagerly hoping it was Hanne, he pulled it from his pocket, but it was not her name that came up.

Ron Hall.

Nevertheless, he picked it up impatiently, hoping that at least the American might have some news of his lover. Or some thoughts on how to get to her.

"Hello, Ron. Good to hear from you. Any news of

Hanne, my friend?"

"Hello, Richard. Yes, that's why I am calling."

"Tell me," Richard said, perking his ears.

"Well, I just got off the phone with Malik Rorsen, you know, the Prime Minister there. The Russians took his entire cabinet prisoner, including Hanne. She is now being kept by herself at the historic Hans Egede House, although Malik and the others have been allowed to go home. This special treatment for Hanne is worrisome indeed. Malik though, is surreptitiously trying to arrange for her escape and extraction. And that is where we might come in to help."

"What are your thoughts, Ron?"

"Well, as you probably know, we have some ships in the Nuuk area, offshore. But if we move any of these anywhere near the coast, I'm sure the Russians will try to counter our moves. And that could be highly dangerous all around, as you can well imagine. Any movement by us would be too obvious and give the game away. And possibly lead to a shoot-out. War. Something we must avoid."

"Hmm."

"So, I was thinking that perhaps if you—that is, Canada—could send an amphibian or seaplane— preferably a private one—to pick Hanne up somewhere near Nuuk, that might work. Still not without danger though, and we would have to choose a spot where the sea is relatively quiet and without ice floes. And not too obvious to the Russians."

"Actually, I was thinking I needed to get to Nuuk myself. Of course, not officially—and what you are suggesting could be the best way. The goal now is to get Hanne out. A dangerous mission, to be sure. But her situation is grave as it is. Ron, let me see what I can do."

"I guess the fallback would be to have Hanne hide out somewhere in Greenland. But that would be very difficult, especially on her. And, of course, this all presupposes that somehow, we can spring her from captivity."

"Of course. Any ideas?"

"I think we need to see what Malik comes up with. He and his people are much closer to the situation and know the lay of the land. A landing at this point by our troops would be highly provocative and would certainly result in a major shootout, with bombs and missiles etc. It could even lead to World War three."

"Yes, we have to avoid that. Let's hope our Greenlandic friends can come up with something."

"Good, I will talk to Malik, and you look into the seaplane idea, Richard."

"Excellent. Thanks, Ron."

℮⫯℮⫯

As soon as he hung up, Richard looked for General Wippinger in his contact list and laid out the situation for him even as he continued his stroll toward the Global Affairs office building. The General said to leave the problem with him for half an hour to an hour and he would get back.

Indeed, just as Richard closed his office door, his cell rang, and it was Wippinger.

"Richard, we're in luck. I can get one of our air force jets to fly you to our base at Goose Bay, up in Labrador—it shouldn't take more than a couple of hours. We can also line up a private plane to take you to Nain further north, another hour and a half or so. The airport there is right on the coast, and my people have confirmed that there is a

Cessna Caravan seaplane owned by the mining company Vale that we can co-opt for your purposes. The Caravan has a range of around two thousand kilometres, so it can certainly get you across Davis Strait to Nuuk, in say three and a half hours, and almost all the way back. But you could rather fly to Iqaluit on Baffin Island on the return trip, which is closer and a surer bet, and we could get you from up there. How does that sound?"

"Excellent. When?"

"Well, I think we should get you to Goose Bay still today. If you can come to Rockliffe airport in say an hour, I will arrange to fly you up to Goose Bay before night falls. And then you will have tomorrow to do the dangerous part of the trip. We will firm each step along the way up for you, Richard, so you don't need to worry."

"I don't know how to thank you, General."

"You just have a safe and successful trip. Good luck."

Chapter 33

Nuuk—Evening, Wednesday, October 1, 202-

It was comfortable in the historic Hans Egede House, even though Hanne was alone, and the inside was small and somewhat dark, and she knew there were at least two, possibly three armed Russian soldiers outside— she had heard them talking and laughing, smelled the smoke from their cigarettes and caught sight of them through the small windows as they were circling the house. An escape would be very difficult under the circumstances.

Hanne could not help but worry about her fate and more broadly, the fate of Greenland, although she did try to distract herself by looking through some of the historic books in the house. There was one in particular on the famous missionary after whom the house was named, who in the early eighteenth century played such a key role in the history of this nation. He and his sons had baptized much of the population, which now was an astounding ninety-five per cent Lutheran, Hanne read.

But she was too anxious to delve into books for long and kept wandering around the house dwelling on what might happen and trying to figure out a way to escape. She had to get away somehow, Hanne knew, otherwise Gusanov would surely have her killed, or at the very least, taken to Russia for a fate she could only imagine. And these brutish Russian soldiers could do whatever they wanted with her in the interim.

The windows were small, and they would be difficult for her to get through. She would have to break one of them, which would make a lot of noise and surely be noticed. There was one though, she thought she might be able to open and squeeze through, but it would still be loud and with the ever-patrolling Russians out there she would certainly be caught. Perhaps when it got dark—the sun was starting to get low in the sky, and would probably set within the hour she thought—and the soldiers might get lazy and take turns patrolling out there, or get drunk, or whatever…Maybe, maybe…

Hanne was thinking along these lines, when she heard a car drive up, and moments after, the front door opened with a crash and in burst her nemesis, Erik Larsen, with a couple of Russian soldiers trailing behind.

"Well, well, if it isn't the beautiful Hanne Kristensen," he said with a chuckle. Looking around, he continued, "And where is my other favorite babe, your friend, Kristi? I thought both of you would be waiting for me with bated breath when those bastard Americans released us. In any case, your former lover, my friend Jens, had to go to the hospital with some crazy virus. Fortunately, though, I avoided those baddies, so rest assured, my dear, I can stand in for him. I'm sure you will like it even more with me, honey. And maybe you'll be better than Kristi, although she sure is one fuck that is hard to beat." And then laughing, he added, "But as her lesbian lover, I'm sure you know that."

Hanne cringed, not deigning to answer, so the Danish

beast continued.

"So, Hanne, it seems my boss, President Gusanov has it in for you. You really pissed him off with your performance at the United Nations. But we'll deal with that later. I am so pleased that our Russian friends here have made it easy for me to take over, putting this stupid Greenlandic cabinet under house arrest. Right now, though, I'm very hungry and thirsty—you must be, too, from what I was told. Haa, haa. Anyway, I'm going to ask this Ivan here to bring us something to eat and drink. Generous of me, no?"

Hanne still did not answer, although it was true that she hadn't eaten anything since her morning cereal. After "Ivan" was sent off to get some food and drink—presumably alcoholic—Erik continued his tirade.

"Well, don't talk to me then, you stupid cunt. But at least point out where the fuck the bathroom is so I can have a dump and wash up."

Hanne waved her arm in the direction of the toilet, hoping he would never re-emerge. She even thought of attacking him in there, but the Russian soldiers were still outside.

e∙∋e∙∋

He took a long time in the bathroom, and when he finally came out, said: "Nice place you have here, Hanne. A bit quirky though, I must say…"

"It's a historic house. The home of the first missionary from Denmark. He converted the entire population to Lutheranism."

"See, Hanne, we Danes were not that bad after all. We brought religion to these heathens. And a lot else."

"Yeah, a lot of illness and suffering too…"

"Now, now, Hanne, let's not get into an argument…" A knock on the front door interrupted, which he greeted with, "Oh goody, here is our Ivan. Let's get at it."

He went to the door and grabbed from 'Ivan' the boxes of take-out and a bag with a bottle of Akvavit and a six-pack of Erik the Red beer, which he took out and plonked on the low coffee table in the room. Before he slammed the door shut, Erik told Ivan that he and his mates were no longer needed and should get the hell out of there since he was entirely capable of guarding this woman. He did not want them around.

The Dane then strutted over to the table, opening the take-out boxes and cracking open one of the beers, saying, "Here, honey. Come and get it. Have one of my namesakes to make you feel better." And when she didn't respond, "Okay, have it your way. I'm going to celebrate my new-found freedom. I'm ready for a good time babe, after being cooped up for days with Jens again and that a-hole, Ogarov. He added, as an afterthought, "Better to be cooped up with you any day." And he let out an obnoxious laugh.

Erik dug in with gusto, lighting into yet another beer, chasing the golden liquid down with a loud burp and a big swig from the Akvavit bottle. Hanne did have a bite or two of the ham and cheese sandwich Erik had ordered for her and washed it down with a gulp of the beer but refused the Akvavit he proffered.

Hanne was dismayed and afraid of what Erik might do, now that he was getting more and more drunk, and stood up to clear away some of the empty bottles and take-out boxes. Walking over to the kitchen counter with her hands full, she heard a clutter behind her as the brute got up, and she sensed him coming toward her. Just as she got to her destination to put her load down, two hands reached around her, grabbed her breasts, and violently whipped her around. Her face was right up against Erik's, and she was disgusted by his foul-smelling breath as he tried to force a kiss on her lips, violating her mouth with his tongue. She pushed against him with all her might, pulling her head away and spitting in his face.

"You bitch," the drunk muttered indignantly as he wiped himself with his sleeve and grabbed after her. "You're going to pay for that." He tore at her clothes, and shoved her against the wall, grinding himself into her from behind. Hanne tried to wrestle herself away, but he was much stronger than she, and the slime tugged her sweater and shirt over her head, pinning her arms with one hand. Within moments, he had ripped her bra off and was molesting her breasts with one hand and now tearing the garments off her arms with the other, totally exposing her upper half. Still grinding her against the wall, he popped open the button on the front of her pants, forced a hand inside and tried to insert a finger or two roughly into her pussy, but with her arms now free, with a superhuman effort using her legs and her entire body, she managed to push hard against the wall and shove him back, liberating herself from his grasp. The drunken sod was momentarily knocked off balance, and in that instant Hanne grabbed one of the beer bottles from the counter and bashed his head with it as hard as she could. He was stunned and tottered, she surprised, and with only the neck of the broken bottle remaining in her hand, when he turned to rush at her again with a loud yell, she shoved the sharp protruding edges into his face, even as she was knocked to the ground, Erik toppling on top of her.

Her assailant, wounded, drunk, furious—and now with one eye literally oozing out of its socket—thrashed at her, yelling, "You bitch, you bitch, you're going to die!" Hanne quickly rolled away, stood up, and grabbing the half-full bottle of Akvavit, smacked the beast on the skull with a hard blow when he tried to get up and reach for her again. This time, her assailant simply collapsed to the floor, as she stood there trembling, still threatening him with the makeshift weapon.

After a few moments, during which tears welled up in her eyes and Erik did not move, she gingerly moved closer to him, still gripping the bottle, and leaned down to see if he was breathing, had a pulse. His face was bleeding profusely where the broken bottle had lacerated it, but she thought she felt a weak pulse in his neck artery, and shallow breaths seemed to emanate from his mouth. She momentarily thought of calling an ambulance, but Botnikov had confiscated her phone, and she did not want to search her bleeding victim for his. Besides, let the bastard bleed to death, she thought, as her anger at the way her countryman had treated her. *Yes, I will leave him here to die!*

But the determination that her attacker was still alive spurred Hanne to action: within moments she had located her torn top, slipped what was left of it over her head, leaving her shredded bra behind, and, remembering that Erik had told the Russian soldiers to leave, gingerly opened the front door and peeked out. Glad that the guards were gone, with one last look at the twisted, bleeding body of her assailant, she left the historic Hans Egede House behind her, and ran as fast as she could, immediately not knowing where to go, toward town.

Chapter 34

Hanne slowed her pace when she saw other pedestrians and cars passing so that she would be less conspicuous. She knew she needed to collect herself, formulate a plan. She could not afford to be caught again by the Russians, who would certainly be on the lookout for her. Perhaps not actively searching yet—not until the morning, anyway, since she was supposed to be ensconced with that brute, Erik, who had told the guards to stay away. But still, if they saw and recognized her, she would be in trouble.

Without her jacket and just in her torn top, Hanne felt the cold of the October evening, and even more so since it had started to rain. But she couldn't go back to her apartment—it could well be under surveillance. Nor to Malik, since there was definitely at least one, possibly more, soldiers there. So where to turn to?

Aniuk, yes, her Inuit friend and colleague would help her! Too bad that Botkinov had taken her cell, because easiest would be to call Aniuk's number which was in her contact list. She did not know her address, but her friend had taken her once to the apartment she shared with her partner—would she remember where it was? Somewhere over by the port for sure—Aniuk's boyfriend, Silla, was an avid fisherman and owned a boat with his brother, she had told her. She needed to head over in that direction, and maybe, maybe the street and house would all come back. She would feel her way there.

☙☙☙

Hanne, bruised and sore, frozen and soaked through to the skin in her light top, leaned against the bell thankfully, grateful that she had succeeded in finding her Greenlandic friend's apartment building—with her name and Silla's clearly displayed and lit up next to the buzzer—and now hoping, praying that she would respond and take her in.

It was a male voice—must be Silla, whom she hadn't met—that answered with an "Aluu!" Greenlandic for hello, and then, "Who is it?"

Hanne gave her name, saying in Danish that she is Aniuk's friend, and needed help. Silla asked her to identify herself one more time just to be sure, and then told her to wait. It was Aniuk who came on the speaker this time: "Hanne, come right up. Apartment 302."

When she arrived on the third floor, Aniuk was waiting, door open, with Silla right behind her. "Oh dear, Hanne, you are soaked. You must be freezing. Come, come in. Silla, this is my boss, the wonderful lady I have been telling you about. Hanne Kristensen. Hanne, my friend, Silla."

"Thank you. Lovely to meet you, Silla," Hanne said, teeth chattering.

"We must get you out of those wet clothes," Aniuk said. "They're torn. What happened?" And she continued without waiting for an answer. "Silla, will you run a hot bath for Hanne, please? I will bring something dry for you to put on."

"Of course." This from Silla.

"Thank you. Thank you. I will tell you all later."

"Hanne, while you wash up and change, I'm going to call Malik."

"Good. We were all taken to Hans Egede House. He was allowed to go back home with a couple of soldiers. They may still be at his place, but if you talk Greenlandic, even if they are right beside him, they won't understand. Oh, but they took his cell phone. All our phones. Do you know if he has another one?"

"Yes, he has a government fixed line. I will call on that." And then she added with a smile, "After all, this is official business."

❧❦❧

Hanne felt refreshed and rejuvenated after the warming bath and happy to see that the clothes Aniuk had laid out for her—jeans, a T-shirt and a sweatshirt—all fit well. When she found her hosts in the kitchen with some bread and smoked fish, some sliced pepper and onion put out on the table, she again thanked them profusely for their hospitality.

Aniuk was eager to report on her call with Malik.

"Hanne, he suggested we get you away from Nuuk as soon as possible. He has been in touch with Ron Hall, your American friend, who is arranging for a way to get you picked up, but we need to get you somewhere less directly controlled by the invading forces. So, Silla and I thought that early tomorrow morning, just as the sun rises, he and his brother will take you in their fishing boat over to Angisunnquaq Island. It is a trip of about seven or eight miles south, and there is a calm inlet on the northern side where we can safely wait. That should be far enough out of the immediate reach of the Russians. Malik did not want us to tell him where we would take you—just in case he is questioned and tortured by these animals—but suggested you call your Ron Hall. To let him know the plan and to have him arrange for them to get you there. Here, he gave me Hall's number just in case. You can call him on this phone. And while you do that, I will have Silla run over to your apartment with my key and pick up some of your own clothes. And warm ones at that, since you will need them on the boat trip."

"Thank you," Hanne said, taking the cell, as she turned to look at Aniuk's partner. "They are in my closet. That would be great, Silla."

"Sure thing."

"And…some undergarments, if possible, please," Hanne continued, blushing as she said this. "Also, I have my old personal cell phone in the top drawer of my night table beside my bed. My passport is there too. And my laptop is somewhere I think in the living room. Could you get those as well please? I hope it's not too much to ask…"

"Sure. No problem."

"Thanks. God, I hope the Russians won't start looking for me before the morning."

"Even if they do, Hanne, Malik will not tell them where you are," Aniuk tried to console her. "We will be well on our way before they get to him."

Hanne dialled Hall's cell number, and fortunately, he picked up right away. Good. He must be prioritizing all calls from Greenland, Hanne thought to herself.

"Hanne, I'm so pleased to hear from you. Where are

you?"

"Hello, Ron. I'm with friends here in Nuuk. Safe for now. They will take me to Angisunnquaq Island early tomorrow morning, seven or eight miles south of Nuuk. You can see on a map that there is a major inlet there on the northern side. Can you arrange for someone to get me?"

"Perfect, Hanne. I have been in touch with your Canadian friend, Richard Simpson, and he has made arrangements to fly to Nuuk by seaplane to see you. He can change his destination and fetch you on that island and fly you out. I will talk to him right now. One way or other we will get you, as long as you can make your way there. Angisunnquaq Island, is it? I will look right now on Google maps."

"Thanks, Ron. I owe you one."

"Anything to help my Arctic heroine."

"Hope to see you soon."

"Indeed. Stay safe, Hanne."

Chapter 35

Hanne woke from the depths of her sleeping pill induced slumber to Aniuk shaking her by the shoulders and telling her they needed to hurry to get down to Silla's boat in the harbor before sunrise. Her partner had gone ahead to meet his brother, Inuk—whom he had alerted already the evening before about the importance of the mission—so they could ready their Cleopatra 33 fishing boat, which, with its twenty-seven-knot top speed, should be able to get them to Angisunnquaq Island in well under an hour. That is, if all went according to plan.

Even though it was still dark, Aniuk and a hooded Hanne scurried along the streets of Nuuk as inconspicuously as possible, to get down to the port. Fortunately, there was no one in the streets and it took them only a few minutes. Inuk was already untying the boat as quick introductions were made and Hanne expressed her profuse thanks to the brothers. Silla manoeuvred the vessel expertly out of the harbor and revved the engine up to full speed as soon as they were clear of the parked boats and in open water, Hanne staying below deck all the while. Only when they were out of easy visibility from land did she come up and watch the steely sea- and landscape emerge with the now rising sun, and the still dark shapes whizz by as if they had a life of their own. She could not help but feel elated that she was leaving the current difficult and life-threatening circumstances in her adopted country behind—at least for the time being—although she was not entirely sure what would confront her going forward. Or, indeed, what she should be doing next, and for that matter, where she should head to—if she managed to get away. Her mind left these thoughts behind and switched eagerly to excitement at the prospect of seeing Richard very soon.

Looking back toward Nuuk, she was delighted to see that the Russian warships offshore Nuuk were receding in the distance. Soon, the Cleopatra entered a channel between two smaller islands, and then passing a headland, they lost sight of the capital. They were proceeding due south and after leaving another couple of small islands behind, Silla came up beside Hanne, and pointing ahead, said: "There, that is Angisunnquaq Island. And we'll be heading straight into a bay on its north shore. That is where we should be meeting your friends."

Not long after, and in the bay but behind a headland that hid them from a possible sighting from the open sea, the boat pulled close in to shore and Silla cut the engine while Inuk released the anchor. Aniuk's partner came back again to where the two women were sitting and said, "We will wait here and keep a lookout," then adding with a smile after a moment of looking around, "We may as well pull out the fishing rods, although that is not how we normally do our fishing. Would either of you want one?"

So, they all tossed a line overboard and settled in for a wait of what could add up to several hours.

Until Richard got there, Hanne was hoping.

છગ્ઝ

It was right around the time the brothers' Cleopatra was slowing down as it approached Angisunnquaq Island that Captain Kolnikov—Botkinov's boss, and, with Admiral Ogarov and Captain Petrov both incapacitated, the ranking officer now in charge of all the Russian forces in, and offshore, Nuuk—left the hospital where Ogarov and Jens Andersen, were being treated for a serious viral infection that, he concluded, must be the same one spreading so virulently among his troops. He had come onshore early in the morning to visit the two and to ascertain to what extent the Admiral might be capable of participating in decision making and leading the forces, or whether it would continue to be up to him to command. Seeing that the Admiral was on a ventilator, while the other patient was still extremely weak, he proceeded to make his way over to Hans Egede House where—as Captain-Lieutenant Botkinov had informed him the evening before—Erik Larsen, the Governor appointed by President Gusanov and the third prisoner released by the Americans, had insisted on being left alone with their captive, who Botkinov told him was the beautiful minister of Environment and Natural Resources of Greenland. This was the woman Gusanov had ordered them to capture and send back to Russia for a show trial and probably execution. Kolnikov had not been very happy when he had heard of Larsen's demand the night before, but as a soldier used to following orders who was he to question it?

When he thought about it though, it was probably no wonder the governor didn't want his soldiers anywhere near there—he was no doubt going to have his way with the poor woman—who, he had heard, was beautiful—in more ways than one. His reputation of mistreating the opposite sex had been making the rounds in the occupying naval force, and although Kolnikov found it disgusting, he felt frustrated that there was nothing he could do about it since Larsen was the governor now, and in fact, appointed by the president.

But he himself did not agree at all with what the Gusanov gang was doing, especially in the Arctic and here in Greenland—he much preferred the previous troika, led by Pavel Laptov, and including his favorite senior officer and mentor, Admiral Maslenkov. Certainly, Laptov had started to do some much needed important things to help preserve nature and the earth. Too bad Gusanov and his gang had ousted him.

And hadn't this Hanne Kristensen been part of Laptov's effort to save the Arctic?

It was time to go check on matters at that Hans Egede House.

℗℗

The captain was surprised as no one answered when he rapped on the door with his pistol, and even more so, when turning the knob, the door opened easily. It was obviously not locked form the inside. Stepping into the dark front room, his surprise gave way to utter shock: there, on the floor, in a huge pool of drying blood, lay the seemingly lifeless body of a man he presumed to be Larsen. The face was lacerated, blue, bloody, and bloated, the head severely bruised and swollen in several places, so the wounded man was not immediately recognizable. Kolnikov called out, asking, "Anyone here?" and sent one of the soldiers who had accompanied him to look around the rest of the house. But there was no one. He mentally noted to himself that this Danish woman—if she had done this all by herself—was a formidable opponent, certainly not to be messed with.

Kolnikov overcame his revulsion and stepped over to the man lying there to ascertain that he was indeed the governor and whether he was dead or alive. Better if the former, he thought, as he brought his face right down to the bloody remains of the victim's visage and simultaneously felt for a pulse. He was astounded that a very foul smell kept coming out of what remained of the man's mouth and nose, and the vein on his wrist did pulsate, albeit very weakly. Against his better judgement, he yelled to one of his men to call an ambulance, ultimately thinking that even if this jerk did die in the time before the emergency crew arrived, the body would have to be taken away somewhere, he didn't really care where.

But Kolnikov did hesitate for a moment as to what he should do about the missing prisoner—Hanne Kristensen—should he just let her escape, or should he make a call to have her apprehended. He knew though, that if he followed his instinct he would get into trouble. After all, he reminded himself once again, President Gusanov himself had ordered the arrest of this woman. Indeed, he could already be crucified for allowing Larsen's injury—and possible murder, since he didn't at all think the Dane would survive—to take place under his watch.

This thing with this woman though was going too far. Probably raped, perhaps tortured—the broken glass and upside-down furniture, blood and torn clothes certainly pointed to trauma. It was indeed lucky for her that she managed to get the upper hand with this despicable Dane and escape. For one, if he had been able to, Larsen would have certainly killed her in his fury after sustaining any injury. And the more he thought about it, deep down, yes, it was this woman Laptov had been working with, the very one they were now looking for, to put that sweeping Arctic Treaty in place. She was the minister of Environment and Natural Resources for Greenland after all, wasn't she?

Once again, he couldn't help but think that maybe it would be good if she managed to get away.

But then, he simply could not risk not taking any action to recapture her. Botkinov and the others here with him would surely tell, and he would be in serious trouble. Court martialled, certainly demoted, in shame. He could not do that to his beautiful young wife and two little children. So, Captain Kolnikov finally decided to do his duty, call and put out an all points alert for his forces to look for Hanne Kristensen. Ships to block the harbor, helicopters and planes to take off and search surrounding areas.

Deep down though, he hoped she would get away.

We'll see what happens, he thought to himself.

☙❧

Richard, sitting in the co-pilot's seat, was glad to spot the Greenland coastline, knowing that if all went well, he would be hugging Hanne very soon. Fortunately, Ron Hall had managed to reach him the night before, just as he was settling in to a room at the Hotel North Two, exhausted after the enjoyable flight up to Goose Bay on a CF-18 fighter jet, to tell him about the change in plans. He had passed the instructions on to the pilot of the Cessna Caravan, who had decided that best would be to approach Angisunnquaq Island from the south, giving Nuuk and the remaining Russian warships a wide berth.

The seaplane flew low over the island, and, as it passed over a headland, it was not hard to spot the action near the entrance of the bay. Two helicopters with Cyrillic markings on them were hovering over what looked like a fishing vessel and a cruiser that could only be Russian, with a rubber dinghy just pulling away from the fishing boat in which he saw Hanne with another woman and three soldiers armed to the teeth guarding them.

"Damn it!" Richard vocalized his frustration, "We're fucking too late."

The pilot veered the plane sharply away from the scene of the confrontation and back over the island. Richard thought for a moment, before saying, "Well, we may as well land in Nuuk. I can get out, you can refuel and go back to Nain. There is no way we'll be able to extract my Minister friend today." And then he added, more to himself than the pilot, "I'll just have to see what is possible once I'm down there."

Chapter 36

Nuuk—Thursday, October 2, 202-

W ell, well, well, if it isn't that Danish slut again," Captain-Lieutenant Botnikov greeted Hanne as she negotiated the last rung of the ladder leading up onto the Russian cruiser's deck. "Or should I say, whoring bitch who tried to murder the governor appointed by my president. You will pay for it, I can assure you." The fleeting thought that went through Hanne's mind was that Erik Larsen did not die, and now she was in even more danger than before.

Botnikov continued more calmly when he saw Aniuk. "And who is this Inuit beauty?" as he reached down to give her a hand, which was refused.

When neither of the women responded to him, in his fury the Russian officer yelled at the soldiers who had gone in the boat to fetch Hanne and Aniuk, "Tie them up in the front under the cannon. I will come in a minute to question the bitches. Unfortunately, though, we won't have much time to have any fun with them. We have Captain Kolnikov's orders to bring them straight to him—at least the Danish whore."

As the soldiers manhandled and pushed her and her

friend along, Hanne was again struck by Botnikov's excellent English, spoken with an American accent (was it indeed Texas?)—very unusual for a Russian soldier—although that said, he seemed like a real bastard. And what was this Captain Kolnikov going to be like, the one she was to be delivered to? Eating away at her was also the question of what would happen to her now, recaptured and having severely wounded that rapist provisional governor, Larsen? Who would no doubt want to kill her with his own two hands to have his revenge. But even more so, she feared for Aniuk, too, whom she had brought into this entire ghastly affair.

The two women were trundled along by the soldiers and then had their wrists handcuffed to a railing just under the cruiser's cannon. Botkinov followed and slouched up to Hanne, grabbing her by the chin, as he asked, "So, Ms. Kristensen, you must tell me what happened at that Hans Egede House. You succeeded in getting me in deep trouble for running away, but even more so for nearly killing the guv, your fucking compatriot. I need some answers, and maybe a little payback." The brute let his hands run down Hanne's front and back, rubbing his crotch up against her, before turning to Aniuk. "And what is your name, you gorgeous little Inuit slut? You, too, are in deep shit, for helping the bitch next to you escape. An accomplice, so we will need to punish you too, my dear."

"She had nothing to do with any of this. You leave her alone, you bastard," Hanne yelled, wishing that she had never involved Aniuk in her escape. She, herself, was no better off than if she had given herself up after the scene in the Hans Egede House, and now her friend and her partner and his brother were also in trouble.

Fortunately, she saw that they were already within view of the other ships lying offshore Nuuk, and indeed

Botnikov too, was cognizant of this. "I have express orders to surrender you to my boss, you stupid cunt," he said as he again grabbed Hanne by the waist with one hand and squeezed a breast with the other, "but nothing was said about the native girl, so we shall keep her for ourselves." Then to the soldier standing there, something in Russian, whereupon the man unshackled Aniuk who was led away by the captain-lieutenant and the soldier, as Hanne thrashed about helplessly, yelling, "Let her go. Please! She has done nothing."

 summary

Richard thanked the pilot of the Cessna, and grabbing his backpack with his few overnight necessities and laptop, jumped up on the shore. Wondering how to proceed, the idea came to him that perhaps he should wait for the fishing boat he had seen Hanne clamber out of and into the dinghy with the Russian soldiers. Surely, the fishermen would make their way back to Nuuk and they would no doubt be able to help: at the very least, they would be able to fill him in on what they knew. So, he clambered up on to the road above, from where he would have a good vantage point of any boat coming in to dock.

While waiting, he had the idea that it might be a good time to call Ron Hall to tell him that the extraction had failed and brainstorm on next steps.

"Richard," the American's voice was excited, "Good. I was hoping you would call right about now. Is Hanne with you?"

"Alas, no. The Ruskis got to her first, just as we were going in to get her at that island. I asked the seaplane to land here in Nuuk and leave me here so I could try and find her, but of course she must be on one of the Russian vessels. I'm sitting in a spot overlooking the harbor, waiting for the fishermen to come back—you know, the ones who had brought her to meet me. They might be able to help me figure out where to start my search."

"Shit!" Richard had not heard Ron Hall swear before. "The Russians will not be easy on Hanne. We need to get to her as soon as possible. Maybe find Malik Rorsen—he might be able to help. Although he, too, is a home-bound prisoner, apparently."

"Well, I'll see what these fishermen can tell me. Then I will try and find Malik."

"Good, Richard. Keep me posted." Hall paused for a moment before adding, "Oh, one piece of potentially good news. It seems that Russia has gone silent, and that usually is the harbinger of political turmoil. All their TV channels are just playing recordings of Tchaikovsky's Swan Lake and other set pieces, some have even gone off the air. So big changes may be coming. Laptov may be gaining ground. We hope."

"But you don't know anything concrete? Can you not get in touch with Laptov?

"No, we've tried. We'll just have to wait and see."

"Thanks."

"Good luck."

☙❧

It was after a wait of a little over half an hour when Richard saw a vessel he thought he recognized as the one that had transported Hanne, enter Nuuk harbor. As it made its way to its docking slot and the two fishermen tied and closed it up for the day, he had ample time to saunter over and, in fact, was waiting just in front when the two Inuit finally clambered over the plank.

"Hello! My name is Richard Simpson, and I'm a good friend of Hanne Kristensen. I saw you out there in your boat when the Russians took her and another lady off your hands—I was in a seaplane you might have seen, coming to rendezvous with her and take her to Canada."

It was Silla who answered: "Yes, we were supposed to deliver her to you. Until the bloody Russians hijacked the mission…"

"Well, we almost succeeded," Richard tried to console the men, but also himself. "Do you know where they might have taken her? And who was the other woman in the boat?"

"That was one of the Russian cruisers out there. They would probably re-join the rest of the vessels sitting offshore. Perhaps they took them to the destroyer or one of the other ships, whichever one has the officer in charge on it. The Admiral, who was in overall command is now in our hospital with that virus." And then Silla added, "Oh, and the other woman out there was my girlfriend, Aniuk. I damn well hope they leave her alone, otherwise there will be hell to pay."

"How did you all get involved in this escape effort?" Richard asked, wanting to find out some of the background.

"Aniuk works in the Environment and Natural Resources Department. Ms. Kristensen came to us last evening in a terrible state. She said this Dane—the one the Russian president had appointed governor here—had tried to rape her but she managed to incapacitate him and get away."

"Oh, God, not again!" Richard was utterly distraught. "This, of course on top of the Russian president putting out that awful statement against her…they will crucify her now that she's in their hands again! Oh, poor Hanne…"

"Well, let's see what we can do," Inuk said. "Maybe there's a way."

"The best might be to try to locate the prime minister. He might have more information on how these Russians are operating," Silla said.

"Agreed. Let's do it!" Richard acquiesced, for lack of any better step to take.

Chapter 37

Nuuk—Thursday, October 2, 202-

Captain-Lieutenant Botkinov preceded Hanne up the destroyer's ladder, with a couple of the soldiers from the cruiser bringing up the rear. His boss, Captain Kolnikov, up at the top, did a double take when he saw the gorgeous Danish woman and it took him almost a minute to recover before he said, glancing toward Botnikov, "Well done, Captain-Lieutenant! I commend you for bringing Greenland's minister of Environment and Natural Resources back to us safely. And a very warm welcome to you, Ms. Kristensen." Whereupon Botnikov glanced at her with a frown—after all, she was a prisoner, and not someone to be welcomed, was Hanne's take.

Indeed, she was sure the handsome captain was being sarcastic, but when he bade Botnikov goodbye and turned to her to invite her into his office, she started to doubt her initial view. And all in perfect English to boot—this time, Oxford, not Texas: what was going on? Zaitsov and these two—were Russian naval officers required to pass an English test? At least the younger ones maybe…

But as the commander of the cruiser made his way back to the ladder, Hanne mustered the courage to say,

"Captain, your Captain-Lieutenant Botnikov and his soldiers are keeping my friend and colleague, a Greenlandic young lady, captive on their boat. He threatened her with what I took to be abuse, and it would be terrible if something untoward should happen to her. Your relations here with the locals would be seriously impacted. She has done nothing wrong, except to help me try and get away. I would be in your debt if you were to order him to release her and take her back to Nuuk or at the very least bring her to be here with us."

The officer was at first taken aback by Hanne's forthright request, but then said, "Just a minute, please," and went after Botnikov. When he came back, all he said was, "Done. Thank you for pointing that out. Your friend will be sent back to Nuuk. I will check to make sure once we are finished here."

As they walked side by side, Kolnikov asked whether Hanne was hungry, and when she said yes, instead of his office, he ushered her down to the mess. There, over a warm bowl of borscht followed by pork *pelmeni*—Russian dumplings—the captain said, "I would like to be upfront with you, Ms. Kristensen. You have been declared an enemy of our country by President Gusanov. Plus, you have now seriously added to your woes by coming close to killing the governor of Greenland appointed by our president. Nevertheless, I must confess, I applaud what you—and our former troika member, Pavel Laptov—were trying to do earlier to save the Arctic. If it were up to me, Russia would never have withdrawn from the excellent Arctic Treaty you and he crafted…and I do respect you for that. However, for us to get to…shall we say…a more comfortable place, Ms. Kristensen, you need to tell me what happened since you were left alone by the captain-lieutenant at the Hans Egede House."

Hanne continued to be surprised by the far better than expected treatment she was receiving from this rather unique Russian naval officer. At least he was giving her a chance…

"Thank you. I shall tell you all as it happened. Yesterday morning, the captain-lieutenant interrupted the start of a cabinet meeting called by Prime Minister Rorsen and took us all prisoner, marching us over to Hans Egede House. As you may know, we were to be hostages in an attempt to force the Americans to release your commanding officer and the two Danes working with you, who, by the way, had been my friends back in Denmark in another era."

"Yes, this was agreed all the way down the chain of command. I am sorry if it inconvenienced you."

Hanne continued, ignoring the interruption. "When word came that they had been let go, Captain-Lieutenant Botkinov allowed all the other cabinet members to return home under guard. Except, of course, for me, since, as you pointed out, your president had ordered my arrest even before all this happened. I was kept there in captivity with two or three of your soldiers outside the house making sure I didn't escape. When the three prisoners from Thule arrived in Nuuk later in the day, as I think you are aware, two of them were taken straight to the hospital, but the third, Erik Larsen, the man appointed provisional governor of Greenland, came to Hans Egede House. He had been looking for Pavel Laptov on orders from your president and thought I might know where he was hiding…or some unfinished business such as that."

"Yes, we have all been searching for the minister…And there are some reports now that he may have surfaced back in Russia. But we will get on to Laptov later. First, I want you to finish telling me what happened."

"Well, Larsen ordered the guards left behind by the captain-lieutenant to get some food and drink for us and then to leave, saying he was perfectly capable of looking after me…"

"Clearly, a mistake. Since he is now in the hospital, and you escaped."

"After drinking several beers and most of a bottle of Akvavit, he viciously attacked me and then tried to…rape me…" Hanne paused, finding the retelling difficult.

"Ugh…"

"Fortunately, I was able to grab an empty beer bottle and I hit him hard on the skull with it. He was stunned but he rushed at me, so I shoved the broken bottle in his face. Wounded and in a fury, he took me down with him, but I managed to roll away and get to my feet. As he started to stand up and come at me again, I bashed him hard on the head, this time with the partially empty Akvavit bottle. He staggered and fell to the ground, and lay there not moving, unconscious and bleeding. But when I examined him close up, he still had a pulse and was breathing."

"So you ascertained that he was alive?"

"Yes. But shocked with what I had done, bruised and sore all over, I nevertheless pulled myself together and gathered up my tattered clothes, put them on the best I could, then checked to see that the guards were indeed not there, then left by the front door. I did not think I could go home or show up at Malik Rorsen's residence, thinking that both places might have been under surveillance. I thought of my friend and colleague—the one you were just getting the captain-lieutenant to release—and although I did not have my phone since Botnikov had confiscated it, I managed to find her place. Aniuk—that's her name—was there and she took me in. Fortunately, her partner and his brother have a fishing boat and they offered to help me get away from Nuuk the next day."

"Did you have a goal in mind where to go?"

Hanne hesitated before answering because she would have to tell about Richard and the entire extraction effort. But then again, it might help her cause if the Russians knew that the plans to extract her involved an international team.

"Angisunnquaq Island," she blurted out. "The Americans and Canadians were arranging for me to be picked up there in a seaplane. But your captain-lieutenant got to us first, and so here I am."

"Well, I am glad, Ms. Kristensen," Kolnikov paused a moment before continuing.

"So…Ms. Kristensen, what do you know about the whereabouts of Minister Laptov?"

Hanne answered with a simple, "Captain, I'm not prepared to talk about that. I know that your President Gusanov has also given orders to capture and bring him back to Russia."

"Well, as I mentioned, I am a great admirer of the minister. I was only asking—and I probably should not be telling you this—because since yesterday, we have not had any communication from headquarters in Russia. Complete radio silence. And I was wondering, could he have gone back and started another…revolution? Could the forces he might have been able to gather to his side be in a deadly fight with the allies of President Gusanov? I know that several of my fellow officers in the Northern Fleet are supporters of Laptov. I might be able to help if I knew where he is now."

"And, Captain, what would you do if you did know? If Pavel Laptov were indeed back in Russia and some of the elements of your military were helping him?"

"I believe we have talked enough, Ms. Kristensen. I am

going to have my staff ready this boat to head back to Russia. Many of our sailors are ill and we seem to serve little purpose here anymore. And you will come with us."

Hanne was taken aback by this. Clearly, just as she was still unsure of this ostensibly friendly captain, he did not totally trust her either. Perhaps the captain was hedging his bets—if there is a confrontation and Gusanov wins, he would please the rogue president by delivering her, but if Laptov looks like he will come out on top, he will join with him and ingratiate himself by freeing her. Clever man!

Chapter 38

Nuuk—Thursday, October 2, 202-

Richard and Silla made their way up the hill to where Silla knew from Aniuk Prime Minister Rorsen's residence was, and the Canadian diplomat was pleased when the two Russian soldiers toting Kalashnikov's just glanced at them as they went to knock on the front door. Even though a captive, Rorsen must be allowed to conduct the business of the country, he surmised, although the ease with which any stranger could approach the prime minister's residence was surprising, even to a Canadian.

In fact, it was Nanurjuk who opened the door, and after the usual Greenlandic greeting of "Aluu," Silla went on to explain in a low voice that they had come to discuss an important matter—the kidnapping of the minister of Environment and Natural Resources and her aide. Nanurjuk immediately understood the meaning of what Silla was telling her, so she invited the two men standing in the doorway to come in and talk to her husband.

Malik greeted Richard warmly, remembering him from the Ottawa signing of the Arctic Treaty and was dismayed when he heard that Hanne's extraction had failed and that now both she and Aniuk were prisoners of the Russians.

"They were taken away in the Russian cruiser, and we don't have any idea of where they are being held," Richard voiced his frustration. "Perhaps still on the cruiser or one of the other boats. How can we find out? What can we do to help them? They may kill Hanne, if we don't get her away fast."

Malik was at a loss for suggestions, other than saying: "They certainly have not brought the ladies on shore. I am quite sure of that—I would have heard. The only thing they might have done is transfer them to another boat. Maybe the big destroyer where the commanding officer must be. We could enquire with the soldiers outside, but of course, they speak none of the languages I know. Do you speak any Russian, Richard?"

"No. It's the last language I would want to learn."

"The one thing I do know from my colleague the minister of Health who was over at the hospital, is that that vile man, Erik Larsen, the pretender of a governor the Russian president appointed, was brought in there this morning with severe wounds. Apparently, he wanted to be alone with Hanne at Hans Egede House, but it seems she must have gotten the better of her and escaped."

"All the more dangerous for her to be back in their hands," Richard worried.

"Well, perhaps we should call Ron Hall and let him know that your attempt to take Hanne away from here has failed," Malik said. "Perhaps he will have a suggestion."

"I talked to him earlier," Richard answered, as the prime minister picked up the phone to dial. "And he told me that matters in Russia seem to be evolving. He had the same thoughts as you on where Hanne might have been taken. But good idea, Malik."

❧❧❧

"Prime Minister Rorsen! Wonderful to hear from you." Malik was pleased to get through directly on Hall's private cell after three rings. "Any news of Hanne?"

"Yes. I am afraid it is not good. In fact, I have Richard Simpson here with me…who I think already told you the mission failed."

"Hello, Richard. Yes. Any further news on her whereabouts?"

Malik waved to Richard to talk. "Hello, Ron. Malik and I have just been brainstorming—we arrived just a little too late, and the Russians in the cruiser grabbed her and her assistant and spirited them away. She's probably still on that boat, or perhaps more likely Malik thinks, transferred to the destroyer where the commanding officer probably is to be found."

"That's not good. Unfortunately, the US is not prepared to start a war to free her. We'll just have to see how this all pans out. In fact, we're following events in Russia very closely. The situation is very murky, but some of the reports we're getting suggest that the continuing catastrophic impact of climate change and the re-emergence of Laptov as a possible leader who might do something about this, is putting pressure on the Gusanov government. It seems that Laptov's forces may be gaining ground."

"Well, that, at least, is good news," Richard said. "Not necessarily for Hanne, though, especially if she is in pro-Gusanov hands. They may just kill her sooner rather than later so there is one less potentially powerful enemy for them on the international front. But, as you say, unfortunately there is very little we can do now. Just wait it out and watch how it develops."

"We will try to approach the Russians in charge here," Malik said. "Although it is very difficult to figure it all out. It seems from what my colleague at our hospital said it may be a Captain Kolnikov—he is the one who visited the very sick Admiral Ogarov—who is now in command, at least around here in Nuuk. I will try to get to him one way or the other."

"Good, Malik." This from Ron. "Keep me posted. Hang in there."

Richard found the discussion totally unsatisfying, other than the vague prospect of some positive developments in Russia, so he stood up to take his leave. Just then, Nanurjuk burst into Malik's home office, with a good-looking Greenlandic twenty-something young lady in tow. Before anyone could say anything, Silla jumped up from his chair, involuntarily shouting, "Aniuk!" as he rushed to embrace the girl. And after the hugs and the introductions, he asked, "How did you get away, my love? Tell us what happened."

"And please, where is Hanne?" Richard added, surmising from Silla's question that this must have been the other woman captured along with his Danish lover.

"That captain or lieutenant or whatever—Botnikov was his name, I think—had his cruiser take us to the bigger vessel out there, since his orders were to hand Hanne over to the commander of that boat. Hanne climbed up the ladder and was hustled away by the men at the top. That was the last I saw of her. This Botnikov wanted to keep me for himself, or so he said, so did not let me go. But fortunately, just as the cruiser was about to pull away, it seems that orders came from the commander that he was to take me back to shore and release me. Hanne must have interceded on my behalf. Which is why I am here, and

Hanne is on the destroyer or whatever that bigger boat is."

"I am so happy you are here with us, and very sorry about Hanne," Silla said glancing from Richard to Malik.

"These Russians are disgusting brutes and I fear for Hanne's safety on that big boat. Malik, please, please, do whatever you can to get in touch with that Captain Kolnikov you mentioned. I'm going to try and find a place to sleep tonight."

"Yes, of course," Malik answered. "I'll keep you posted."

"You are welcome to stay with us for the night," Aniuk said, as she, too, got up to leave.

"Thank you, but no. You two need to be together alone tonight. After all that has happened," Richard answered. "The last thing you need is a stranger in your apartment. I will find a place—what is the hotel, the Hans Egede?"

But just as he got up, Nanurjuk burst in again, so excited that she had trouble putting words together. "Malik, it seems that the big Russian ship is leaving the fjord and going out to sea! Come look!"

And they all rushed outside, to catch a glimpse of the destroyer, most probably carrying Hanne, picking up speed as it distanced itself from Nuuk and made its way out toward the open ocean.

Chapter 39

Kolnikov showed Hanne to his tiny cubicle and said, "I am afraid you are not going to have much privacy on this boat. Either you sleep in the bunk room with all the men, or perhaps safer would be for me to vacate my room here—occasionally intruding to use the facilities and get my stuff, if you don't mind. I can sleep on a mattress in my office next door. In any case, I need to leave you now, but we will touch base later."

"Thank you, Captain. You are very generous. I really do appreciate your kindness and understand what you need to do. Perhaps it will all turn out well for everybody."

Kolnikov looked at her for a long time before going out the door and closing it behind himself.

Hanne was glad to be alone. She immediately took out her phone, knowing she owed Richard a long overdue call and needed to do it while there still might be reception.

"Hanne," she heard the excited voice of her Canadian lover, "I'm so happy you called. Where are you? How are you? So many questions…"

"Everything is fine, Richard. I'm on the destroyer just leaving the Nuuk area, heading out to sea. Captain Kolnikov—who fortunately, is not like the other Russian soldiers—has decided to return to Russia and he's taking me with him. I'm not quite sure, but he seems to have expressed favorable comments about Pavel and Admiral Maslenkov—and Pavel indeed mentioned him to me earlier as probably one of his supporters—so he may be keen to join up with them. But if Gusanov stays on top, the captain may just hand me over to the bad guys, so the situation is still somewhat tenuous."

"Did anyone harm you, my dear? I heard that that brute Larsen attacked you. Are you okay?"

"Yes, thanks. I managed to fight him off. In fact, he was badly wounded when I left him."

"I heard. Good for you. He's in the hospital here now. Do you know where in Russia they are taking you?"

"No. But probably to Severomorsk or Murmansk—the Northern Fleet's home base."

"I'm going to try to come there somehow."

"Richard, don't do anything stupid. Let's wait till this all settles out."

"I can't. I need to see you and hold you in my arms. Take care of you. If anything happened to you, I would never forgive myself."

"It's just a little longer, Richard. I'm sure things will work out. I love you."

"And I you. Very much."

❧❧❧

A knock on the door, and Kolnikov entered. "Ms. Kristensen, I know you and Pavel Laptov became friends. Is there any way you can get in touch with him? I am aware that this is a highly unusual request to be making, but an unofficial contact might give us better information than what we can get through our official channels. Which is nothing, I must say. Our internal communications are down, totally. I would be grateful. You can use my phone."

"Thank you. But my friend did manage to get my private cell phone from my apartment before we made the escape attempt, and I do have Minister Laptov's number in it. So, I can certainly try, I guess. Do we still have reception, because aren't we going out to sea?"

"You'll be fine for now, so please make the call."

Hanne scrolled down to find Laptov's number and pressed the green telephone icon.

It took only four rings before Pavel's gravelly voice came on the line. "Hanne, what a surprise! Where are you? How are you?"

"Pavel, is this a good time to have a brief chat?"

"Well, it is the middle of the night, my dear, so you caught me at probably the only moment I am free to talk."

"Sorry, Pavel…"

"No, it's perfectly fine. So where are you?"

"Pavel, I am on one of your destroyers sailing toward Russia. The commander, Captain Kolnikov, is here with me, and urged me to call because he is unable to contact his superiors and has no news of where matters stand."

"Captain Kolnikov! Yes, I remember him. He is another of those superior officers Admiral Maslenkov and I decorated with the prestigious medal *For Service in the Submarine Force.* An excellent soldier and a good man. Put him on the speaker."

"Well, Kolnikov, I am pleased that you are rescuing my favorite fair maiden. Thank you."

"Minister, my pleasure indeed. And I am delighted and honored to be talking to you. It seems that our country is going through troubled times again, and we in the Northern Fleet—at least those of us deployed to Greenland—need some direction. As you may have heard, Admiral Ogarov is out of commission."

"I am glad to hear that he is still not able to command. He was always a bit of a Gusanov man. Never did like him. Much better to have you steering things, Kolnikov. And just to let you know, we have managed to free Admiral Maslenkov and he is now in command of the navy as far as I am concerned. He is currently involved in discussions with other senior officers in the military, who we know favor our cause. We are pretty well in control here in Severomersk and Murmansk now and will be moving on St. Petersburg in the next few days. And then after that, the Kremlin, where the Gusanov gang is holed up. They are still trying to direct matters from there."

"Minister Laptov, we are just leaving Nuuk, heading east. We can come to wherever we are of most use to you. My sailors and I are delighted that you are back in the driver's seat, and we fully support your cause. The world, the Arctic, and Russia, need you to take charge again and oust that renegade Gusanov and his gang. "

"Thank you for that, Captain. We certainly need all hands on deck. I will consult with Admiral Maslenkov and have him get in touch with you via official or unofficial channels. And we can always communicate via Hanne, if there is reception," Laptov said, laughing. "For now, I think perhaps it would be best if you headed for St. Petersburg. It would be good to have your support there from the water side. I am sure Admiral Maslenkov would agree and might deploy other vessels to join you. As I say, we will be in touch."

"Excellent, Minister. Thank you."

"And Captain, make sure nothing happens to my friend, Hanne Kristensen. I hold you personally responsible. We need to get our country back on track. And then the Arctic comes next. We have a lot to do. And Hanne, take care of yourself. Stay out of the way of these warriors."

"You be careful, too, Pavel. And good luck!"

ℰℬℰℬ

"Thank you, Hanne. That was important," the captain, stood up to leave.

As he did so, Hanne addressed him: "Captain Kolnikov, if we're going to St. Petersburg, we will need to pass close to NATO countries, which might not welcome the intrusion of an unannounced Russian ship in the Baltic, especially during these strained times. I would be happy to talk to my American friend, Ron Hall, who is a close advisor to President Barlow, to get them to brief their northern NATO colleagues. I've been meaning to call him anyway."

"Sure, that would be helpful. Thank you. And thank you again for getting in touch with Minister Laptov. I have to go and talk to my officers now, so please excuse me…" He was obviously impressed that Laptov and she were on first name terms.

"No problem, Captain. I will let you know how my chat goes," Hanne said, smiling.

She found Hall in her contact list and dialled. Fortunately, the call went through, and she heard the American voice say, "Hello, this is Ron Hall." And then he must have recognized the number. "Hanne, is that you? Is everything all right?"

"Ron, great to talk. Yes, all's well. I am on what I think is a friendly Russian destroyer. We—the captain, who is a Laptov supporter, and I—just talked to Pavel, and it seems they are making headway against the Gusanov regime.

Admiral Maslenkov has been freed and they are now getting set to move on St. Petersburg. We're heading there now to give them support."

"That sounds terrific! So, you've left the shores of Greenland?"

"Yes. Captain Kolnikov saw no reason to stay any longer. Many of his men are infected with that new virus, and with events developing in our favor in Russia, Gusanov's aggressive expansionism seems to be coming to an end. So, it's all good, and you certainly won't need to intervene in Greenland. Between evolving events in Russia and the virus…"

"That is good news indeed."

"But, Ron, as now we will be entering the Baltic, can you alert your NATO allies that we are a friendly Russian destroyer? The *Admiral Levchenko*. They should certainly not molest us, and if possible, give us all the help they can."

"Consider it done, Hanne. And good luck. It seems that with you in the picture, things always turn out for the better."

"Thanks, Ron. I will try to keep you posted."

Chapter 40

North Atlantic, Friday to Sunday, October 3-5, 202-

Hanne was glad she had asked Aniuk to have Silla get her laptop, so now she was able to catch up on the massive load of emails that had collected in her inbox since she was last able to look at it. But more importantly, with the hope that Laptov would prevail and the possibility of peace and positive action in the Arctic, she would take some time to review the Arctic Treaty she and Pavel, with the help of many others, had drafted. She wanted to see how much updating it might need for the new realities.

The trip across the North Atlantic took two and a half days through rough seas and some bad weather, but she was glad to be left alone by Kolnikov and his men, getting together with the captain only for meals. She would go up on deck for air and exercise two or three times a day, weather and seas permitting, but otherwise stayed in Kolnikov's minute room except for when the captain came to get her at mealtimes. Of course, when she did leave the room, she inevitably had to endure the lusting stares of the Russian sailors, who nevertheless must have had a talking to by the captain to stay away from her. She was infinitely grateful to the officer for his protection, civility and generosity and resolved to commend him to Pavel Laptov and Admiral Maslenkov when they finally met up.

They must have been approaching Europe, because on the second day out of Nuuk on one of her deck walks, Kolnikov came up behind Hanne, and pointing far out to sea in a southwardly direction, said, "See that? That is one of the Orkney Islands. Scotland. And soon to the north we will see the Shetlands. Also, part of Scotland. We are a little over halfway to St. Petersburg and getting close to Norway, and then to your country. In fact, we will pass right by your hometown, Copenhagen. Probably early morning, tomorrow."

"Wow! Amazing."

"In fact, I was thinking that maybe it would be best for you to get out there. I am not sure what we will encounter when we get to St. Petersburg, but if we get into heavy fighting, I would prefer you not to be on board, if you don't mind, Ms. Kristensen. It would give me one less thing to have to worry about. And make it easier for me to fulfill my pledge to Minister Laptov."

"Hmm…Captain. I hadn't really thought about it."

"It would be the best, I think."

"Perhaps you are right," Hanne conceded I wouldn't mind catching up on some things back home, seeing my family and a few friends." And here, Hanne was thinking primarily of Kristi…

"Good, then. So, just be ready before dawn—let's say 5 am tomorrow. We will make arrangements to drop you off. A quick trip in a rubber dinghy and you will be on shore without us having to go into port with all the officialdom that entails. I presume you will not have any trouble calling a taxi—perhaps you can book it even before you leave the boat."

"Good idea. And thank you, Captain."

☙☙☙

Hanne had trouble sleeping the last night on the boat and was outside on the deck at five sharp. She was pleased to see the silhouette of her native city and noted that indeed, they were very close to shore. Kolnikov's sailors had already lowered a dinghy, and the captain was at the top of the ladder as she approached.

"I must thank you for all you've done for me, Captain," Hanne said, with difficulty holding back the tears. "You have been terrific, and I owe you in many ways. As does Greenland for your service." And, on an impulse, she threw her arms around his neck and embraced him.

"Well, Ms. Kristensen, I am pleased to have been of service." The captain was surprised by the sudden expression of affection. "The world owes you a lot for the treaty you devised. Let's hope we can put it all back, in place. And good luck to you." With that, he let go of Hanne and gently nudged her toward the ladder.

Chapter 41

Copenhagen, Sunday, morning, October 5, 202-

It took the dinghy only a few minutes to get to shore, and, as she clambered up the ladder to the dock, Hanne had the clear impression as she looked around that the water level here, too, was much higher now than it used to be. She was pleased, though, that, at this early hour, she was not confronted by any official as she made her way to the taxi she had ordered waiting at the top. Once inside, she directed the driver to take her to Kristi's address, which she knew off by heart. Hanne had given up her apartment when she left her Danish government job and was offered the position of minister of Environment and Natural Resources in Greenland, leaving a few of her essential belongings—such as several changes of clothes—with Kristi, and dispersing the rest among family, friends and charities.

The taxi sped through familiar streets as it approached Kristi's building, and getting more and more excited as it got closer, Hanne conjured up an image of her lover lying naked in her king size bed, with her just slipping in beside her, embracing passionately and then…

That would be the most favorable scenario, she decided

with a smile.

Alternatively, Kristi could be out, sleeping at one of her other friend's places—male, she thought, hoping, she did not fully understand why, that she would, at least, be her only female lover. In which case, she would just stay in Kristi's bed until she came home and slid in beside her, smelling of sex and her wonderful self…

Or the third possibility: that her lover was there, in her bed and fucking with someone, as Hanne entered the bedroom…Would she lie down beside the two and engage in a threesome, like the last time, when Jens was still in the picture? That had been wonderful sex…but would she dare again? Or would she just stand there quietly, and watch, as her Kristi copulated with someone else? There was something to that as well, a bit of kink…voyeurism, but…it would be hard not to join in.

Not wanting to wake or disturb the occupant or occupants, Hanne found the key in the usual hiding place and quietly entered the apartment. She smiled as she was struck by the familiar images and smells and went into the living room to put the backpack with her belongings down before heading ever so quietly to the closed bedroom door. Gingerly, she opened it at first a crack, peering in, and then fully and stared at the slept-in, unmade bed. At least there was no one in it, so the decision on what next was not hard.

"Okay, Kristi my dear, I will take a much-needed shower and wait for you between the sheets," she said to herself as she went to retrieve her backpack.

୧୬୧

Hanne was glad to settle into Kristi's rumpled bed, and, closing her eyes, could not help but feel the erotic vibes from her friend even though she was not there. She stroked herself, at first gently and then ever more vigorously, bringing herself to an anticipatory climax. Later, she was sound asleep when she felt the gentle touch on her naked shoulder and opened her eyes to see Kristi's beautiful face smiling at her.

"Hello, love," her friend said, caressing her cheek. "I have been dreaming of this moment ever since we parted in New York." Lips touched sensually, then opened, tongues toyed, as Kristi, who had undressed before waking her friend, threw the sheets off Hanne's naked body, and the two embraced, pawed, kissed and licked all over, before first Kristi went down on Hanne and then vice versa, bringing each other to a fever pitch of orgasm the likes of which only a woman could do for a woman.

They did not stop there but took delight from rubbing their pussies against each other's thighs, as they kissed with open mouths, tongues violating buccal cavities, before again proceeding to mutual cunnilingus. Hanne was sure that she had never had such good sex, never prior to this, not even with Kristi. Was it the separation, was it all that she had just been through in Greenland, was it the mind-fucking build-up she had engaged in just before, that made it so special? She was not sure, but she did not care. It was time to enjoy any and all of the carnal pleasures her lover brought to her.

Sometime later, as they still lay in bed in each other's arms, although it was getting close to noon, Kristi asked Hanne to tell her what had happened since the two parted in New York. When she finished the story, and after Kristi's exclamations of "Wow! You've been through such a lot, you poor dear," followed by hugs and kisses, Hanne asked Kristi, rather coyly, "And who were you fucking last night, before you came home this morning smelling of sex and jumped into bed with me?"

"Well, my dear, I thought you would never ask. Why don't you try and guess?"

"Was…it…male or female? Or something else?" Hanne asked, willing to play the game.

"Male. I like to alternate between sexes."

"You bisexual whore, you. At least someone I know?"

"Yes, someone I met through you."

It could certainly not be Sven who was dead, and Erik and Jens were still in the hospital in Nuuk as far as she knew. Besides, Kristi hated them with a passion. Some of her work colleagues? No, for sure not. They were boring bureaucrats.

"My father?" she blurted out, jokingly. "You wouldn't dare, you slut!"

"No, not my type. Besides, he is an old codger. "

"Was it Karel then, my brother-in-law? You wouldn't dare break up his marriage to Beatha?"

"He is handsome, but no, not family. Yours or mine."

Then she had a thought. "Captain Zaitsov? The handsome Russian submarine commander? He's here? Well, well, well…you really had the hots for him, didn't you?"

"Sure, Hanne. But he's busy trying to help your friend Pavel engineer a coup in Russia. You must know that."

"Yes, of course. Just checking…" Hanne racked her brains. She could neither figure nor remember whom else she might have introduced to Kristi. "Okay, I give up."

"Well, you dolt. How about Anders Jakobsen?"

"No, you dog, you, not my favorite detective! Why you little slut…" and Hanne knelt on all fours, grabbed a pillow and beat Kristi's head with it. "He is one handsome dude. You lucky little cunt."

"Well, we could have a threesome one of these

days…or nights, if you'd like."

"Oh, I'm so happy for you, Kristi," Hanne said, ignoring the comment and hugging her friend again. "I was hoping that something would develop between the two of you. That is just wonderful, dear!"

"Yes. We're quite in love. But I, not as much as with you."

"Have you told him about us? I mean, of course he knows we're friends, but the rest? That we're lovers?"

"No, silly. Of course not. I was waiting for us to do it together."

"Whew! I'm not sure that's such a good idea."

"Well, we're going to have to do it, because I am not giving you up. For any man. They—that is Anders—can have me, but only if I can continue having you."

"How far along are you, relationship wise? Any talk of marriage? Kids?"

"We're serious, that's for sure. He hasn't bought me a ring yet, but he has skirted around the topic. And I have met his parents, and he mine."

"Wow, you guys are moving right along. How are the oldies?"

"Lovely. He comes from a wonderful family."

"So happy for you."

"And, my dear, what about that Canadian Richard dude you have been fucking? Aren't you quite keen on him, you horny bisexual cunt?"

Hanne again whipped a pillow across Kristi's breasts, even as she blushed.

"Yes, my dear. He has declared that he wants to marry me. Several times."

"And have you accepted?"

"No, not yet. I haven't been able to decide…I can't seem to give you up either. Plus, I'm so busy, and our lives are in different places. It would be difficult right now…”

“Baloney, Hanne. If you love him, if you want the man as a partner, if you want to have children with him, you make it work.” Kristi said, putting on a serious face before adding, “But only if it doesn’t impinge on our love.”

“Well, that’s one of the things I haven’t been able to figure out, dear. How to tell him, and more importantly, how we will make it work.”

“I have an idea!” Kristi sat up suddenly. “We double date in our sexiest gear and lay it all out for the guys. We love them, and would be happy to marry them, have kids and all, but only if they let us fulfil our love for each other whenever and however we wish and for as long as we wish. Surely, they will be open-minded enough! They can always join in, we can add. If they truly love and want us—and how could they resist two such gorgeous and sexy ladies—they will say yes. If for no other reason than not to have to give up the tremendous loving they have been enjoying with us…”

“Okay. That might be a way. It really does sound good, Kristi,” Hanne answered, with a little laugh. “Let’s give it a try. Richard wants to come and be with me wherever I am right now, so I can just call him and have him come here. And we can lay it all on them then. How about it?”

“Terrific, Hanne. Do it!”

“Fine. I’ll call when he’s up. It’s just after noon here, so maybe early afternoon—around three—would work.”

“Well then, it’s Sunday. Shall we have lunch at Amalie? Anders is not available, since Sunday is when he visits his parents who live in the country, but you and I can celebrate your return to your hometown, Hanne. A little champagne and a bite or two will work, won’t it?”

“Sure. That sounds lovely. But I will have to make a few phone calls. Including to my parents, whom—you just reminded me—I must go see.”

❦

First, Hanne called her parents, who were delighted that she was in the capital, and would come to see them. They agreed that she would go by the home and have dinner with them the very next day. That would work out well since Kristi had a date with Anders then to go hear an all Sibelius concert at the DR Koncerthuset, with a late dinner after.

With that out of the way, next, she considered calling Pavel, but decided it would be better to text him and let him call back. She wanted him to know that she had just gotten off the destroyer in Copenhagen and that way he would know roughly when to expect Captain Kolnikov and his small force offshore St. Petersburg. She ended the text message with a request for him to call her when possible; clearly, she wanted to know how things were evolving in Russia.

For Ron and Richard, she would wait since it was still a bit early in those capitals, but Malik was probably up— it would be just before 8 am in Nuuk, she decided. Knowing him, he would be up, even though it was a Sunday, so perfect time to call.

“Hello, Malik,” Hanne was glad when after three rings, Rorsen picked up. “Surprise, surprise. I’m in Copenhagen…”

“How did you manage that, Hanne? So good to hear from you. I thought they were taking you to Russia.”

“Well, it turns out that Captain Kolnikov is a supporter of Minister Laptov. And he knew that I had played a role in the Arctic Treaty and surmised that Pavel and I were friends. So, as soon as it seemed that Gusanov was losing control and that there was a chance that the 'good guys' would take over, he felt he no longer had to follow the orders from the rogue president. In fact, it was he who suggested I get out in Copenhagen, which we were passing because Pavel had asked him to come help liberate St. Petersburg. I guess he did not want me to be in the way if there was any fighting…"

"So Laptov is that far along?"

"Yes, it would seem. They have liberated Admiral Maslenkov—actually, according to Captain Kolnikov, many key officers in the Northern Fleet were supporters of the Admiral and Laptov—and when Laptov reappeared on the scene this became evident. So, it seems they have a chunk of the armed forces on their side, and they are now moving on Russia's second city."

"Good for them. I wish them continued good luck. That also explains why the Russian vessels offshore Nuuk are all leaving. In fact, my colleague overseeing the Queen Ingrid Hospital told me late last night that that Captain-Lieutenant Botnikov, the one who disrupted our cabinet meeting, went by with some of his soldiers and demanded the release of Admiral Ogarov and the two Danes. Yes, Hanne, including the governor, that one who accosted you and then you wounded, sending him to the hospital."

"Wow, Larsen, too?" Hanne interrupted, perking up. "Not good. Those two should be in prison."

"They would be if I were in control. Presumably, they were all taken to the boats and are heading back to Russia. It all seems murky though—are they going to join up with Gusanov and his forces, or is this on the orders of the new regime under Admiral Maslenkov?"

"Good questions, Malik. It remains to be seen, I guess. Let me know though if you find out anymore. I really don't want my two countrymen to come anywhere near me."

"Understood, Hanne."

"In any case, Malik, I think I will stay here in Copenhagen for a little while to see how things pan out in Russia. If Pavel manages to oust these rogues, we will want to reinstate the Arctic Treaty as soon as possible. I know he will want to bring Russia back into the fold. And the sooner the better, with the way climate change is ravaging the world. I have started to review the treaty and it may be best to have an updated, stronger version—but I need to think a bit more about it."

"Hanne, take all the time you need. And don't just worry about work—you have been through a lot and need time to look after yourself!"

"Thank you, Malik. I will not be away for long, but I appreciate your understanding."

"And keep us posted if you learn anything. It would be great if Pavel takes the reins, but if he doesn't, we should know as soon as possible so we can prepare for the worst here in Greenland."

"Of course. We are all rooting for Pavel!"

Chapter 42

Seated at Amalie's, Hanne ordered the "Herring from Christians," a special recipe from an island near Bornholm, saying that she had been really missing this Scandinavian favorite fish concoction, while Kristi settled for the hand-shelled shrimp. They sprang for a bottle of Pol Roger Brut Réserve, wanting to celebrate Hanne's escape from Russian captivity and the trauma inflicted on her by her countryman, Erik Larsen, and of course, the glorious reunion of the two lovers. Both dressed in mini-skirts and low-cut tops, they enjoyed being the center of attention in the restaurant.

When the two were on their second flûtes of champagne, a middle-aged woman who had been sitting with her back to them in the far corner of the restaurant got up and approached their table. Hanne did a double take: it was Lise Frondholm, Denmark's Minister of Climate and Energy, who had been her boss when she was still working in Copenhagen. She had a big smile on her face, as Hanne stood up to hug her.

"Well, well, if it isn't the beautiful Hanne Kristensen! My favorite former colleague in the Department. How have you been?"

"Hello, Lise. Lovely to see you."

They mutually introduced their partners, after which Hanne continued, "You must have heard that the Russians tried to invade my new country. But it seems they're leaving now."

"Well, that is good news. Hanne, you must tell me all about it. Maybe over lunch or dinner one day soon. How long are you here?"

"Thank you. I'm not quite sure, but probably at least for a week…oh, and Lise I would very much like to talk to you about the Arctic Treaty."

"Hasn't it become null and void since Russia pulled out of it? They were a key player…"

"It seems now, that if Pavel Laptov can regain control, they will come back into it. And I would like to make some changes to reflect the need for all participants to be much more active on climate change."

"Good idea, Hanne. Let's talk about it over lunch next week. Or, if that doesn't work, come by the office for a coffee. Call my secretary and we'll set something up."

"Terrific. Thanks. Great to see you."

"Equally. Bon appétit."

✃✄✃✄

It was when they were just outside Kristi's building that Hanne's cell rang. Instinctively, she knew who it was. Pavel returning her call. She had to take it.

"Hello, Hanne. Glad I caught you."

"Thanks for coming back to me. How are things going?"

"Well, we are meeting with the leaders of the Western

Military District tomorrow at a secret location. If we can get them on our side without a battle, and if the troops follow their commanders, we will essentially control St. Petersburg and, perhaps more importantly, also Moscow. We will have to see though, how things will pan out, especially in the capital."

"Excellent news, Pavel. Thank you for telling me. Captain Kolnikov and his destroyer should be offshore St. Petersburg probably by tomorrow morning, if not sooner."

"Good. That will help put pressure on the officers in charge of the District. They are all sitting at the headquarters in the General Staff Building, so right in St. Petersburg. Admiral Maslenkov has also ordered most of the other vessels deployed under Gusanov to Greenland to come help in the Baltic or back to home base. So, the Western District commanders will certainly see our resolve. And, I am told that they too, are now quite concerned about climate change. The sea level rise in St. Petersburg has been noticeable, by all reports."

"Must be those melting glaciers in Antarctica…But good luck to you, Pavel. Once you are back in control, we will get all the original signatories of the Arctic Treaty to sign a new and stronger version to help combat climate change. I have some thoughts on this, and when you are ready, I can discuss them with you."

"Thanks, Hanne. I look forward to that day. Meanwhile, stay out of trouble."

"I can hardly wait. Take care."

∽∾∽

Once inside the apartment, Hanne thought that while the conversation with Pavel was still fresh in her mind, she should pass what she had learned on to Ron Hall. When she told Kristi this, her friend, already half naked, said, "Sure, go ahead, my dear. I will change into something more comfortable and wait for you in the bedroom. I need some more lovin' very soon to make up for all those lost weeks, days, hours…"

Where else? Hanne thought, *my friend is an insatiable sex addict,* as she plunked down on the sofa and dialled Ron on her cell. *So much the better*… The American picked up right away, seeing the caller's number.

"Why, Hanne, so good to hear from you again. Where are you?"

"Hello, Ron. In Copenhagen. Captain Kolnikov dropped me off here, not wanting me on board his destroyer in case there would be fighting when they got to St. Petersburg. But I just talked to Pavel, and he thinks that they may be able to convince the leadership of the Western Military District, which is headquartered in St. Petersburg, to join up with them. Then there would be no fighting…no civil war."

"Yes, that would be great…"

"In fact, apparently Admiral Maslenkov has ordered the entire fleet surrounding Greenland to return home—either to help in St. Petersburg or back to Murmansk. Would you, Ron, be able to confirm that they are indeed leaving? Malik Rorsen is keen to know, too. Surely you have surveillance videos or satellite images! I would be really grateful if you would get back to me on this. And, if I may ask, I would love to know especially if the cruiser and the frigates offshore Nuuk are heading this way…toward St. Petersburg."

"Of course, Hanne. I will get the reports from the Joint Chief of Staff. But why particularly the boats off Nuuk?"

"Well," —and Hanne had not dared verbalize this

before— "to tell you the truth, I'm very concerned that those two Danish bastards who were working for the Ruskis may be on one of those vessels. They've both tried to kill me, and I don't want them here in Copenhagen."

"Understood. I will get you whatever info we have. Also, we will train our satellites on the St. Petersburg area, so we should be able to see if any conflict erupts there. Let's hope that Laptov and Maslenkov can convince their fellow officers to support their cause."

"Yes, of course. Pavel believes that most of the officers in the military are sufficiently concerned now about the damage climate change is causing, that they will see that the retrograde policies of Gusanov do not match up against those of a government led by him and his pro-democracy allies. We shall see…"

"That makes sense, Hanne. Take care of yourself. I will be back to you shortly."

"Terrific, Ron. Thank you!"

禄

Hanne's next call had to be to Richard. She had put it off long enough, but now it was time. She knew that as soon as she told him everything, he would want to jump on a plane and come to Copenhagen. Was she ready for that? She wasn't sure, but certainly to be loved with such intensity by a handsome, smart and talented man was intoxicating.

So, without dithering further, she scrolled down to Richard's number and pressed the dial icon.

"Richard, hi," Hanne opened the conversation.

"Hanne, my dear, I've been anxiously waiting for your call. Where are you?"

"Copenhagen. The captain of the Russian destroyer dropped me off here on the way to St. Petersburg, where the next key confrontation between the Russians could take place."

"And how are you? Have you recovered from your ordeal?"

"I'm doing okay. Glad to be away from the tense situation in Greenland. Although now it seems to be more or less finished…the Russian invading forces are withdrawing."

"That's good news. I'll make arrangements to come to Copenhagen as soon as possible. Unless of course, you're coming back this way…"

"I'll probably be here at least a week. Perhaps longer. If Laptov comes out on top in Russia, we will want to reinstate the Arctic Treaty as soon as possible. Likely a stronger version, seeing what is happening with climate change. Can you help with that?"

"Of course. Let me know how. I will come as soon as I can, dear, and we can work on it together."

"Thanks, my love. See you soon."

"I can't wait. Take care of yourself. I want to marry you as soon as I can. And start having children with you."

There it was again, the proposal. Well, maybe very soon, it will be in person. Hmm, a diamond ring would not be bad! She would enjoy a wedding, but how practical would marriage between a woman working in Nuuk and a man in Ottawa be?

One last thing before she would join Kristi in the bedroom: a call to her former boss's secretary about lunch or coffee—she may as well meet her sooner than later. And it was good that she jumped on it, because in fact, Lise Frondholm had some time free the very next day, and then not again for a while. *May as well let the Danish government buy me lunch tomorrow*, Hanne thought to herself as she hung up.

And then she was done for the day, ready to join her lover for a late afternoon tryst, then a shower and dinner ordered in, with lots of catching up—physically, emotionally—and talk about the past, present, and future.

Chapter 43

Copenhagen, Monday, October 6, 202-

Monday was a workday for Kristi, and Hanne was glad to have time to herself so she could do a little work on the treaty in the morning before meeting with her former boss, and then head off to see her parents. Kristi had a concert/dinner date with Anders, so they would not see each other until much later that night. If at all. After a quick peck from her lover, all dressed to go to the doctor's office where she worked as a nurse, Hanne stretched and luxuriated in bed for a little while longer. After all, she had been through so much and needed to catch up on her rest.

She took pleasure in the fifteen minutes or so of just lying there and contemplating her life rather unproductively, but then decided to get up and start the day. Following her ablutions and a soothing, warm shower, she put on one of Kristi's bathrobes and fixed herself a light breakfast of muesli and berries, accompanied by a cappuccino. She settled on the sofa with her laptop and turned the TV on low, in case anything of importance was in the news, as she tackled the signed version of the Arctic Treaty. Yes, it could use some strengthening, especially regarding the need to share information on environmental matters and to cooperate maximally on combatting the causes and effects of climate change. She drafted some language but knew that it would have to be put into the appropriate legalese and would no doubt be rewritten many times to please all the participating parties. But at least some of the key ideas were jotted down in a document and she would start refining them by trying them on her former colleague and friend over lunch.

In the background, the announcer trumpeted the withdrawal of the Russian forces from Greenland and switched to a special report on why this was happening. The in-depth piece correctly identified the new virus and Greenland's clever move to obtain vaccines quickly for its population while letting it rage among the invaders as possibly one of the key factors. But it failed to point out the growing dissatisfaction in Russia with the current regime's lack of focus on climate change as a significant threat to humanity, in contrast to the demonstrated actions and policies pursued by the previous government under Laptov. Strange, too, Hanne thought, that the focus in the report was on the virus—the emergence of which was to a large degree a consequence of climate change—rather than on the existence threatening cause itself.

Just as she was clearing off the dishes, a call came through on her cell. It was a little after 8:30 am. Lise Frondholm's secretary. "Ms. Kristensen? Hello. The prime minister has asked for Lise's presence at a working lunch today. Could you come by say at ten-thirty rather? She could give you half an hour over coffee."

"Yes, of course. I'll be there. Thank you."

Hanne hurried to get dressed and replanned her day. After the meeting, she would do a little shopping—it would be nice to take her parents something. Chocolates at the least, a bottle of wine maybe. Then she thought she might look at augmenting her wardrobe since she was sure Richard would come soon and she only had the clothes she had arrived in and the few items she had left at Kristi's. She also gave some thought to what she would say to her former boss, the minister of Climate and Energy for Denmark.

ℯᔆℯᔆ

"Hello, Hanne. Thanks for agreeing to come in earlier," the Danish minister started the meeting "We'll do a leisurely lunch the next time. Oh, and by the way, congratulations on your powerful statement to the United Nations General Assembly. That certainly put all those mighty nations interested in Greenland's resources on the back burner!"

"Thank you, Lise. On that topic, I was thinking, as I was walking over, that perhaps the now independent Greenland should work with Denmark and other countries—maybe Canada, Finland, Norway and those that would be more interested in helping us preserve our environment and way of life—when it comes to the extraction of our resources. Clearly, the deal with China will not work—they were going to give us a lot of money in return for having license to plunder our riches."

"I guess that is their standard procedure…"

"Not on. I guess we were a bit naïve. Lise, I know there are a lot of hard feelings here in Denmark about Greenland's earlier unilateral declaration, but I'm sure we can find a way to work together that will benefit both our countries. After all, we have known each other intimately for several hundred years."

"Hmm. Perhaps. An interesting idea, Hanne."

"Let me think about it a bit more, and flesh it out. I will also try it on Malik Rorsen, the prime minister. He and I have become good friends. And maybe a few other people, too."

"Good, Hanne. I will chew on it as well, and let's see where we get to."

"Now, Lise, on the Arctic Treaty—if Laptov manages to come out on top, he will want to bring Russia back into it. I have spoken to him, and he likes my idea of strengthening the climate change provisions, given what all our countries are now going through. We will have to get everyone to sign on to an amended treaty."

"I am totally in agreement with that. Do you have new wording to propose? Or is it too early?"

"I have put some ideas into a draft—it's very preliminary though. But I can send it to you, not as a formal proposal, but just so you see where I am going with this."

"Terrific, Hanne. I will look at it and come back with some thoughts."

"Thanks, Lise."

"Hanne, may I ask a personal question?"

"Sure…of course, Lise."

"How are you? I hear that you have been through a lot since the Russians moved in on your country…" The Danish minister seemed genuinely concerned.

"Well, I must admit, Lise, it hasn't been easy. But I'm fine. Thank you for asking."

"Good. As a friend, let me know if there's anything I can do to help."

"Thanks, Lise." And with that, Hanne knew that her time was up, so she took leave of her friend and former colleague.

❧❦❧

As she left the building where she had spent several years working, she thought of how little they had understood about climate change and its ravages even just a few years ago. Since then, the Department had become much more focused on what the government could do about the causes and effects of this existential disaster, and rightly so. She was bemused by the thought that, in those early days, Jens, Erik, Sven and their Green Liberation Front were the ones crusading for the environment, while she, and the Department were focused more on the energy and mineral resources that could be extracted from the earth, albeit paying at least lip service to sustainability. How things have changed!

She loved to walk, so she made her way to the Strøget, the main shopping street in the capital, and lost herself in the abundance of supply and choice after the more austere availability of goods in Nuuk. It did not take her long to fixate on an expensive box of Belgian chocolates for her mother and a bottle of Chateau Lagrange 2015, Bordeaux St. Julien she knew her father adored. As for herself, she picked out several comely ensembles and some casual attire, but also made her way out to the Victoria's Secret shop in Ørestad to make sure she would have something attractive for Richard. And, also, of course, for Kristi. She knew she loved that kind of thing.

Satisfied with her purchases, Hanne made her way back to her friend's place to drop the packages and then set out for the Sølund Nursing Home, the wonderful new retirement home her parents had recently moved to, armed with the chocolates and the bottle of wine.

Her parents were delighted to see her: they had not been happy to see her go off to Greenland, nor that she broke up with Jens right around the same time.

"Are you back for good now, dear?" her mother asked.

"No, Mama, I am still the minister of Environment and Natural Resources for Greenland. And I'm loving the job. I will have to go back soon. Maybe ten days or so."

"Didn't the Russians invade soon after you all declared independence from Denmark? What a mistake that was…" This from her father, an ardent Danish nationalist.

"No, Papa, it was not a mistake. It was an important move for Greenland, and yes, the Russians did come for a few days, but they have now gone." She wanted to change the subject, so she said: "And, I'm sure you will be pleased that I have a man again."

"You're back with Jens!" her mother blurted out. She had rather liked her weak and despicable former boyfriend. "That is great news, Hanne, dear."

"No, Mama. I met a wonderful Canadian diplomat. We are very much in love. He has asked me to marry him."

"A Canadian?" his father asked. "What's wrong with Danish men?"

"Nothing, Papa. Only that I love this Canadian."

"Well, you better not move there," the old curmudgeon said.

"We'll see, Papa, where we end up." Hanne was getting more and more exasperated, as she always did, the more she talked to her parents.

"At least you will get married finally and start to have children. The sooner the better at your age," her mother kept up the pressure. "When can we meet this…Canadian?"

"Well, he's coming here in a few days, so hopefully he

will have time for us to come by. I would like to introduce him," Hanne answered, even though she was not sure that this was a good idea. Alas, but ultimately a necessary one.

"Mmm. This crispy pork is delicious," Hanne went to change the subject again.

The rest of the meal, they spent talking about family, the nursing home and other matters, and Hanne was glad when she saw that her mother and father were getting tired, and perhaps fed up too: it was time for her to leave. Another exasperating visit with her parents, but a necessary one.

Chapter 44

Copenhagen, Monday, late evening, October 6, 202-

Hanne was glad to get back to Kristi's after the rather full and exhausting day. It was past nine, and with a concert and dinner on the agenda, Kristi was certainly not going to be back until closer to midnight, although it was a work night for her. Hanne thought she should move her stuff into the spare room and eventually bed down there in case Anders came up with Kristi, just to give her the options. As she made the move, a message came through on her phone: it was Richard, giving his ETA as 7:10 am on Wednesday. Excellent—she was indeed dying to see him. She was sure Kristi would not mind him staying in the apartment but thought she better check before telling him where to come, once he arrives.

Pleased that Richard would soon be with her, Hanne took time to luxuriate in a hot shower to soothe her aching body: she had walked an awful lot, but at least she had managed to get some exercise. Coming out of the shower, she towelled herself down, creamed her body, especially her tired legs, then put on the bathrobe and made herself comfortable in front of the TV in the living room. She wanted some entertainment, so she turned it on to stream Episode 1 of Season 4 of *Borgen,* a series of which she had avidly watched the first three seasons when still living in Denmark. The first episode was so engrossing, that she kept going with Episode 2 right after. Finally, when this too, finished, she was tired enough so she decided that it would be best to go to bed without waiting up for Kristi. Who knows, her friend may have ended up at Anders' place.

Hanne finished her evening ablutions, plugged her phone in by the queen size bed Kristi had in the spare room, turned off the light and stretched out naked between the soft cotton sheets, thinking that her life had, all in all, turned out pretty well so far. She certainly could not complain.

Soon after, she must have dozed off, for the next thing she woke to, were some voices—at first, she thought she was dreaming, but as she came to, she thought she recognized them. No not Kristi, the other one maybe Anders—but, in fact, both male. And yes, as her heart skipped a beat in fear, the voices were those of…Jens and Erik, definitely, though his somewhat distorted because of the no doubt still raw facial wounds she had inflicted on that bastard. They were the last people in the world she wanted to see. Quickly, she grabbed her phone off the night table and messaged Kristi: *Help! Erik/Jens creeps are here in yr. apt. H.*

Frantically, she looked around: the closet, yes, maybe she could hide in the closet. She jumped out of bed with her phone and plunged into the tight space, closing the door behind her, hoping against all hope that the intruders would not find her.

"Maybe in this room," Hanne heard Erik say, as he kicked open the bedroom door. "Well, the bed certainly sems to have been used here, too. Yes, hmm…it is even warm. And there is an aroma here…The smell of…pussy. There must have been a woman in between the sheets until very recently. I'm getting warmer…" And Hanne heard the Danish monster's steps as he approached the closet door, then flung it wide open, and reaching in, grabbed her by the arm and pulled her naked body into the room, at the same time exclaiming, "Well, well, well. What do we have here, if not my favorite Danish whore, the one pretending to be some minister in Greenland's illegitimate government. The very one needing *mucho* payback. And ready for it, I see." A chuckle before he continued, "Fancy meeting you here, Hanne. But of course, this is the apartment of your cunt-licking lesbian friend, isn't it?" And when she didn't answer, he continued, "And pray tell, where the fuck is she now? Somewhere close?"

Again, Hanne didn't answer, so the brute resumed his monologue, as he shoved her over onto the bed, "So Hanne, since we have a little time, perhaps we should continue where we left off the last time before you hurt me so badly. And then, if you are a good girl, maybe your old boyfriend, Jens, will deign to fuck you before we mess with your face and body. Like you did with mine." He must have seen the fear on Hanne's face because he backed off a bit: "But there is a lot we need to do before we take that step…"

Hanne cringed at the top of the bed and looked around hoping to find something she could use as a weapon, just as Erik started to unbutton his pants. Stepping out of them, yelling. "Come, Jens, you better hold down this babe just in case, while I fuck the shit out of her, then I'll do the same for you. The bitch can get violent and she's surprisingly strong." Hanne struggled as Jens went to grab her arms, and Erik, by now completely naked, member erect, pulled her down on the bed forcing her legs apart.

Just as the brute was about to enter her, Hanne thought she heard a door open and Kristi's ebullient voice yell, "Hanne! We're home, where are you?"

"Holy fuck!" This from Erik. "The other twat is here. Go get her, Jens." And as he turned around and released his grip on her leg, Hanne managed to land a hard kick on Larsen's already lacerated head. The wounded man let out an unearthly scream and fell down on the bed on his side, both hands moving up toward what was left of his face. When Jens hesitated to go get Kristi, Hanne rolled off the queen, and ran out of the room, pulling the door shut behind her. She was glad when Anders rushed over and helped her with the handle, although knowing the door opened inward, she was not sure how long they would be able to keep the two vile Danes inside. Kristi, too, came over, having fetched her cell form her room where she had left it before going out, even as she was calling 112 to get the police to come as fast as possible. While Anders held the knob, the two ladies pushed a large armoire in front of the door. "Phew, that should help," Anders said, "but I hope the cops get here fast. Very fast."

"Hanne, you poor thing! These bastards have mistreated you again." Kristi hugged her still naked friend. "But come, put my bathrobe on at least," she added, as she saw Anders look Hanne up and down. "Are you okay?"

"Yeah. Thanks. You got here just in time. The asshole Erik was trying to rape me again, with the help of his stupid friend. But fortunately, I'm…I guess intact."

"We'll get the two assholes put away forever!" Kristi was outraged.

Hanne heard the bedroom door beginning to open, and then the banging on the rear of the armoire. "What the fuck, Erik! They have barricaded us in with some huge piece of furniture."

"Well, let's push the thing over." Erik retorted, and Hanne could hear the two monsters grunt and groan as they put their shoulders to the armoire. Anders, Kristi and she picked up chairs holding them in front of them, legs pointing outward, and stood by the front door to prevent their escape. Several tries and the two traitors managed to topple the dresser with a loud crash. But as they clumsily clambered over it, Hanne heard the sirens approaching, and then, when the two rushed at them, the footsteps of the policemen as they ran up the stairs. They held them off long enough for the officials to burst through the door, each holding a H&K 9 mm pistol. Seeing what was going on, the police contingent moved toward Erik and Jens, and when Anders—whom the officer in charge recognized— said, "Arrest them, Sergeant. They are traitors, rapists, evil criminals," the four agents moved in to handcuff the two intruders. As he was led away, Erik looked at Hanne with his one good eye full of hate and said, "Don't worry, bitch. We will come and get you wherever you try to hide." And it was only when the two sell-outs were outside the apartment, that Hanne, snuggling on Kristi's shoulder, broke down and cried.

Anders gently ushered the two women over to the sofa, and helped them sit down, saying, "Kristi, take care of Hanne. It might be best if I left the two of you alone—you both need rest, so will go home now and see you both tomorrow. We will need to go to the police station to press charges—I am going to talk to my friend, Sergeant Gundersen, and suggest a time. Say 11 am—I'll see if that works for them, and I will let you know."

"Yes, I will come too. I'm sure the clinic will understand."

"Good, then, I'm off. I love you." Anders gave Kristi a

kiss and then turned to Hanne. "Bye, Hanne. I hope you can get some sleep."

Chapter 45

Kristi cuddled Hanne all night, and for once, they did not engage in sex. Hanne was just happy to be held by her friend, tenderness and skin-to-skin contact being what she needed after the second violent assault by Erik.

The morning came, and waking, Hanne looked over at the gorgeous body beside her and said, "Thank you, Kristi. You are the best…friend and lover anybody could have. We will have tonight to fulfil our desires."

Kristi moved closer, giving her a kiss. "Good. And I love you too." And then stretching, she glanced at the alarm clock before saying, "Hanne. Will you be all right here by yourself until we meet up at the police station? I probably should go to work, but will join you there."

"Sure, Kristi," Hanne returned the kiss, before continuing, "I need to make a phone call or two anyway."

"Excellent. Just take your time, have a nice breakfast and we'll meet up later. Not sure if I can do lunch, but we can see. Perhaps Anders will join us too." Hanne watched, as Kristi's sleek body unwrapped itself from the sheets and made its way to the bathroom. She herself decided to close her eyes for a few more minutes and think through what she needed to do this day before Richard arrived.

ᔛ

She caught up on her emails while she was having her breakfast of muesli with a cut up banana and cappuccino, and after clearing the dishes away and making herself a macchiato for an added hit, she settled in the living room, TV on low, to make her calls.

First, Pavel.

"Hanne, I'm glad it's you," the Russian said. "You help take my mind away from all the military and political games I have to play these days."

"Thanks, Pavel," Hanne didn't know exactly how to respond. "You're such an inspiration, and what you are doing is so…so very important for the future. Of Russia, of course, but also the Arctic…indeed the whole world. A democratic, friendly Russia can make such a difference…as opposed to the inimical and destructive dictatorship of this vile Gusanov regime."

"Well, Hanne, we are making some progress. But it is slow going. The leadership of the Western Military District is now on-side with our goals. The timely appearance of Kolnikov's destroyer and the other vessels from Greenland no doubt helped, although the high-ranking officers in St. Petersburg were already fed up and now are keen to join us to depose Gusanov and his gang. They are just taking the measure of the troops and hopefully, we will be in a position to move on Moscow."

"Excellent…"

"The aim is to muster a force large enough so that anyone thinking of opposing us will think twice. And if the gang in the Kremlin doesn't give in, we will have the forces there ready to attack, and hopefully, any conflict can be limited in scope."

"That sounds good, Pavel. Outright civil war would not be good."

"Yes, to avoid at all costs."

"Keep me posted, please, Pavel, would you?"

"Of course, Hanne. You are my voice to the rest of the world…"

"We're all rooting for you."

"Thank you."

☙☙☙

Next, it was a good time to call her boss.

"Hello, Malik."

"Good you called, Hanne. I have some news to report. It now seems that the Russian military operations here have ceased. The vessels and the troops have all left Greenland's territory and waters. Including up at Citronen, I am told. Thank God, for that. And thanks to you and your friend, Pavel Laptov. And Ron Hall, of course, with the vaccines."

"I'm happy things seem to be returning to normal, Malik. Pavel seems to be making headway in Russia as well. The important Western Military District has now joined up with them and they are moving on Moscow."

"Well, that's good, but things are unfortunately not quite all normal. Remember that Professor Li? He flew in unannounced yesterday and insisted on meeting. The Chinese want to have another discussion on 'how we can cooperate.' I told him that any in-depth discussion will have to await your return."

"Interesting. But Malik, I've been thinking—why don't we link up rather with some of the more environmentally focused countries like Canada, Norway, Finland, Sweden and yes, even Denmark, to develop a plan to extract our resources sustainably and in an environmentally friendly way? We could all benefit from this. This could even be an Appendix of the Arctic Treaty if we can get all the countries to agree—although I think Russia and China, maybe the USA, would be tough nuts to crack. So perhaps we start with something separate and bring others in later."

"Hmm, Hanne. Certainly, worth thinking about. No doubt the devil will be in the details, so we will need to flesh the proposal out more."

"Yes, I know. But let's think about it. Maybe also see what the cabinet says?"

"Good, Hanne. But I also want to hear how you are. I know you have been through a lot lately and I worry about you."

"Thanks, I'm fine. That bastard, Erik Larsen came at me again, but now the police have him in custody. Along with the other Dane, Jens Andersen. Too bad they managed to escape the last time. I'm going to the police station later today to press charges and insist that they be held in a high security prison."

"Well, let me know if there is anything I can do to help."

"I will be meeting with my Canadian friend Richard Simpson tomorrow. We will work on the treaty and the…proposal. Also, I will talk further with some of my Danish contacts here. Once we have something a bit more concrete, I'll come back to you and then we can get others on board."

"Very good, Hanne. But take care of yourself. These are still difficult times."

"Thanks, Malik."

∽∾∽

Hanne spent some time noodling some thoughts about how bringing in some of the other more environmentally friendly nations to help Greenland develop its resources might work. The goal would be to replace the five hundred million euros that Denmark used to contribute each year to Greenland's budget—the twenty-five billion dollars from China would have done that in spades, and then some—to help develop resources that would ultimately provide revenues to make Greenland a self-sufficient state. Perhaps some kind of a multilateral fund, with contributing countries getting some of the benefits along the way from the resource extraction. And her department ensuring that it is all done sustainably and in an environmentally friendly manner. She would discuss this further with Richard, maybe Lise—and there is also that Norwegian Government Pension Fund, the largest international investor in the world, that she should approach at an early date. They are an environmentally focused investor.

Lots to think about, lots to do.

But it was time to get dressed to meet Kristi and Anders at the police station to put Erik and Jens away, hopefully forever. She put on jeans and a tight red turtleneck, boots, a jacket on top—after all it was October and around ten degrees Centigrade according to her phone. She wanted to walk to get some exercise and air and to be able to think.

It took her slightly longer than she had calculated, so Kristi and Anders were already at the station talking to the sergeant from the night before when she was led in. After the customary hugs for the friends, Gundersen—that was his name, she remembered—led them into a small office, where they all sat down around a table, he behind a laptop.

"So, I take it, the two men we took into custody last night brutally attacked you, Ms. Kristensen?"

"Yes, and this wasn't the first time."

"But you are all right?"

Yes, other than the trauma of an attempted rape…"

"In fact, Henrik, you will see in the records that these two men were arrested several months ago in Greenland for bombing a mine, and then for an attempt on Hanne's…Ms. Kristensen's life," Anders took over. "And then they managed to escape, turned up in Belarus, and joined the Gusanov gang in its efforts to destabilize the west. Erik Larsen was appointed provisional governor of Greenland by the rogue Russian president, having turned traitor and sold out everything we stand for. He also had tried to rape M. Kristensen earlier, but Ms. Kristensen was able to escape his clutches and in fact, seriously wound him, hence the ugly facial disfiguration. As I said last night, he is a murdering rapist and a traitor, and Jens Andersen is his accomplice. The two deserve to be put away for life."

"Well, well, well. Those are very serious charges," Gundersen replied, typing something on his laptop. "We will hold them in custody and seek to arrange an early trial date. Ms. Kristensen, you will be prepared to testify?"

"Of course."

"So, will I," Kristi said, to everyone's surprise. "Larsen and I went out a few times, and in the end, he was an abusive sexual molester." Hanne knew about the relationship that ended up very badly, but it was certainly new to Anders and Gundersen.

"Also," Hanne added, "I can get some depositions from friends in Greenland who were witness to some of their actions or their consequences." She was primarily thinking of Malik and Aniuk.

"Good. That may help at the next stage after we have the initial court session. We'll let you know when we have a date. And thank you, it is important to put these evil social pariahs away for as long as possible."

☙❧☙

Outside the police headquarters, Anders asked, "Lunch anyone? I'm starving and would be happy to invite you both for a bite. Especially since I won't be able to join you later today since we have an office strategy session and dinner."

Kristi jumped in: "Too bad. I was hoping to, but we are short-staffed, and it was already a stretch for me to come for this long. I had better get back."

"Hanne?" Anders looked at her questioningly.

"Yes, why don't you, Hanne? It could be fun for Anders and you, my two soulmates, to talk about beautiful me," Kristi said with a little laugh.

"Sure, why not. And we promise we will only talk about you—no, not the weather, the state of the world, politics, or any of those boring topics—only little old you." Hanne teased, giving her friend a hug, as did Anders.

"Anders, remember, I am staying with you for the next few days starting tomorrow, while Richard is here," Kristi said, as she stepped away. "But maybe we can all have dinner together tomorrow to celebrate."

"To celebrate what?" the detective asked, but Kristi just laughed mysteriously and continued on her way.

"We'll no doubt find out. Kristi often has these little surprises." Hanne had a suspicion, but she wasn't going to tell.

⁕

Since it was a sunny October day, they walked down to the Kayak Bar on the waterfront, one of Hanne's favorite places to hang out, and after ordering mussels with fries and a beer each, they settled in to watch the boats pass by.

"So, Hanne, Kristi tells me that you and Richard are planning to get married," Anders launched into the elephant-in-the-room subject. "Is that what was behind Kristi's suggestion that we celebrate tomorrow evening?" Anders, being a detective, did not take long to ferret things out.

"It seems that we're moving toward it, Anders," Hanne answered with a little laugh. "Although Richard has only asked me over the phone, and I have not formally accepted yet."

"So, it may all come together in the next few days. That is very exciting, Hanne!"

"Well, marriage could be rather complicated for us at this point, given our lives." Hanne avoided a straight answer.

"But wonderful…and I am sure you can make anything work as long as you love each other."

"Yes, of course. And we may just do it. But what about you and Kristi, Anders?"

Hanne saw Anders blush as he hesitated before answering. "We are very much in love—I am sure you can see that when we are together. But it has been a whirlwind affair so far, and I haven't yet dared asked her…"

"I know men are generally slow to move forward to tie the knot, but I'm quite sure you'd be pleasantly surprised at the answer. Since you are both here in Copenhagen, it wouldn't have the complications that a step in that direction by Richard and me would. All the more reason…" Hanne suddenly thought that maybe she had better step back…let Kristi and Anders move at their own pace.

"And thank you, Hanne, for introducing us in the first place. Kristi has been the best thing in my life so far."

"May it continue that way. She is also one of the two best things in my life." Hmm, Hanne was pleased—perhaps it was not a bad idea, by alluding to Kristi alongside Richard, for her to set the stage for the discussion Kristi had suggested they might have with the two men in the following days.

The rest of the lunch was spent in getting to know each other and Hanne's view of this smart, handsome detective grew immeasurably, as did, no doubt, his of her. It was past two pm when Anders, looking at his phone, finally said, "Gee, I had better get back to work. Time just passes so quickly when you're having fun," as he signaled to the waitress to bring the bill. After settling, they stood up, gave each other the customary Danish goodbye hug, and saying how much they looked forward to the dinner the next day, went their own way—he, back to the office, and she, to meander back to Kristi's to make some calls, work on the treaty and the proposal and prepare dinner for when Kristi came home.

Chapter 46

Copenhagen, Tuesday afternoon and evening,
October 7, 202-

After the long walk back to Kristi's, during which she made a detour to Hav Torvehallerne, the famed seafood shop, to pick up some special Norwegian lobster tail to make a celebratory dinner for just the two of them, Hanne enjoyed a long shower, washing her hair in the process. Refreshed and dressed in the usual comfy bathrobe, she settled in one corner of the sofa in the living room, legs drawn under her, to make a few calls and do a little work.

For a start, good time to phone Ron Hall. She hadn't talked to him since Sunday, and then only briefly.

"Ron, glad I caught you."

"Hanne, as always, I'm pleased to hear from you."

"Lots to report. First, Laptov seems to be making progress in Russia. He has the Western Military District—you know, the one that includes Moscow and St. Petersburg—on board. And they're amassing a huge force on the periphery of Moscow and demanding the surrender of the rogue regime in the Kremlin…"

"Yes, we've noted the troop movements. And that the

Greenland naval force arrived offshore St. Petersburg. Wow, that is fast action on Pavel's part…"

"Well, it seems, Ron, that many even in the Russian military are now aware of how important action on the climate is—and Gusanov was just not cutting it. By contrast, Pavel's policies are very environment focused. Maslenkov commands a lot of respect, too, among the military."

"Excellent. Of course, we will continue to follow what is happening in Russia and do let us know if you learn anything."

"Ron, you probably won't know but the two rogue Danes who were meddling in the situation in Greenland— one of whom made a violent, personal attack on me—have now been arrested here in Copenhagen and will be put away."

"Yes, they were those abhorrent, sell-out lackeys of the Gusanov regime, weren't they? Well, I'm really glad we're done with them. Thanks."

"Also, Ron, I've been thinking about getting an updated Arctic Treaty signed, if and when Laptov is back in the driver's seat in Russia. Several of the provisions dealing with climate change and environmental issues need to be strengthened. I'm working on this and will be trying a draft on my friends in the Canadian and Danish governments in the next few days. Then with Laptov. I would also like to send you a copy for your comments."

"Sure, Hanne, I look forward to it."

"Lastly, since Greenland's situation with respect to China has changed after our speeches at the United Nations and rejection of their offer to take over resource extraction in our country for a cool twenty-five billion, Greenland needs to make alternative plans. Although I just learned from Malik that the Chinese now have come back with another delegation to Nuuk again wanting to negotiate further on their plans."

"Yeah, I'm not surprised…"

"My thought, Ron, is that Greenland should rather team up with a group of the more environmentally friendly nations in the Arctic Council—such as Canada, Norway, Finland, the United Kingdom, and perhaps, dare I say it, even you—to create some kind of fund to help with the mining of some of the valuable minerals in and offshore our country. I don't want to touch any oil and gas leases, since fossil fuels are a no-no. But the rare earths for sure, copper and zinc and maybe uranium, in return, of course, for a share in the benefits. I'm sure the rare earth deposits we have would be of immense interest to the US among others."

"What a great idea, Hanne. Why don't you flesh it out, and we can have a chat about it. I'd be happy to take the concept to the appropriate people in our government. And maybe also to key companies that might be interested."

"Yes, I thought that perhaps some kind of public/private fund might be the best way to go."

"Well, you're certainly a busy lady, Hanne. Keep up the good work. But above all keep out of trouble. There are many evil forces out there that do not like what we're doing."

"Fortunately, I have some good friends. We'll talk soon, Ron."

⌘

Hanne spent the rest of the afternoon working on the treaty provisions, and then fleshed out some thoughts on the proposal to replace the Chinese funding. She was quite happy with the amendments to the treaty she had drafted, but the funding document still needed more thought and work. Input from Richard over the next couple of days should help get both to a ready enough stage to show to Lise Frondholm, then to Malik and Pavel, and maybe Ron. Eventually the Norwegians, and once close to final, they could invite the Brits, the Swedes, the Finns and the Germans and French into it. Others might line up as well, if the existence of the funding proposal became more widely known. But those aggressive Russians and the greedy Chinese would definitely be kept out.

Happy with the work she had done, Hanne turned her attention to making dinner. Since it was their last night alone without male companionship for they did not know how long, she wanted to prepare something special for her best friend and long-time lover. The menu Hanne had thought up started with *Leverpostej*, Danish liver pâté, with fresh warm French baguette and a flûte or two of a vintage 2022 Veuve Clicquot Brut Rosé. Next would come the main course of two broiled Norwegian lobster tail each, prepared with garlic, paprika and lemon juice and served with baked potato and a green salad, the rest of the baguette with lots of butter—so something simple, but delicious. For dessert, she was going to bake a *Lagklage*, or Danish layer cake, which Kristi had said her grandmother had made on special occasions. It was her favorite. Very rich and sweet, but so be it. (*We'll certainly work it all off in bed later*, Hanne thought to herself with a smile.) Accompanied by a bottle (she had another one in reserve) of delicious Meursault Premier Cru "Charmes" 2019, followed by an Oremus Tokaji Aszu 5 Puttonyos 2010 with the dessert (or the champagne, if any was left).

With everything ready, table set and she all showered, creamed and ready for a night with her lover, Hanne had just put on her sexy, plunging, easy-to-take-off, blue drape dress she knew Kristi loved, when she heard her friend turn the key in the front-door of the apartment.

"Whew, what a day!" Kristi shouted from the corridor. "I'm going to shower and…wow, don't you look beautiful, you sexy thing!" Kristi entered the bedroom with lust in her eyes, scarcely able to keep her hands off. "…put something more comfy and appropriate on."

"Wonderful," Hanne said as she finished combing her hair. "Then we can start the evening off with some champagne and pâté, followed by…"

"Gorgeous love making…" Kristi interrupted, stepping out of her shoes. "I want an orgasm."

"Before we go on to the lobster tail with Meursault…"

"More loving and at least two orgasms each…" She wriggled out of her skirt as she said this.

"And the *pièce de resistance,* the surprise dessert of the evening…"

"Licking your breasts, your pubis, your clit until you dissolve in orgasmic delight…" Kristi threw her top on the bed, then her bra, and wrapped her arms around Hanne's neck.

"Now, now, Kristi," Hanne, gently freed herself. "Do hurry up and take your shower, so we can do this properly."

"Well, okay then, Madame Minister. You are the boss. And I'm hungry as hell. Not just for the lobster tail, but also the Hanne tail."

The rest was drowned out by the sound of the cascading water in the shower and Kristi's humming of *We all live in a yellow submarine.*

❧❧

Hanne had the Veuve Clicquot in the ice bucket, two chilled flûtes on the silver tray with the plate of pâte and the basket with the warm sliced French baguette wrapped in a napkin, waiting on the coffee table as Kristi came out in her sexy red miniskirt and see-through low-cut white tank top showing off her tanned legs, neck, shoulder, arms, with much of her chest revealed as well.

"We are beautiful, aren't we?" Hanne took her hand, drew her into her body and they kissed passionately. "Okay, love, time for a little refreshment." She took the bottle out of the bucket and popped the cork—which Kristi's eyes followed, as she said with a little laugh, "That will be you having an orgasm in a few minutes,"—then pouring the pink bubbly into the two glasses. "*Santé*," she said, as she handed one to her lover, picking up the other one, clinking glasses. They each took a swig, then put the flûtes down, as, still standing, Kristi moved in, and embracing her friend, this time gave her a champagne suffused kiss.

They continued necking as they sat down on the sofa, occasionally surfacing for a nibble of the pâté on a slice of bread, or a sip of the champagne, peppered with a few breathless words, but by the time it was time to move on to the main course they were both naked and sated with an orgasm each, there on the sofa.

It was time to regroup.

The two lovers went to find their bathrobes, and Kristi, first out, lit the candles, as Hanne fetched the lobster and baked potatoes from the oven. They lingered over dinner, with lots of reminiscing, laughter, and delight in the food and the loving times they had had, and at least one more session in the bedroom. So it was close to midnight when they repaired back to the living room and Hanne brought the *Lagklage* and the Tokaji to the coffee table. Kristi clapped her hands in delight like a little child, and said, "Oh Hanne, you're amazing! You fulfill all my desires, all my wishes. You can read my very soul, my love."

"And you mine, Kristi dear. How will I be able to live without you?"

"And how will I, without you?" Kristi embraced Hanne as she said this. "Well, we won't have to. Because, as we discussed the other day, we will tell our future husbands—that is, if Anders ever asks me to marry him—that we will only do so if they let us continue to have our little romantic interludes for as long as, and whenever we want. We'll lay down the law maybe, already tomorrow, over dinner."

"It is a novel idea, but why not?" Hanne said. "In some ways, it's sort of bisexual bigamy for both of us, when I think about it. Although we are not formalizing our relationship, so that makes it okay. But still pretty racy, *n'est-ce pas?*"

"Well, we have always been ahead of the times..." Kristi added with a chuckle.

"Oh. Kristi, my love, I think I may have planted the idea with Anders that he had better hurry up and pop the question, so watch out, dear."

"Thanks. We'll see what happens."

"Well, it has been quite a day, and it's past time to turn in. Richard is arriving tomorrow early, and I need my beauty sleep."

"And I have to work tomorrow. Bright and early."

They lay down naked together in Kristi's king-size bed, but after a hug and a kiss, they were both fast asleep. It had been an action-packed day.

Chapter 47

Copenhagen, Wednesday, October 8, 202-

Hanne woke to the ding on her phone indicating that a message had come. She came to slowly, knowing it would be Richard and read it just as it dinged a second time. "Just landed. On time. Should be there in an hour or so." Maybe an hour and a half, Hanne thought to herself. We had better get going.

"Kristi, let's get moving. Richard just landed. He'll be here in a little over an hour."

Kristi looked at the alarm clock. "Oh no, it's past seven. I have to be at the clinic ready to go at eight. But can we have a quickie?"

"Kristi…how about just a nice hug."

A passionate embrace later, they were both in the shower together washing each other's bodies erotically, and despite Hanne's misgivings that they were cutting it close, it did not take long for them both to reach orgasm. Fulfilled, they hurried—Kristi put on her work clothes, Hanne just her bathrobe—and went into the kitchen to prepare breakfast. Kristi had a quick cappuccino and a banana, then gave Hanne a kiss, saying, "I've got to run, babe. But have fun…with your man," as she gave her a lurid smile.

"I shall, and we'll see you later at the restaurant."

"Yes, Restaurant Barr. Anders made a reservation for eight. Oh, but I may come back earlier to pick up a few of my things."

"Good. We may or may not be here. But we'll see you at Barr if not before."

∽∾∾

Hanne just finished putting out a few items for breakfast—smoked salmon, anchovies, rye bread, muesli, raisins, prunes, some fresh fruit—and was sipping her second cappuccino when the downstairs bell rang. Heart a-flutter she ran to the speaker and pressed the buzzer. Of course, it was Richard. It took the elevator a few minutes to bring him up, but Hanne had the door to the apartment open, and jumped into his arms right there, in the corridor when he reached her.

"God, I've missed you so. I love you," Richard muttered between kisses.

"I missed you, too, darling. Terribly."

They disengaged and Richard picked his bags up as Hanne led the way. "How nice of Kristi to let us stay here."

"In fact, she's letting us have the apartment for a few days. She's moved in with her boyfriend."

"Terrific. We'll have our privacy then."

"Wow, what a lovely breakfast you've put out. Thank you, Hanne. But perhaps—that is if you don't mind—first I'll take a quick shower…And then, would you like to climb back in bed with me?"

"Of course, dear. How can I refuse?"

❦❦❦

The sex was good, but with Richard out of practice, a bit too rushed, and Hanne thought to herself, not as good as with Kristi. But it will no doubt improve as they get used to each other's bodies again.

When they disengaged, Richard jumped out of Kristi's king size bed, went to his suitcase on the luggage rack and came back with a small box. He handed it to Hanne, saying, "This is for you, my dear. As I said over the phone several times, I would like you to be my wife. Will you marry me?" And he went down on one knee, naked, beside the bed.

Hanne reached out and stroked his cheek as she opened the box and pulled out a ring. "Wow, this is beautiful! Thank you," she said, as Richard gently took the white gold masterpiece studded with diamonds and sapphires out of her hand and slipped it on the fourth finger of her left hand. "And it fits perfectly. This ring used to be my mother's and before that, her mother's, so it is a family antique."

"Thank you! I love you," Hanne said, throwing her arms around his neck and kissing him.

"But you still haven't answered me, Hanne. Will you marry me?"

"Of course, Richard. I love you, as I just said, " and she pulled his face to hers and gave him a passionate kiss again. "But there is one condition…"

"What?"

"Not now. Maybe later," Hanne mouthed, as she stroked his penis, kissed his chest and stomach and moving down on him, made Richard forget about the condition as he shuddered in ecstasy.

∽∾∽

Over a leisurely breakfast, Hanne brought Richard up to date on all that had happened and her thinking on the treaty and the funding proposal. While Richard read both her drafts sitting on the sofa, Hanne cleaned up, and then went to join him.

"So? What do you think, husband-to-be?"

"The treaty points are excellent. It does bring more focus on climate change and what needs to be done. I'm not sure China and some others will like it, though. They were already hesitant because the treaty puts a huge limitation on the use of the Transpolar Sea Route. They were rather glad when Gusanov blew up the original treaty…"

"But they are only Associated Parties, and it's even more evident now that the Arctic Ocean will not refreeze and will need to be protected."

"I agree. We must do everything possible. And if we can get the USA and Russia to sign again as Contracting Parties, China will have to comply or risk having any of their offending ships entering the Reserve being taken into custody or sunk. I doubt that they would want to start a world war over this."

"I agree."

"I can have our lawyers review the amendments you propose, so they are more in legalese English," Richard said with a little laugh.

"That would be terrific, to have native English-speaking lawyers take a look. Thanks. And then we can try it on some of our other friends among the Contracting Parties."

"The funding proposal, too, is interesting. I'm sure my government would consider putting up a hundred million as a start to keep the Chinese from massively infringing on our hemisphere and colonizing a neighbor. Especially, if as you say in here, some of the proceeds from an environmentally friendly extraction of Greenland's natural resources—say, the rare earths—would accrue to us. I can take it to the right people in my government. I will also explore some private financing opportunities—we have several companies actively involved with rare earths and other minerals."

"Good. Thanks, Richard. Now, shall we get dressed? I want to show you around my hometown. And later we will meet up with Kristi and her beau for dinner. How's that for an action-packed day?"

"What about that condition, you mentioned?"

"Later. And you're not getting another blowjob, now, you pervert…" Hanne said, running into the bedroom to get ready for the day.

❧❧❧

They arrived a few minutes after eight at the restaurant, and Hanne immediately saw Kristi and Anders holding hands at a table in the far corner, Kristi radiant in a bright pink, low-cut short dress, Anders unable to take his eyes off her. Hanne could tell, as they approached, that her friend was admiring the ring on the fourth finger of her left hand. So, good, her suggestion had sparked Anders into action. Indeed, the bottle of champagne with four glasses confirmed that they were in a celebratory mood.

The girls hugged, and the men shook hands as they were introduced. Everyone sitting, Hanne blurted out, "Well,

well, it seems you guys both had the same idea!" And she flaunted the ring on her finger. "Yes, yes!" Kristi could not keep back her joy. "Anders asked me to be his wife, and I accepted. I'm so happy." She too showed her ring around

"Richard asked me to marry him. Formally, this time." She didn't add though that they were naked and in bed. "We too, are very happy. And of course, I agreed." Hanne took Richard's hand, smiling at him, before she continued, looking at Kristi. "But I accepted with one condition…"

"Me too." Kristi blurted out. "I had a condition, too."

Just then the waiter came over to pour the champagne for the newcomers and to take their order. Once their choices were made and communicated, Richard turned back to the subject at hand. "Well, cheers. And congratulations all around. But you two conniving little witches must tell us what your conditions are, don't they Anders?"

"I'm dying to hear." Anders put his arm around Kristi, thinking that it was all probably a big joke.

"So, you guys know that Hanne and I have been the best of friends since childhood…" Kristi weighed in.

"Yes." And, "Of course."

"And…we are not just friends, but also lovers. We were each other's very first sex partners…" Hanne could see that both the men did a double take: Richard gulped, and Anders turned as white as the tablecloth. Then, simultaneously, both downed the bubbly in their glasses.

"And the sex is so…so good, and we still love each other." Kristi said with a nervous little laugh.

"So, the condition, dear fellas, is that we will marry you, but you have to let us continue with our relationship whenever, and for however long we want." There, Hanne blurted it out, and then took a sip from her flûte.

Anders asked, "So you two are…bisexual?"

"Well, I guess you might say that," Kristi answered, with a little laugh. "But only with each other—I mean the bi-part, the lesbian part if you want to call it that."

"Phew, this is all hard to take in." This from Richard.

"Whoo…I knew you were very, very close friends. But I never would have suspected." Anders, too, had difficulty coming to terms with what he was hearing.

"Well, there you go." Hanne weighed in. "We love each other very much, but we also love you guys. And we're not prepared to give any of it up just yet."

"I mean…I guess it's all right." This from Anders. "Now that we are going to be man and wife, I guess it will be okay. You will just go off with Hanne whenever she comes to town. Is that it?"

"Here and there. Yes, or we can invite Hanne to stay. Richard too, if he comes. We're all friends," Kristi brazenly said.

Before the men could jump in again, Hanne said, "So guys, let's just see how it plays out. We haven't had any problems with accommodating everyone so far. So, let's keep doing what we've been doing, perhaps adding a few twists here and there. We just have to make sure we're all upfront with each other."

"That sounds fine," Richard agreed. "Hanne, you and I will likely not be together all the time anyways, since our jobs, for now, are in different countries."

"And Kristi and I are in different parts of the world, too," Hanne added. "So, it will only be rarely."

The waiter brought the food and the wine, so the conversation came to a natural end, and when they resumed talking, it was back to planning the weddings.

"Shall we have a double wedding?" Kristi proposed enthusiastically.

"Well, Kristi, let's not jump the gun." This from Hanne.

"I first need to introduce Richard to my parents and then I'd like to meet his parents. And I want to get this treaty that we have been working on signed first…but you guys can go ahead."

"We should talk about it, sweetheart," Richard cuddled up to Hanne.

"We, too, need to see what will work for us. And our families," Anders, too, took the sensible approach.

Chapter 48

Copenhagen, Thursday, October 9, 202-

Morning came, and Hanne sneaked out of bed, leaving Richard still sound asleep. Quietly, she put on her bathrobe and tiptoed out of the bedroom, peeking back at her husband-to-be as she closed the door. What with all the catching up they had to do, both physically and emotionally, the loving punctuated by much needed talk to bring them up to speed with each other's lives, and Richard's jetlag plus the obvious exhaustion from work, it was no wonder, Hanne thought, that he slept like a log. *And, actually, it's great that he will be back in form later that day.*

After fixing herself a cappuccino, Hanne turned on the TV with the news channel in the background as she dialled Lise Frondholm's office to see if she might wish to join Richard and her for lunch to talk about the treaty. She was in luck. They agreed to meet up at twelve-thirty pm at Selma, a restaurant that had made history when Michelin awarded it a *Bib Gourmand* several years back. Opening her laptop, she sent Lise an email with the current draft of the treaty as well as the funding proposal document, hoping her ministerial colleague would have a chance to read both before lunch.

Hanne looked up from her laptop and ratcheted up the volume on the TV when she noticed tanks rolling across the screen. "Events in Russia are evolving rapidly." The reporter said in a grave voice. "Troops from the Northern and Western Military Districts are now surrounding Moscow, under the command of former troika members Pavel Laptov and Admiral Maslenkov, and the Western District's Colonel-General Zhevkin. Laptov has issued an ultimatum to President Gusanov and his allies, who are holed up in the Kremlin, to surrender or be taken by force. It is not clear whether Gusanov still has the full support of any units in the military and indeed, of the elite Presidential Regiment, which historically has been charged with protecting the president and key government officials. Laptov's re-emergence seems to be partly due to the recognition by the highest ranks of Russia's military leadership that the Gusanov government has been woefully inadequate with its lack of policies on climate change—which, as we all know, is devastating parts of Russia, as it is the entire world. This acknowledgement has been a long time coming, but Pavel Laptov's history as a polar explorer and activist for the Arctic, has finally hit home certainly among the Northern and Western Military Districts commanders. They, no doubt, are first-hand witnesses to the devastation of the melting polar icecap, the thawing permafrost and the all-consuming wildfires that Russia's north has experienced over the last few years. We will keep you posted as this situation develops, so stay tuned."

A good report, Hanne thought to herself. And good for Pavel. She decided not to bother him with a phone call, but to wait until the provisions she had added to the treaty had been more or less agreed at least by the Danes, the

Canadians, the Americans, the Norwegians and, of course, Greenland. They could then arrange a signing—perhaps even in Moscow, if Pavel's hold on power was firm enough by then.

Caught up with the essential emails, Hanne next called her parents.

"Hello, Mom."

"Hi, darling, are we going to see you today?"

"Well, I was thinking that maybe I would bring Richard by, if that's all right…"

"Who's Richard?"

"Richard Simpson, Mom. My new boyfriend. The one I told you about. He has asked me to marry him. I think you will like him…"

"Is he Danish?" Obviously, she had forgotten the whole conversation from the other day. Alzheimer's.

"No, Canadian. And I love him…"

"I can hardly wait to meet him."

"We'll come by and have dinner with you at the home. Is that okay?"

"Lovely! See you at six."

It was time to start getting ready to go to lunch, so Hanne quietly opened the bedroom door, wanting to go take her shower. Richard stirred, and seeing her, reached his arms out and said, "Hanne, my love…"

So, instead, she shed her bathrobe and slid in under the sheets beside him.

"Hello, Mr. Sleepyhead," Hanne said, giving him a kiss, before continuing: "I was going to wake you after my shower because we need to think about getting over to Selma, the restaurant where we are having lunch with Lise Frondholm, my former boss. I would like you to meet her and we can discuss the treaty amendments and my funding document."

"No, Hanne…let's first make love," Richard said drowsily, enveloping her in his arms. "There is so much catching up to do. And I'm so out of practice…"

"Well, as your eyes are open, and you are ready to go, we may just be able to fit in a short practice session, dear, if you insist." And she reached down to his member which was already erect. "Practice makes perfect. And provided that you promise you will be in form later."

"I was hoping that would be the case," Richard said, caressing her breasts and kissing her passionately.

ℝℝℝ

Hanne timed their arrival perfectly and they were already sitting at the table looking at the menus, when the Danish minister of Climate and Energy breezed in.

"Lise, I'm so glad we can finally break bread together," Hanne stood up to greet her former boss. "Meet my friend, Richard Simpson. Assistant Deputy Minister for Arctic Affairs in Canada's Global Affairs Ministry." She deemed it a bit premature to introduce him as her husband-to-be to her former boss.

"Delighted," Lise shook Richard's hand, "Lise Frondholm, Minister of Climate and Energy here in Denmark. No doubt, we have a lot to talk about."

"Indeed," Hanne said, as they all sat down.

Small talk and ordering out of the way, Hanne thought it was time to get down to business. "Lise, did you have a chance to read the email attachments I sent you this morning?"

"Yes, Hanne, thank you. I did glance at them before coming here. Certainly, the tightening up of the treaty is a good idea, and I think your proposed amendments should go a long way to deal with the issues around climate change. I have, in fact, passed the document to my colleagues and our legal department and will come back with comments if they have any."

"Well, Richard has sent it to his colleagues in Canada, who will probably put it in better English legalese," Hanne said with a little laugh. "But the substantive concepts should not change. I shall send you the updated version as soon as we have it back."

"As for the funding proposal, again the idea is good, but we will need to flesh it out more and understand the cost-benefit involved for us. And, indeed, for each participating country. Once we are all agreed at the ministerial level, perhaps we should have our bureaucrats negotiate the details. I'm sure there will be lots of back and forth."

"I second that." This from Richard.

"Good idea. Ron Hall, the US president's advisor on Arctic affairs in the National Security Council is now trying both on his government. Lise, I know you are close to our Norwegian, Finnish, and Swedish counterparts. Would it be possible for you to approach them on this? And of course, the treaty?"

"Sure, I was going to suggest that. Leave it with me."

"Terrific. Thanks, Lise."

⌘

Lunch finished late, so Hanne and Richard chose not to go back to the apartment, but instead sat on a bench in the nearby beautiful Orsteds Park, before they would have to make their way to the Solund Nursing Home, just across Dronning Louises Bridge over the Sortedams Sø. Hanne wanted to call Malik, while Richard needed to check emails and see whether his bureaucrat colleagues had made any progress on the treaty and Hanne's proposal.

"Hello, Malik."

"Hanne, so pleased to hear from you. We have a lot to talk about."

"Yes. We are very close to having agreement on the treaty amendments—at least among ourselves, the Dames and the Canadians, and I'm sure the Americans. My former boss, Lise Frondholm will be sending the draft to the Norwegians, the Swedes, and the Finns for their buy-in. Also, the draft funding proposal document I have prepared along the lines we discussed. But on that, there obviously will need to be lots of negotiation."

"What about the Russians? How is your friend Laptov making out?"

"Great. They have now apparently surrounded Moscow and presented an ultimatum to Gusanov and his gang who are holed up in the Kremlin. It seems that the Russian military is siding with Pavel since the policies of Gusanov on the Arctic and the environment are so destructive."

"Yes, I saw the reports. Let's hope that Laptov is able to gain control soon."

"And then I would propose that we have the Arctic Treaty signed almost immediately. The sooner the better, so the provisions—especially those on climate change—can start to be enforced."

"Where would the signing be?"

"My thought is that perhaps it should be in Moscow. That way, we could all show our support for Laptov and his government—and the sooner it's in place the better."

"Well, keep me informed."

"Sure, and thanks."

As Hanne finished her call, Richard said excitedly, "See the latest news report, Hanne? On Russia."

"No, what?"

"Apparently, the Presidential Regiment—that's the elite guard in the Kremlin—has done the unthinkable. They, too, have turned on Gusanov and arrested him and his closest lackeys. And they have now handed those criminals over to Laptov's troops, who are already in the Kremlin. Laptov will be making an announcement in the next couple of hours. Very exciting."

"Amazing! That is really good news. Boy, things are moving fast…"

⁊⊙⁊

They walked over to the nursing home, checking their phones for news from Russia every few minutes, and arrived a little early.

Hanne's mother was a little flustered when she came out to the common room, her curmudgeon of a husband dragging behind, to meet her daughter's husband-to-be.

Hanne and Richard both stood up from the couch and she leaned forward to hug her parents, even as she said, "Hi Mom. Hello Dad. Meet Richard. Richard Simpson. My future husband." And she looked at Richard with a big smile on her face.

"So pleased to meet you, Mrs. Kristensen. And Mr. Kristensen," Richard shook the hands of the oldies. "And, as Hanne has said, I would very much like your approval and blessing on my proposal of marriage to your beautiful daughter. I love her very much."

"We are delighted…" Hanne's mother started to say, as a bleep on Hanne's phone distracted them.

"Richard, it's Pavel! He's about to make a statement," adding, as an afterthought, "Mom, Dad. This is so, so important. My friend, Pavel Laptov, is back in power in Russia. The Arctic, everything I have been working on…hangs in the balance…"

"Is it more important than your marriage?" Hanne's mother asked, but it was only she and her husband who heard this, since Richard and Hanne had moved over to an alcove in the far wall to listen to Laptov's speech on her phone, leaving them standing by the couch. "Well, I never…" Hanne's father was outraged. "How rude is that?"

ა৩ა৩

"My beloved people, the people of Russia! As you see from my surroundings, I am back in the Kremlin, having re-taken control of the government with my well-respected friends, Admiral Maslenkov and Colonel-General Zhevkin and the help and support of the forces of the Northern and Western Military Districts and the Presidential Regiment. This has been necessary largely because former President Gusanov and his government were so antithetical to taking necessary action to protect our environment and our peoples, and especially, the Arctic, which is so important for Russia. Our country, indeed, the world, is severely under stress as a result of climate change and this cannot go on. It became very clear for me, as for all of us who have joined in this bold move to oust the previous government, that President Gusanov's policies and actions were posing an existential threat to our nation, to the very survival of our peoples and our environment. No doubt many of you have experienced these stresses first-hand over the last few years, and these have only become more and more accentuated over the last several months,

weeks, and days. His invasion of Greenland, a newly independent northern nation, further threatened the Arctic and was unconscionable. We could not wait any longer, hence our move. We will be putting forward a clearer statement of our policies in the very near future and we will assemble a slate of well-respected leaders to form our government. Once we are back on the right track, we will recommend a date for a general election to the Duma. We trust you will support us. Thank you."

"Wow! What a powerful statement." This from Hanne.

"Let's talk about it later. I think your parents were not impressed with the way my proposal to marry you went," Richard said, glancing over at the two oldies fuming over on the sofa. "We better go make amends."

"Sure. Yes, you're right." Then, approaching the sofa, "Mom, Dad. So sorry about that interruption, but it's the best news possible for my work. Our work." And she took Richard's hand, as he sat down beside her.

"Well, I am glad. But Richard, do tell us about yourself…"

Richard did and the oldies mellowed to him over the dinner of pork, potatoes, and broccoli. By the time dessert came, they were talking about the wedding and the timing

"Well, we hope it's soon," Hanne's mother said. "You need to get cracking with a family, my dear."

Hanne laughed, "Of course, Mom. But first, we have to get this treaty signed, then I want to meet Richard's parents and family…we all have to compare calendars to see when we can do it. We are both very busy at work."

"So…what then, next month?"

"Let's see. But probably not much before Christmas. Maybe next year."

"Who will be your maid-of-honor?" Hanne's mother asked. "Will it be Beate?"

"No, Mom. I think I will ask Kristi," Hanne said, looking at Richard. "My oldest and best friend. She's getting married too, and she will, I'm sure, ask me."

"Hmm…" From Hanne's father. "But shouldn't it be your older sister?"

"Leave it, Jørgen." Hanne's mother put her hand on her husband's knee. "That's wonderful. Who is her beau?"

"Anders Jakobsen." She didn't want to get into a whole conversation about Kristi and Anders, so she moved on. "Mom, it's getting late, and we need to go. We have a busy day tomorrow."

"Well, thanks for coming by. And wonderful to meet you, Richard. At least, two, was it—wasn't that how many children you wanted?"

As they parted with hugs, Hanne saw that her parents were content, if not overjoyed, and accepted Richard as possibly a good choice for her. Even if he was not a Dane.

ↅ◌ↅ◌

Back at Kristi's, Hanne first sent a brief a message to Pavel, saying: "*Glad to see you're back in charge. Have sent draft of amended treaty to key participants. All seem keen. Will send final draft to you tomorrow. We can proceed with treaty signing when you are ready. In Moscow? Hanne*".

Next, she called Malik. Saying basically the same thing, that the others she had contacted about the treaty were supportive of her draft amendments, and she had been in touch with Pavel about a signing. Probably in Moscow, also to show international support for the new Laptov government. As for the funding proposal, the representatives of other countries were supportive, but it would require more discussion and negotiation.

"That's fine. Just let me know when the signing will take place, and if I can't make it, I would be happy to have you sign for Greenland. After all, the treaty is your masterpiece." Hanne was pleased that Malik's support seemed to be unconditional.

Then Ron. The same short briefing to bring him up to date on where matters stood. And to see where he was with his colleagues in the USA.

"We're getting close. I think there is general buy-in at the department level that the amendments you suggest are a needed and welcome improvement. We just need the sign-off from the President."

"Thanks, Ron. I hope to be able to send you a near-final draft tomorrow."

"That's terrific, Hanne. I look forward to it."

While Hanne was making her calls, Richard followed up with his legal department, who told him that yes, they would have a draft ready the next day, which, in principle, Canada's minister for Global Affairs and the prime minster would be prepared to sign.

"That is good news indeed, Richard. Thank you for all your help on this." Hanne was happy. It all seemed to be coming together.

Chapter 49

In Russia, after a couple of weeks of demonstrations largely in support of Pavel and the end of the Gusanov regime, the Federal Assembly—the joint session of the Duma or Lower House and the Federation Council or Upper House formally voted to reinstate the pre-Gusanov provisional government until orderly elections could be organized across Russia in the six months to one year time frame. The troika they voted for included Pavel, then Oleg Kasyanov, the widely respected economist and finance technocrat, and, replacing General Morozov, the previous Chairman of the Joint Chief of Staffs who had become tainted by going along with, if not supporting Gusanov, Admiral Maslenkov.

It was auspicious that the date of the inauguration of this new trio was the anniversary of the October Revolution (according to the old Julian calendar in use in Russia at the time) when the Bolsheviks seized power in St. Petersburg in 1917, an important date in Russian history (even though per the Gregorian calendar in use now, it is celebrated on November 7). The treaty signing was arranged for the same date, as all the Arctic Council leaders were invited to the investiture celebrations.

Including, Hanne was pleased to learn, the premier of China, as she was—probably in vain, she recognized—still hoping to make the Chinese accept the importance of the treaty.

During the two weeks leading up to the inauguration and signing, Hanne did a whirlwind tour, touching base with all the key governments participating in the treaty, as well as the Secretary General of the United Nations. Of course, she started with home base: Malik was delighted to see her, and in fact, called a special meeting of the cabinet to approve formally Greenland's signature and to recognize Hanne's role in getting it done.

Since she was already on the other side of the Atlantic, it was easy for her to make a stopover in Ottawa on her way to New York and then Washington. Richard and she had only been separated for less than a week, but they were delighted to be able to spend a night together, and it was useful for Hanne to meet Richard's colleagues in Canada's Global Affairs Department, who all celebrated her preeminent role in the treaty. Of course, Richard was also personally invited by Pavel to the inauguration and signing, so when they parted, they knew they would be meeting in another week or so.

In New York, Hanne personally thanked the Secretary General, Sung Chi Park, and the President of the General Assembly, Hele Mägi, for allowing her and Malik to make their statements in front of the 193 other members of the United Nations, which she allowed had been an important international condemnation of Russian and Chinese aggression in Greenland, and one that had in fact helped lead to the demise of the Gusanov regime.

In Washington, she was happy to see Ron Hall, who insisted she have an audience with President Barlow. The president also showed his gratitude for her role in getting the Arctic Treaty back on track and helping to bring about global peace, while she thanked him for the timely supply of vaccines that helped the population of Greenland fight the virus that weakened the invading Russian forces.

The US was followed by Iceland, Norway, Sweden, Finland, then London, and back to Copenhagen, where she was delighted to be able to spend some time with Kristi, as Anders discretely left them "to do their thing". Once again, it was wonderful, and she and her friend expressed their hope that their future husbands would learn to live with the somewhat exotic arrangement they had imposed on them.

She also met with Lise again and thanked her for her help in bringing the other Arctic nations to the table. Frondholm, for her part, expressed her agreement that with this new version of the treaty, the Arctic and the nations involved would have a much better chance at surviving. She was delighted that she had such a talented friend as her ministerial counterpart in Denmark's former colony of Greenland.

⌘⌘⌘

Hanne met up with Richard at the Four Seasons in Moscow, and they managed to arrange to have rooms on the same floor. Although invited to the inauguration and signing, Malik was not up to traveling as he had a minor health issue that required hospitalization. So, Hanne was the senior Greenland representative, and she was joined by Kirima Hanseraq, its ambassador to the United Nations. After checking in, Hanne and Richard agreed to meet up for drinks and dinner in the hotel's main restaurant, the Silk Lounge. Happy and having caught up over a sumptuous meal, they sneaked back upstairs with Richard joining Hanne in her suite for a celebratory night of champagne and great loving.

The inauguration was splendid, although since it was a "special" change of government, at Pavel's express request, more muted than the grand ceremony usually celebrating the event. Nevertheless, there was a grand procession through the Spassky Gate to the Grand Kremlin Palace and then into Alexander Hall, where the Russian Standard of the President and the Emblem of the Russian President were on display. There, the Constitutional Court formally proclaimed the inauguration of the governing troika. This was followed by the Russian national anthem and short speeches by all three leaders and as the orations ended, and the inaugurated leaders filed out, "Slavsya" from Mikhail Glinka's first opera *A Life for the Tsar* was played by the military band and a twenty-one gun salute was fired.

The treaty signing had been organized to take place immediately after this, and all the prospective signatories had been invited back into Alexander Hall, where enough copies of the document had been placed on several long tables for all parties to end up with one, plus five extra copies to house with the reinvigorated Arctic Council.

Pavel, as the host, signed first, then Richard for Canada and Lise for Denmark, and Hanne signed right after the Finnish prime minister. She was proud to have her name on the document that she had masterminded with these exceptional officials from all over the world, a document she knew would do good for the world and help preserve the Arctic as much as possible. Although she knew in her heart of hearts that there was no stopping climate change, only slowing it down. And she was even prouder that she got to keep her own pen this time, not one given to her by Pavel as in the first signing of the treaty, which then had become null and void when Gusanov withdrew Russia. Hopefully, this one was there to last.

Chapter 50

Copenhagen, June 20, the following year

After a lot of to and fro, and much planning, Hanne and Richard finally decided to have their wedding in June of the following year. With all the pressures of the last few months, it didn't make any sense to rush into it, but rather to plan a blast of an event that many of their family and friends could attend. And because Hanne's parents were not very mobile, the venue they chose was the historic Brøndsalen next to the beautiful Frederiksberg Gardens, which was easily accessible from anywhere in Copenhagen.

A lot happened though, in the intervening months. Kristi and Anders had a small, quiet wedding still in November; they simply could not wait, and with Hanne very busy back in Nuuk dealing with the myriads of issues stemming from climate change and, of course, putting in place the funding proposal for Greenland's sustainable resource use plan, she was barely able to get away to be Kristi's maid of honor. But she would not have missed this for anything in the world, and with Anders at the all-night bachelor party the night before, and Richard there too, the two ladies had a lovely night together full of all the pleasures they had been enjoying ever since puberty.

But Richard and Hanne's wedding turned out to be the event of the year: she had invited all the friends she had made designing and putting the treaty together, and the Brøndsalen wedding venue had never seen such a gathering of distinguished guests. There was a delegation from Russia, headed up by a last-minute acceptance by Pavel Laptov himself, and including Captains Zaitsov and Kolnikov from the Russian navy. Malik Rorsen and the entire Greenland cabinet, (minus of course the caretaking deputy prime minister), and from Hanne's adopted country, also Aniuk and Silla, Aani and Biina. The United Nations was represented by Hele Mägi, President of the General Assembly, and the United States, by Ron Hall among others. Lise Frondholm, of course was there too. As the local hostess, Lise gave a short, laudatory speech, and she was followed by Malik and last of all, Pavel—everyone praising Hanne's courage, hard work and devotion to her job and most of all to the cause of helping combat the effects of climate change and save as much of the Arctic environment as possible. The best speeches, though, were those of Richard and Kristi, who praised her for the amazing woman she was, but also were able, with their intimate knowledge, spoof her appropriately.

The wedding feast was delicious with lots of champagne and wine; later there was much dancing, and only in the wee hours did the bridal couple manage to break away and ride the short distance to their small but comfortable nearby Hotel Josty in a horse-drawn carriage. Richard carried Hanne in his arms up the stairs and into the bedroom of their suite, where the two lovers continued the magical night *á deux*.

This was certainly a year Hanne would never forget!

Epilogue
THE ARCTIC TREATY

The Governments of Canada, the Kingdom of Denmark, the Republic of Finland, Greenland, Iceland, the Kingdom of Norway, the Russian Federation, the Kingdom of Sweden, and the United States of America, hereinafter referred to as "Contracting Parties",

And

The Governments of the Democratic People's Republic of China, the Republic of France, the Federal Republic of Germany, the Republic of Italy, the Republic of India, Japan, the Kingdom of the Netherlands, the Republic of Poland, *the Republic of Singapore*, the Kingdom of Spain, the Republic of South Korea, *Switzerland* and the United Kingdom, as well as the European Union, hereinafter referred to as "Associated Parties",

Taking into account the relevant provisions of the 1982 United Nations Convention on the Law of the Sea ("UNCLOS"),

Recalling the 1996 Ottawa Declaration on the Establishment of the Arctic Council,

Recognizing that it is in the interest of all mankind that the Arctic shall continue forever to be used exclusively for peaceful purposes and shall not become the scene or object of international discord;

Recognizing also that it is in the present and future interests of all mankind to preserve the Arctic environment and to create a zone free from resource extraction, industry, *nuclear proliferation* and unlimited *tourism and* maritime traffic;

Convinced that the establishment of a firm foundation for the continuation and development of international co-operation within the context of the Arctic Council will promote these objectives and the progress of all mankind and further the goals and principles embodied in the Charter of the United Nations;

Have agreed as follows:

Article I

1. All sea, ice or land territories in the Arctic above 80°North latitude falling outside the Exclusive Economic Zones ("EEZ") of those Contracting Parties that extend beyond this latitude (See Annex 1 Map) will be declared a World Heritage Site and a World Nature Reserve (the "Arctic Nature Reserve" or the "Reserve").

2. Above 80°N latitude, no extensions of EEZs pursuant to UNCLOS will be permitted. In this respect, this Treaty supersedes the provisions (paragraph 76) of UNCLOS that permit such extensions provided certain conditions are met. Extensions agreed during the course of the year of the signature of this Treaty pursuant to UNCLOS will be rescinded.

3. Any Contracting Party may unilaterally extend the Reserve to include land, sea or ice-covered territories within its jurisdiction or EEZ as far south as the Arctic Circle, with appropriate notification to the Arctic Council. The provisions of this Treaty will apply to such extensions of the Reserve. Such extensions may be unilaterally revoked by the original proposing Contracting Party or its jurisdictional successor with a one-year period of notification to the Arctic Council.

Article II

1. The Reserve shall be used for peaceful purposes only. There shall be prohibited, inter alia, any measures of a military nature, such as the establishment of military bases and fortifications, the carrying out of military maneuvers, as well as the testing of any types of weapons.

2. Under no circumstances will nuclear weapons be permitted in the Reserve. Nuclear explosions in, under or above the Reserve and the disposal there of radioactive waste material shall be prohibited.

3. The present Treaty shall not prevent the use of military personnel or equipment for scientific research, monitoring of compliance with the provisions of this Treaty pursuant to Article VII or for any other peaceful purpose.

Article III

1. No exploitation of resources shall be permitted in the Reserve. Specifically, there will be no mining or extraction of fossil fuel resources, commercial fishing or hunting permitted in the Reserve.

2. *In the event that a Contracting Party extends the Reserve pursuant to Article I, paragraph 3, it shall only establish industrial facilities and / or power plants within the Reserve if a majority of Contracting Parties vote in its favor at a meeting of the Council. The Council shall also vote on grandfathering any existing such facilities, and should such a facility not be approved by a majority, the Contracting party shall, within a reasonable timeframe to be determined by the Council, cease the operations of such a facility.*

3. Notwithstanding the provisions of paragraph 1 this Article, the historic rights of indigenous peoples to hunt and fish for their livelihood will be grandfathered within the Reserve, unless the Contracting Parties, in consultation with the Permanent Participants of the Arctic Council, determine that a particular species is endangered.

Article IV

1. Any ships over 300 tonnes entering the Reserve will need to register with the Arctic Council and provide information on its
   a) flag
   b) purpose
   c) destination
   d) ice class
   e) cargo
   f) the amount of oil or other fuel it is carrying

    g) passengers and staff

2. Only ships meeting stringent design standards to maximally protect the environment will be permitted in the Reserve. The minimum design criteria are set out as Annex 2 to this Treaty.

3. Ships carrying hazardous material will be prohibited entry into the Reserve.

Article V

1. Freedom of scientific investigation in the Arctic, and co-operation toward that end, shall continue, subject to the provisions of the Treaty and notification to the Arctic Council.

2. In order to promote international co-operation in scientific investigation within the Reserve, the Contracting Parties agree that, to the greatest extent feasible and practicable:

    a) information regarding plans for scientific programs in the Reserve shall be exchanged to permit maximum economy and efficiency of operations;

    b) where practicable, scientific personnel shall be exchanged for expeditions and research within the Reserve;

    c) scientific observations and results from the Reserve shall be exchanged and made freely available;

    d) *specifically, information on warming temperatures, icecap melt, sea level rise, thawing of the permafrost, wildfires, inundations and flooding and any other climate change caused effects will be communicated to the Council and all Contracting Parties to this Treaty on a priority basis;*

e) *the Contracting Parties agree to cooperate maximally to combat these effects and the causes of climate change, to discuss these at each session of the Arctic Council and to make public their efforts to do so.*

3. In implementing this Article, every encouragement shall be given to the establishment of co-operative working relations with those Specialized Agencies of the United Nations and other international organizations having a scientific or technical interest in the Reserve.

Article VI

1. Each Contracting Party shall contribute the sum of USD 10 million within one month of ratification of the Treaty to finance the costs of carrying out the provisions of this Treaty.

2. Each Associate Party shall contribute the sum of USD 2 million within one month of ratification of the Treaty to assist in the financing of the costs of carrying out the provisions of this Treaty.

3. The Arctic Council shall, on an annual basis, assess the adequacy of the funding, and, if necessary, call upon both Contracting and Associate Parties to provide additional funding on a pro rata basis.

Article VII

1. A permanent Arctic Council Secretariat will be created to carry out the provisions of this Treaty. It will be the task of the Secretariat to carry out the provisions of this Treaty and to ensure compliance with it within the Reserve.

2. Each Contracting Party shall make available at its own

cost a minimum of five and a maximum of ten of its nationals to serve on the Arctic Council Secretariat. The particular expertise of the individuals provided will be determined between the Director of the Secretariat and the Contracting Party.

3. Associate Parties may, at their discretion and cost, provide up to two individuals to work with the Secretariat. The particular expertise of the individuals provided will be determined between the Director of the Secretariat and the Contracting Party.

4. Notwithstanding the provisions of this Article, and with notification to the Arctic Council, aerial or maritime monitoring may be carried out at any time over any or all areas of the Reserve by any of the Contracting Parties.

5. Each Contracting Party shall inform the Arctic Council, the responsibility of which will be to notify all other Parties, of

   a) all expeditions to and within the Reserve, on the part of its ships or nationals, and all expeditions to the Reserve, organized in or proceeding from its territory;

   b) all stations within the Reserve occupied by its nationals and

   c) any military personnel or equipment intended to be introduced by it into the Reserve subject to the conditions prescribed in paragraph 3 of Article II of the present Treaty.

Article VIII

1. In order to facilitate the exercise of their functions under the present Treaty, and without prejudice to the respective positions of the Contracting and Associate

Parties (together the "Parties") relating to jurisdiction over all other persons in the Reserve, personnel of the Secretariat provided by Parties shall be subject only to the jurisdiction of the Party of which they are nationals in respect of all acts or omissions occurring while they are in the Reserve for the purpose of exercising their functions.

2. The Parties concerned in any case of dispute with regard to the exercise of jurisdiction in the Reserve shall immediately consult together with a view to reaching a mutually acceptable solution.

Article IX

Any or all of the rights established in the present Treaty may be exercised as from the date of entry into force of the Treaty whether or not any measures facilitating the exercise of such rights have been proposed, considered or approved as provided in this Article.

Article X

Each of the Parties undertakes to exert appropriate efforts consistent with the Charter of the United Nations, to the end that no one engages in any activity in the Reserve contrary to the principles or purposes of the present Treaty.

Article XI

1. If any dispute arises between two or more of the Parties concerning the interpretation or application of the present Treaty, those Parties shall consult among themselves with a view to having the dispute resolved by negotiation, inquiry, mediation, conciliation, arbitration, judicial settlement or other peaceful means

of their own choice.

2. Any dispute of this character not so resolved shall, with the consent, in each case, of all Parties to the dispute, be referred to the International Court of Justice for settlement; but failure to reach agreement or reference to the International Court shall not absolve Parties to the dispute from the responsibility of continuing to seek to resolve it by any of the various peaceful means referred to in paragraph 1 of this Article.

Article XII

The present Treaty may be modified or amended at any time by unanimous agreement of the Contracting Parties. Any such modification or amendment shall enter into force when the depositary Government has received notice from all such Contracting Parties that they have ratified it.

Article XIII

1. The present Treaty shall be subject to ratification by the signatory States. It shall be open for accession as an Associated Party by any State which is a Member of the United Nations, or by any other State which may be invited to accede to the Treaty with the consent of all the Contracting Parties.
2. Ratification of or accession to the present Treaty shall be effected by each State in accordance with its constitutional processes.
3. Instruments of ratification and instruments of accession shall be deposited with the Government of Canada, hereby designated as the depositary Government.
4. The depositary Government shall inform all signatory and acceding States of the date of each deposit of an instrument of ratification or accession, and the date of

entry into force of the Treaty and of any modification
or amendment thereto.

5. Upon the deposit of instruments of ratification by all the
   signatory States, the present Treaty shall enter into
   force for these States and for States which have
   deposited instruments of accession. Thereafter the
   Treaty shall enter into force for any acceding State upon
   the deposit of its instruments of accession.

6. The present Treaty shall be registered by the depositary
   Government pursuant to Article 102 of the Charter of
   the United Nations.

Article XIV

The present Treaty, executed in the English and
Russian languages, each version being equally authentic,
shall be deposited in the archives of the Government of
Canada, which shall transmit duly certified copies thereof
to the Governments of the signatory and acceding States.

In Witness Whereof, the undersigned Plenipotentiaries,
duly authorized, have signed the present Treaty.

Done at Ottawa this twenty-first day of September, two
thousand and fourteen.

Annex

Hanne's Map of the Arctic Nature Reserve

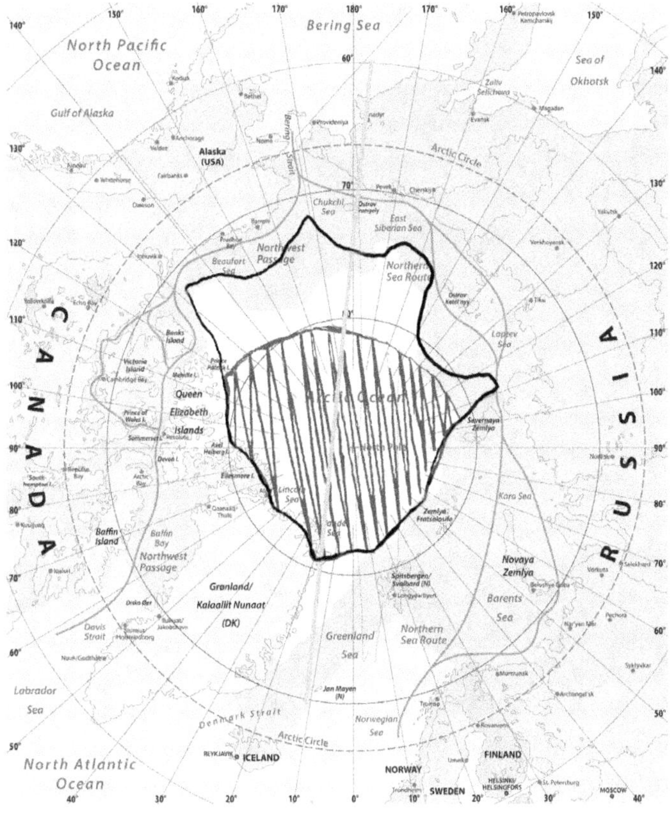

The Arctic Nature Reserve proposed in Hanne's Draft Arctic Treaty is the area cross-hatched in grey, bounded by Latitude 80°N, except where the EEZ of a country protrudes above this Latitude, in which case the EEZ becomes the boundary.

The solid black line shows the EEZ boundaries, the

wavy black the relevant section of Latitude 80N that serves
as the Reserve's boundary.

Distances are not exact.

Author's Note

My life-long fascination with the Arctic stems from the two summers I worked up north for the Geological Survey of Canada as a summer student. I was majoring in Geology at the time at Harvard College and I loved the challenge of working in this remote land, in what is now Nunavut, using Baker Lake as our base, but flying out in a Cessna seaplane to study a geological phenomenon called an esker. These are amazing glaciofluvial deposits that snake all over Canada's northland and were used by the native Inuit population as highways since they were raised above the taiga, which during the summer was largely marshland because of the melting permafrost. I was very taken by this unique but fragile landscape and the exposure I gained to the Inuit way of life, with its many adaptations to be able to survive in their harsh, but beautiful world. At Harvard, I switched to a then just emerging field of study, Human Ecology, with the support of Professor Roger Revelle. This eminent scientist was one of the first to warn about climate change and the dangers created by the burning of fossil fuels—many will also know him as the mentor for Vice President Al Gore.

Later, I became concerned about Russia's buildup of its military capabilities in this fragile environment, and the more research I did into the melting of the polar icecap, the consequent freeing up of the Arctic Ocean and the vast riches it held, the idea for a thriller set in the north started to take shape in my mind. The central position of Greenland, with its track toward independence from Denmark, also became an element in this emerging concept. A visit to this northern island with my son in 2010 crystallized the outlines of the plot for *Arctic Meltdown,* which I rushed to self-publish as an e-book in 2011, as reports of the melting of the polar ice cap and the militarization of the Arctic were already then starting to be more and more in the news. Ten years later, my thriller publisher, Black Opal Books, released an updated second edition of *Arctic Meltdown,* as I was already formulating the ideas for this sequel, *Arctic Inferno.*

Behind the writing of both these novels is my grave concern that with the melting of the polar ice cap and the lack of any serious international governance or treaty, the Arctic could become the setting for very destructive and prolonged military conflict, given its wealth of natural resources, as well as the prospect of a significant shortening of trade routes. Some kind of international accord to protect this fragile environment is essential, and I offer my heroine, Hanne's contribution, as one perhaps naïve, but possible way to move down this path.

Geza Tatrallyay, Barnard, Vermont

About the Author

Born in Budapest, Geza Tatrallyay escaped with his family from Communist Hungary in 1956 during the Revolution, immigrating to Canada. After attending the University of Toronto Schools and serving as School Captain in his last year, he attended Harvard College, graduating in 1972 with a B.A. in Human Ecology, and, as a Rhodes Scholar from Ontario, obtained a B.A./M.A. in Human Sciences from Oxford University in 1974. He completed his studies with a M.Sc. from London School of Economics and Politics in 1975. Geza worked as a host in the Ontario Pavilion at Expo 70, the world's fair in Osaka, Japan, and represented Canada in epée fencing at the Montreal Olympics in 1976. His professional experience has included stints in government, international finance, and environmental entrepreneurship. Geza is a citizen of Canada and Hungary, and, as a green card holder, currently divides his time between Barnard, Vermont, and San Francisco. He is married to Marcia, and their daughter, Alexandra, lives in San Francisco with her husband David, and two sons, Sebastian and Orlando, while their son, Nicholas, lives in Nairobi with his Hungarian wife, Fanni, and his granddaughters, Sophia and Lara. Geza is also the author of five other novels, three memoirs, five poetry collections, a short story collection, and a children's picture storybook. His poems, stories, essays, and articles have been published in journals in Canada and the USA.

www.ingramcontent.com/pod-product-compliance
Lightning Source LLC
Chambersburg PA
CBHW072013190726
48293CB00001B/264